The Fake Child

THE LADY MORTICIAN'S VISIONS SERIES

HELEN GOLTZ

Atlas Productions

The Fake Child – The Lady Mortician's Visions, book 2.

PUBLISHED BY: Atlas Productions

First published 2023.

Copyright © Helen Goltz

Proofread by Crystal L. Wren, COL Proofreading Service.

Cover design by Karri Klawiter, Art by Karri.

PLEASE NOTE: This book is written in British-Australian English.

Chapter 1

ONDAY 2 JUNE 1890. Brisbane, Australia. Fair to gloomy, showery weather to prevail, 22 degrees daytime, 13 degrees this evening.

Phoebe Astin liked winter; it was a good season for a mortician and it was better for the bodies that arrived at the office of *The Economic Undertaker* on their way to burial. The cooler weather preserved them for longer and allowed herself and her brothers, Julius and Ambrose, to not bury with urgency. Because Brisbane's winter climate was mild at best, and summer's most hot, that brief window of time when there was a chill in the air excited her. Phoebe wiped the Life-Glo tint powder from her hands and studied the face of the lady lying on the table in front of her. A little more powder, she decided with a frown. But then again, the colour appeared to be balanced, but the face was not quite restful. That was normally the sign of a troubled death, but from what Phoebe understood, Mrs Henriette Tochborn had died in her sleep after a short illness and she was of a respectable age to depart this world.

She spoke to the lady herself who sat on the winged-back couch against the wall and asked about the loved ones waiting for her. Phoebe smiled and contributed comments as she worked. She welcomed the spirits visiting on their way to the next world, and liked to hear their stories, but not all deceased that came into *The Economic Undertaker* appeared before her. There was one regular visitor, Uncle Reggie, but he had not graced her with his presence this morning.

Phoebe frowned again, why did Mrs Tochborn's death expression appear anxious? With a small sigh, she looked up and asked directly, 'If I may, Mrs Tochborn, now that you are at the end of your journey and can reflect on your life, would you say it was a happy one? You had a very good death, I believe?' Phoebe invited the lady's reflections. But when Henriette Tochborn hesitated, Phoebe understood, the lady harboured a secret.

'It was a mercifully quick death, is that not what we all want?' Mrs Tochborn agreed with a smile. 'And yes, young lady, I was blessed with a life of good health, wealth for comfort, and good companionship. Some would say I was very lucky.'

'Indeed,' Phoebe agreed. 'But in matters of the heart? You do not have to say of course, but I sense you carry pain within. If it helps to leave it here with me, I invite you to do so.'

She saw the kindly expression Mrs Tochborn gave her.

'What an astute and thoughtful young lady you are, understanding so much for one so young. And, might I say beautiful too, locked away here in your cool, little room.'

Phoebe laughed lightly. 'I like my cool little room. I have plenty of company and plenty of peace. The outside world is often too much. The living can be demanding,' Phoebe said in a rare show of vulnerability.

'I know only too well.' Mrs Tochborn rose and came to stand on the opposite side of the table from Phoebe, looking down at herself. The two ladies were of similar height but Mrs Tochborn was slightly stooped as if defeated. 'I don't look restful, do I?'

'No, that is why I asked after your last days. I would hate to distress your relatives and friends at your showing if they noticed the same.'

'I suspect they will not notice, not for a moment; I have looked that way for several decades. They might be more surprised to see me at peace.' She laughed but Phoebe could

3

not find humour in such a sad thought. 'Do not be concerned, I am happy at last, young lady,' she declared and smiled.

'Then I shall capture that look upon your face now if I can.' Phoebe studied her and then the strained look on the body's face.

'I have found my child.'

'Your child?' Phoebe snapped to look at Mrs Tochborn. A mother who outlived her children was not uncommon with the many illnesses at play and the many children in a family. But it was no less devastating; it was life and Phoebe had prepared them all, the young, the old, the unexpected. 'Has only one of your children passed?'

'I only had one child, the child that was never really mine to begin with.' Mrs Tochborn cocked her head to the side, studying Phoebe. 'You don't know who I am then?'

'Forgive me, no.'

'How refreshing when I feel like I have lived my life under a microscope.'

Phoebe did not speak as she ran Mrs Tochborn's name through her mind trying to recall why she should know it.

'My child, my only child, a boy...' The mature woman rubbed her throat as if pulling the words from within. She swallowed and recovered herself. 'My son and I are reunited at last, at long last. It seems he was dead all along, and now, my dear, I know the truth. The sooner I am buried and leave this world, the better.'

Phoebe knew there was more to come; if Mrs Tochborn truly felt that way she would be gone now, but here she was in spirit in the rooms of *The Economic Undertaker*.

'But you are not resolved to move on?' Phoebe asked with no subtlety as time was of the essence at this stage of life, some might say the dead had run their race and life was over. She added in a low voice, full of concern, 'What can I do for you, Mrs Tochborn? What are you needing? If I can help, I will.'

The mature lady's lips thinned and Phoebe saw the bitterness first hand that featured on the face laying before her.

'I want justice. For the boy, for me. Will you help me, Miss Astin, will you?'

Chapter 2

DETECTIVE HARLAND STONE LEFT his superior's office on the first floor of the Roma Street Police Headquarters and returned to his office on the level below with the file for his next case tucked under his arm. He had a skip in his step; the case was a difficult one and he suspected as the youngest of the ranking senior detectives, he had been given it when no other detective wanted it for fear of failure. That suited Harland Stone just fine. Last month, he and his partner, Gilbert Payne, had recently tasted success with the capture of the murderer, Frederick Beaming, so he welcomed an unconventional challenge for their next. Since the Beaming case concluded, they had closed two small investigations and finished a mountain of paperwork. He was itching for a challenge; this new case might be just that.

He wandered down the hall, greeting the occasional officer and fellow detective. Harland Stone was an odd mix of man – tall and solid, fit and handsome, but rugged with an edge of refinement. His habit of boxing for sport told on his face where he had taken a few hits, notably his nose, but his mannerisms were contained, his speech implying a private school education. Harland entered his office, his mind already full of the case.

'Ah, you are in, Gilbert.' He greeted the young man who was proving to be useful in ways he did not expect. The awkward Detective Gilbert Payne with his straight, short, neatly-parted hair, and his shoes polished to such a degree you could see your reflection, was not promoted from merit but by favour which did not go down well amongst the ranks – not that it was unusual, mind you. Harland did not care if they were considered the odd couple and laughed at behind their backs. He had accepted the role and moved to Brisbane with a handshake agreement that he would take Gilbert as his protégé. They would not only make the best of it, they would excel.

'Good morning, Sir, have we a new assignment?' he asked seeing the file in Harland's hand.

'Yes, and a challenging one, Gilbert. We shall sink our teeth into it and do our best.'

'Do you think they are trying to derail us, Sir?' Gilbert asked and Harland laughed. He had discovered that while the policing instinct might not be one of Gilbert's strong suits, the young man was a fact gatherer and Harland would take advantage of that. Gilbert was also disarmingly honest, speaking before thinking, which was not always a useful trait in this line of business when speech was silver and silence was golden.

'They might be trying to derail us but I prefer to think they are giving us a difficult case because of our recent success. We will do our best for the victim.'

'Indeed, Sir,' Gilbert said with a conspiratorial smile on his face. 'My father and mother are still talking about our role in the arrest of Frederick Beaming. To hear them, one would think we should be knighted.'

Harland chuckled and sat behind his desk as Gilbert joined him, taking the seat in front.

'I am not sure my friends will let me live it down if I am Sir Harland Stone.'

Gilbert saw the name on the top of the file and gasped. 'Tochborn!'

'You recall this case?'

'Yes, Sir, do you not?'

Harland shrugged. 'Bits and pieces over the years, but I confess I lost interest with the passing of time.' He flipped the file open and inside were news cuttings, illustrations, and portrait photographs, some several decades old. He separated the news clippings on the top from the handwritten notes below.

'I will brief you as I was briefed and then we will divide the file and begin work.'

Gilbert nodded, pen and pad at the ready. Harland held the portrait of a young boy – no more than four, dressed in a sailor suit – and handed it to Gilbert who said in a low voice, 'Oh, I remember this boy.'

Harland lifted another image from the file, turning it over to see the writing "James, aged 10."

'The family must have had money,' he mused passing it to Gilbert. 'Not many families could afford to sit for portraits several decades ago when there was food to be put on the table.'

'They paid that big ransom, so they were flushed,' Gilbert recalled. 'My mother tells me I was three or so when this boy was taken from his home. My mother was distraught that I might meet the same fate,' Gilbert said as he looked from one image to the next. 'My father would have gladly seen me taken and not paid the ransom.'

Harland gave a small smile, not quite sure if Gilbert's comments were in jest or a painful recollection.

'Right then. So that is James Tochborn, an only child who would be 30 years of age today if he were still alive, and some would have us believe he is… he is closer to my age than yours,' Harland observed.

'Were your parents not terrified at the time, Sir, especially since you would have been his age when he went missing?'

'My mother was, and I too, like James was an only child. My father sent me to boarding school to ensure I was surrounded by boys and good security. It appears to have worked since I am still here.'

Gilbert chuckled at that logic and they returned their attention to the file. Harland continued his brief.

'James's parents were Henriette and Leo Tochborn, both now deceased. Mrs Tochborn died several days ago, aged 64, a natural death.'

'Bet that's a relief for her to be gone,' Gilbert said still studying the photos.

Harland nodded and continued, 'James was ten when he was kidnapped from his garden on New Year's Day while riding a bicycle – his Christmas present. No witnesses and staff claimed to not have seen anything. A large ransom was demanded the day after his disappearance. It was paid but James was never returned.' He pushed the array of news clippings over his desk showing various stages of the investigation. 'There were four main suspects and three of those are now deceased.'

'That's inconvenient.'

'Yes, except we are not investigating the disappearance again.' He grabbed some of the papers that were on the top of the file and moved them nearer. 'We are investigating perjury, fraud and false identity by two claimants. Two cases, civil and criminal, will soon begin and Mrs Tochborn's remaining heirs are determined that the two young men claiming to be James Tochborn, will not see a penny of her fortune.'

'Goodness gracious, that's a grubby affair!' Gilbert exclaimed.

'And I suspect a dangerous one too, Gilbert. The claimants came forward in January this year when a story ran in the newspaper marking the 20th anniversary of James Tochborn's disappearance.'

'I remember the hue and cry when the claims that James Tochborn was alive were made but it died down and I confess I did not pursue an interest,' Gilbert said.

'Nor I. One of the men is a butcher and very capable with a knife, the other is in an asylum and has some firm support for his claims. And all the while, Mrs Tochborn lies dead while the fight of her life is just beginning.'

Gilbert sat back, and Harland could tell the young man's mind was racing. 'So where has James Tochborn been all this time if he was indeed alive and what was he doing? Why did he not come forward before this article ran on the 20th anniversary and claim his name and rightful place in the Tochborn family?'

'And who kidnapped him in the first instance? Can he not point a finger at them? He was ten at the time and should recall his captor.' Harland closed the file. 'First Gilbert, I shall leave you to assemble information and prepare for our interviews with the men who claim to be James Tochborn so we may call on them as soon as possible. The asylum may have visiting hour requirements and if an appointment is needed, advise we are detectives and require urgent access. Then, please arrange for us to meet tomorrow with the family members who intend to fight the claimants. You will find their details here.' He handed over a sheet of paper from the file.

'Yes, Sir.'

Harland studied the young man. 'I want you to play to your strengths, Gilbert.'

'Yes, Sir.'

Harland waited and sure enough...

'What does that mean, Sir?'

He smiled. 'I believe we have different skills that are well matched if we develop them. I am capable of analysing and assembling a picture in my head of circumstances, cause and effect.'

Gilbert nodded. 'Yes, Sir, I believe that to be true.'

Harland hid his amusement as he was not seeking his junior's endorsement but Gilbert's response was true to his nature.

'What have I skill-wise then?' Gilbert frowned.

'You are strong on fact and detail. A good trait for a detective.'

Gilbert gave a small smile of pleasure and then grimaced. 'Thank you, Sir. So how do I play to my strength?'

'As you gather information from those people we meet or interview, use your strengths to notice detail. Have they contradicted themselves? Are there similarities between parties or in their alibis or actions? Do you see inconsistencies? Do not hesitate to say. Any small matter can help as we saw with Miss Norris in our last case. She was dismissed when she came forward with some minor details, but I believe it led us to the killer faster.'

'Yes, Sir. I understand and will do my best.'

'I've no doubt, Gilbert. I am going to the morgue to ensure Mrs Tochborn's death was, without a doubt, of natural causes.'

'Why do you think otherwise, Sir?' Gilbert looked alarmed.

Harland rose, and Gilbert followed, gathering several papers and returning to his desk.

'It's just a precaution before we get into the case in great depth. I understand Mrs Tochborn was convinced the butcher was her son. Thus, if a family member decided Mrs Tochborn's death would put an end to the butcher's claim before it started, perhaps she was a victim of foul play.'

'Yes, I see, dastardly!' Gilbert agreed.

And with that, the two detectives – the most celebrated at the station for now given their recent victory and the most regarded with amusement – got to work and the investigation began.

Chapter 3

WITH LIGHTNING-FAST REFLEXES, JULIUS Astin grabbed for the edge of the coffin and caught it as the wiry young man, just into adulthood and holding the front corner of the coffin, stumbled, dropping his load. Julius winced at the pull to his shoulder but kept the coffin from falling. It was not the first time his quick instincts had saved a coffin toppling and a body rolling out.

'Sorry about that, lost my footing.'

Julius gave him a nod and moved away as the young man stepped back into place.

'You idiot, John, hold her steady, it's not like she's a heavyweight,' a gruff voice rang out from the back of the coffin parade.

'I'll give you steady in a minute, Ed,' he yelled back.

Julius restrained from looking at Ambrose who had struggled to compose himself several times and the funeral party had barely left the house.

'Think you can lift her to the hearse or do you need help?' Ed continued his ragging from the rear of the coffin. 'Maybe one of the ladies can take your place.'

'Leave your brother alone, Ed, it's your gran's funeral. You can pick on him tomorrow,' a woman who appeared to be the mother of the four men and the daughter of the deceased, reprimanded Ed.

'Yeah, shut it, Ed, or you'll be next in the hearse and buried before Gran,' the wiry man called John who had nearly dropped his deceased grandmother yelled over his shoulder.

Julius stood by the hearse, relieving Ambrose of the duty as his brother tried his best to contain his humour but was not winning; his laughter covered as best he could with coughing, his eyes watering.

Julius hit him on the back and turned to the man nearest him as the coffin was loaded into the hearse. 'Apologies, allergies... some of the flowers can be overwhelming.' Julius had a raft of excuses up his sleeve for such occasions.

'Yeah, I know what you mean,' the man who looked to be the eldest of the four pallbearers said. He yelled over the coffin, 'We should have saved our money, it's not like Gran's here to see the flowers anyway.'

The flowers were the least of Ambrose's problems by this stage as mirth overtook him again.

The eldest man continued, 'The dust is worse than the flowers, living here near the railway, don't know why Gran liked it so much.' He shrugged and stood back after a good shove saw grandma placed inside the hearse. 'Probably something for the old girl to watch when she was bored.'

'Is that what she died from, Alf?' Ed asked. 'Railway dust?'

'Nuh, just old age,' the fourth brother who up until now had said nothing retorted before Alf could reply.

'She was a decent old girl,' Ed said and sighed, as he and the brothers joined the women in their line behind the hearse.

Julius glanced at the ladies of varying ages dressed in black, all wearied, and not perturbed by the undignified banter of their relatives in the funeral party; he relaxed somewhat. Most funerals managed by the Astin brothers and their grandfather, Randolph, were scripted and dignified. This, however, was not one of them and the four brothers having seen to the placement of the coffin firmly into the hearse now looked impatient.

'How long will it take until the earth's tossed on top of Gran?' John asked.

'You can't ask that,' Ed berated him and the youngest, and most impatient brother shrugged.

'Thought you were in a hurry to get to the pub for the wake, Ed,' he mumbled.

'I am, but you got to do some things right by the dead,' Ed retorted.

Julius moved past them. 'We'll be at the cemetery in about 20 minutes—'

'Can we go faster? Aunty Flo is only minding the kids for an hour,' one of the ladies reminded them.

'Well, she can bring them to the wake,' a younger woman said beside her.

Julius nodded. 'We will get a move along then.' He looked as if he might succumb to laughter, and Ambrose could no longer restrain himself. Out of sight of the party, they exchanged a quick grin.

'Please let it be over,' Julius muttered near his brother's ear as they moved to the front of the hearse to begin the journey. They took their seats and Julius grabbed the reins.

'I wouldn't worry about going too slow,' Ambrose suggested, glancing behind at the impatient faces.

'Good Lord,' Julius muttered and started at a faster pace than normal. The party happily kept up talking amongst themselves like they did this every day which set Ambrose off on another round of fresh laughter, hidden from the party behind except for his shaking shoulders. 'This has to be up there with our most unorthodox funeral and we are not even at the cemetery.'

'Heaven help us there,' Julius said with a glance skywards.

Within ten minutes they arrived and poor gran was placed unceremoniously in the earth. With a decent amount of prodding, the priest was hurried along by the grandsons of the woman being interred.

'Gran wasn't much for the church,' Alf told the priest who gave a surprised nod, and Julius saw his eyes scan the size of the four men, and he hurried the blessing. The men shook the priest's hand, before moving to do the same with Julius and Ambrose.

'Beautiful service,' one of the daughters said to Julius, giving him a special smile and holding his hand longer than necessary even though she was old enough to be Julius's mother.

'You're welcome, Madam,' he said, as a younger woman, a sister to the four brothers he suspected, took his now freed hand as well.

'It was so respectful, Gran would be pleased,' she said affecting a demure look and agreeing with her older relative, surprising Julius who thought it a circus.

'Thank you, Madam, I am pleased we could be of service at this... uh, sad time,' he said seeing the brothers were already well on their way out of the cemetery. He extracted himself from the lady just in time to catch one of the children who was leaning over the edge of the plot with no supervision and almost toppled in.

'Careful young lad,' Julius said setting him back on his feet.

'For goodness' sake,' the woman who had put on airs and graces for Julius lost her charm and berated the boy in a loud voice. 'How many times did I say don't go near the bloody dirt hole in case Gran pulls you in?'

The boy looked up at Julius. 'Will she be a skeleton yet?'

Ambrose walked away, unable to control himself any longer, and Julius was saved from answering but gave a brief shake of his head in the negative and a wink to the boy who reciprocated with a big toothless grin as he was dragged away to follow the rest of the party to the wake. The mourners were gone, and Julius and Ambrose thanked the priest again on their behalf and permitted the gravediggers to fill in the plot.

The two men were still laughing at the absurdity of it when they walked into the office of *The Economic Undertaker.* Julius quickly sobered and asked his grandfather in a low voice, 'Are there customers?' He glanced at the meeting room and the coffin display room.

'All clear, a family has just left after booking the top package!' Randolph exclaimed. There was little difference between the packages, they were all affordable and the middle package being exceedingly well-priced was the most popular. Families like to think they did the right thing by their deceased.

'I have just made tea, come and take a cup,' Mrs Dobbs – their self-appointed kitchen manager – invited the family and Phoebe joined them.

'All go to plan, lads?' Randolph asked as he did after most funerals.

Julius and Ambrose burst out laughing again and seating themselves, regaled the party with stories from the event.

'I have never seen Julius come so close to throwing up his hands and telling the mourners that he'd look after gran if they wanted to go straight to the wake.' Ambrose laughed.

Julius grinned. 'Poor gran will be turning in her grave. But good luck to them; on with living then.'

'Speaking of the living,' Phoebe cleared her throat lightly, 'a client who has just left the ranks of the living has come to see me.'

'Uh oh,' Ambrose said and Phoebe nodded.

'Mrs Tochborn, the deceased, would like our help.'

Chapter 4

D R TAVISH MCGREGOR WAS a social man despite the fact his chosen occupation in the morgue saw him working with people who did not talk back. The sight of Detective Harland Stone at his door cheered him up to no end.

'Ah, are you looking for a body or me?' he said in a thick Scottish brogue.

Harland laughed. 'Both. But you will do, for starters. Busy morning?'

'No, which can only be a good thing, can it not?' Tavish said and ran a hand through his reddish hair which was best described as unruly. He gestured to a seat and the men sat opposite each other, a small table between them. 'I would offer you a cup of tea but we would have to go to the canteen and it is truly awful. I have a tipple...'

Harland gave a shake of his head. 'I will abstain as I have a new case. I may need it later in the day though.'

'That so? Are you still enjoying your success? Are ladies throwing themselves at you now that you are the face of the detective branch?'

Harland brushed off his comments with an awkward laugh. 'Hardly.'

'And where is that young partner of yours? An interesting young lad. Mind you...' Tavish kept talking without waiting for an answer as if he needed to release a certain number of words a day and took every opportunity to do so. 'If you wanted to bring that lovely journalist with you next time, you'd be twice as welcome.'

'Miss Lewis? Why do you not invite her to an evening at the theatre or to dinner then? I assure you, while she kept to the terms of our agreement on the last case, I am not actively seeking newspaper coverage.'

'More is the pity.' He sighed dramatically. 'You did well last night in the ring.' He swung easily to the next topic of last night's boxing bout.

Harland automatically touched his jaw. 'It felt good to let off a little steam and I don't think I look worse for wear this morning.'

Tavish shook his head. 'No worse than usual,' he joked. 'Your opponent was a tough one. Have you boxed him before?'

'No, but I have been studying him. I knew his moves.' Harland moved slightly and winced at the pain and memory of the blow. 'He's got a good right jab.'

Tavish grinned. 'We thought you were down for the count at one stage there, but Julius did not falter; he was quite convinced we'd make our money back on you.'

'I must thank him,' Harland said looking pleased. 'Speaking of our funeral parlour friend, I am here about the dead... Mrs Henriette Tochborn.'

'Ah that poor lady, it's a blessing she's gone after the life she had. Always being in limbo looking for that boy and a widow to boot.' Tavish shook his head. 'But you've missed her.'

Harland looked surprised. 'Has she got up and walked out?'

'As good as,' Tavish laughed, 'Ambrose picked her up yesterday. Miss Astin was to prepare her for viewing at the family's request.'

'Hmm.'

'That is it? Just hmm... not "oh good I shall have an excuse to see Miss Astin" or similar?' he teased.

Harland gave the coroner a wary look. 'Tell me, was it a natural death? Was there nothing suspicious?'

Tavish rose and went to a filing cabin, opening it and rifling through the files in the 'T' section, pulling one free and returning with it. 'I confess I did not do an autopsy or toxicology test as Mrs Tochborn's death was not suspicious.

I thought her a little discoloured but she was ill and on medication; her doctor confirmed she had been ailing and he was anticipating her death.'

'Of course,' Harland said frowning. 'I wanted to ensure that the family members who did not approve of her pending support of the butcher's claim that he was her son, did not hurry her out the backdoor in an attempt to stop the claim on her estate.'

'I see.' Tavish ran a hand over his light red beard and nodded. 'Yes, although I believe the doctor to be a credible man. It would not hurt to have a second look.'

'There might be another problem...'

'And to think I was so pleased to see you,' Tavish joked. 'Tell me then.'

'If Mrs Tochborn was... let's say poisoned, the most likely suspects would be the family and they will not be keen to approve an autopsy.'

'Yes, that is a problem, unless let's say there is enough suspicion from a detective to request it, and then they have no say in the matter.'

Harland smiled and nodded. 'I shall do them the courtesy of asking permission first and failing that, I will request it. I need to know as soon as possible as it will change the course of our investigation.'

'I believe the viewing is not for a few days, so perhaps ask Miss Astin to keep the body as cool as possible. If you can get Mrs Tochborn back to me with haste, I'll perform the tests.'

'Thank you, Tavish. I hope to speak with her family over the next day or so, Gilbert is arranging it now. I shall ask the Astin family to send her back to you immediately.' Harland rose and Tavish followed suit.

'Now I have given you an excuse to see Miss Astin, so next time, I expect you to bring Miss Lewis,' he said and gave Harland a grin.

'It is not I who has lost my heart to Miss Astin.'

Tavish scoffed and did not ask to whom Harland referred – it appeared Bennet's enthrallment with Miss Astin was known to all except possibly her brother Julius.

'I like Bennet a great deal but I doubt Miss Astin will have him,' Tavish said. 'They have nothing in common and he is also too handsome and potentially rich.'

'An unattractive combination,' Harland agreed with a grin and wished him good day, not interested in involving himself in the gossip of attachments. But he was rather pleased to have the opportunity to visit the office of *The Economic Undertaker*.

Lilly Lewis – looking resplendent, dressed in a shade of lemon, her chestnut hair neatly coiffured in a becoming style – was not in a state of panic but it was fair to say worry gnawed at her. Mr Alex Cowan, her editor at the newspaper, *The Courier*, had a saying and he looked at her and her fellow reporter, Fergus Griffiths as if he were about to apply it.

'Well, Lewis, Griffith, you have done an excellent job on the reporting of the *Uncemented Bride* murder case and the Albert Street thefts,' he said of their latest assignment. 'I confess, I did not think you both had it in you,' he said in his usual gruff manner, before sitting back and taking a long draw on his cigar. Lilly quickly inhaled the air before he exhaled and filled it with the pungent smell; his office always had a grey tinge of smoke and grime and Mr Cowan, who was middle-aged and of robust weight, seemed to blend in.

'Thank you, Mr Cowan,' Lilly said and was about to speak when he cut her off.

'I thought you would be back writing hatches, matches and dispatches,' Mr Cowan chuckled, 'and you, Griffith, back on the shipping news. But fair is fair, and credit due.'

Fergus thanked the editor and as Lilly went to speak, Mr Cowan cut her off again with the saying she was hoping to avoid, 'But you are only as good as your next story. So, what have you got for me?' He looked from one to the other expectantly. 'My best investigative writers do not wait for me to give them a lead, and given you two are my youngest and basking in the glory of the moment, I am ready to be impressed, again!'

Lilly glanced to her writing partner who looked equally as stricken as she felt, before returning her gaze to Mr Cowan. They had been given little time to prepare for the editorial meeting, having just filed their last story on the Albert Street thefts yesterday and the pair reasonably thought they had the morning to sniff out another good story. Not so; they were summoned to the editor's office bright and early.

'Mr Cowan, we have a hot lead but I do not want to give you a half-story. Allow us one day to glean the depth of it and we shall pitch tomorrow morning,' Lilly stated more confidently than she felt. She had nothing and caught Fergus's shocked expression. If Mr Cowan asked for a hint or demanded to know immediately, they were in dire straits. She prayed her editor would indulge them. To Lilly's relief, he chuckled.

'Well, I remember, young Missy, that last time you came to me with the same sort of deal. You had all your sources lined up before persuading me to let you run with the story, so alright then. This time tomorrow.' He waved them off sitting forward to continue with his work before calling another victim to his office. The pair thanked him and hurriedly departed.

When they were out of earshot, Fergus said. 'Have you got something?'

'Of course not, but I wasn't going to tell Mr Cowan that. We have just bought ourselves 24 hours, that should do it.'

'For the love of God,' Fergus muttered. 'Where to start?'

'Fergus, you have been deskbound to long,' Lilly scolded him. 'We shall separate and seek stories. We are, after all, investigative journalists are we not?' She raised an eyebrow but did not wait for his agreement. 'Let's come together this afternoon, say 3 o'clock to compare notes?'

'Right.' He looked doubtful. 'Where are you going?'

'I am going to see my contacts. The morgue, the funeral parlour, the brothel – do not ask – and see if I can dig up a story. I suggest you head to your shipping contacts and see if there is a story of murder or mayhem to be had at the docks.'

Fergus brightened. 'Good thought. Here then at 3 o'clock.'

Lilly grinned and ignoring Lawrence Hulmes and his persistent dinner invitations – of which he just offered one and she retorted she had no appetite, to the amusement of her colleagues – she was out the door and on the hunt for a story.

Chapter 5

CONSCIOUS OF THE HOURS spent outside of the office already, Julius requested his sister delay her telling of Mrs Henriette Tochborn's story for a brief time while he caught up on some business matters. They agreed to meet after Ambrose and a lad from the stables picked up a pauper's body from the hospital, and Julius co-signed some cheques for his grandfather and confirmed orders. He also wanted to visit Miss Violet Forrester next door in the mourning wear clothing store he had founded and opened one month ago to the day. He was always looking for a reason to visit the beautiful manageress but Julius was mindful not to make it look as if he were checking up on Miss Forrester and her staff of two.

'That's the lot, lad,' his grandfather said presenting the final cheque. 'Will you take the first monthly accounts to Miss Forrester?'

Julius nodded. 'Is she expecting me?'

'She is. I sent a note this morning with Mrs Dobbs who dropped it in with a cake for the ladies.'

Julius could feel his grandfather studying him and sighed. 'Go on, Grandpa, say what you wish to say so I can get on with my business.'

Randolph chuckled. 'If you insist. Please do ask Miss Forrester if you may court her and hurry up about it. Your brother, sister, and I believe you are a most suited pair and a beautiful lady like Miss Forrester will not be long on the market.'

Julius's jaw tightened; he was not one for discussing matters of the heart, or matters resulting in any heightening of emotions, and did not welcome the family speaking of his relationship status in his absence.

'Miss Forrester has made it perfectly clear to me that she welcomed the professional opportunity and was fearful of losing her position if it became otherwise.'

'Then perhaps you need to make it clear to her that it would not be the case. Why would she lose her position if you were to become involved? Would it not reinforce her standing?'

'If we were not to last, she fears her dismissal.'

31

Randolph scoffed. 'You would not do that and she would always have our respect.'

'Yes. You know that, as do I, but Miss Forrester has no grounds to trust me, yet. She barely knows me.'

'You have secured an apprenticeship for her brother, Tom, with Lucian,' Randolph said of his nephew and Julius's cousin whose carpentry business successfully produced coffins and wagons for *The Economic Undertaker* and other businesses. 'And you placed her as manageress securing her independence. How can she not trust you?'

'Because she is an intelligent woman who has had her share of misfortune. She does not want to put her life in the hands of a man, or any person, who could take away her security in a heartbeat.' Julius's voice was low and he appeared disappointed with the situation at hand. 'I cannot blame her; in her position, I would be as wary.'

Randolph started to speak but decided against it. Julius took the opportunity to conclude their business.

'Thank you, Grandpa, for your concern.' He hurriedly changed the subject. 'And thank you for your support, the last month was most profitable and only good reports from our clients.'

'A pleasure, lad. I enjoy the work and staying busy as you know, even though your grandmother would like me to attend more of her charity events with her.' Randolph smiled mischievously at his grandson. 'Thank you for sparing me from that.'

Julius grinned. 'We need you,' he assured his grandfather. 'The customers like to see a mature face and have a calm influence guiding them through a difficult time. I need you.'

'I am sure you would do just fine—'

'No, I need you,' Julius reinforced with a rare show of vulnerability. 'I do not have to worry about the business when you are at the helm.'

Seeing his grandfather's pleased expression and reading the concerned look that followed, Julius gave in to him. 'And yes, I will think upon your words, I assure you.'

Randolph gripped his grandson's shoulder. 'She likes you lad; I do not doubt that.'

'I am likeable,' Julius agreed, his smile disappearing as quickly as it appeared.

Randolph's voice softened as he regarded his eldest grandson with great affection. 'You are that, but Miss Forrester likes you in a way that a woman likes a man. I have seen when you are both together how you try not to look at each other, or conversely are unable to remove your gaze from each other. Nor do you seem to be quite yourselves in each other's company.' Randolph held up his hand cutting off Julius's embarrassed protest. 'Yes, I know Miss Forrester has only been here these six weeks past, but I have observed her with Ambrose and Phoebe; I know her character enough to claim that observation.'

Julius was angered slightly, a flush of red appearing above his collar; his grandfather had been observing him at an unguarded moment. 'You know I hate to be studied.'

'It is my privilege as your grandfather, and we are alone now so we can talk of such things.' Randolph lowered his voice. 'Do not deny it to me, Julius, I know you better than anyone and in the absence of your parents, it is my responsibility to see to your happiness, even if you are a man now.'

Julius ran a finger around his necktie, loosening it slightly. He recovered himself. 'I will take the papers to her now. Can we not speak of this again?'

'I cannot promise that, as I am keen to press your suit for her hand. But I will not speak of it again today.' Randolph chuckled as Julius rolled his eyes again like a boy.

With the papers in hand, Julius thanked his grandfather, gave him another sidelong glance which caused more merriment, and departed. Before arriving next door, he straightened, his heart rate increasing at the thought of Miss Forrester waiting for him, with her pale blue eyes, delicate figure and warm brown hair that he hoped to loosen from its clasp one day. Miss Forrester impressed him with more than just her beauty. She had made a great success of the business in the first month, appeared to be kind to her staff, and delighted the customers.

As for Julius, he was conscious every moment of every day of her proximity. Everything his grandfather had said was true of his own emotions, and he hoped and prayed Miss Violet Forrester reciprocated his feelings. The thought of her with another man was unbearable.

'He is coming,' Mary whispered hurriedly on sighting the tall, striking form of the business owner and her employer, Julius Astin, walking towards them.

'Do not be concerned, Mary; I am expecting him to deliver the monthly accounts. No cause for alarm,' Violet assured her young seamstress, despite her own racing heart. She smiled for reassurance, knowing Mary was a nervous little thing who almost didn't make it through the job interview. But she was a hard worker and a very capable dressmaker.

'Phew, that's a relief then.' Mary returned her attention to the bench and the black fabric she was cutting. She had relaxed and become more herself over time in the company of Violet and Mrs Nellie Shaw – the mature fitter and sewer – who acted like a mother hen around both girls. There was no competition between them and nothing but affection, which is what Violet sought in her appointment of the ladies.

The door opened cautiously, and Julius glanced in, his eyes adjusting to the inside surrounds before settling on Violet.

'Good morning, Mr Astin,' Violet said rising from behind the table where she worked on a black Singer sewing machine. A similar model was set up on a nearby table. She ran her hands down her pale grey skirt and gave him a demure nod. 'It is safe to enter.' She saw his smile which always charmed her, changing his countenance so completely. 'Mrs Shaw is in fitting a lady,' Violet said with a nod to the closed fitting room door, 'but we can meet in the staff room if that is suitable?'

'Indeed,' Julius said entering fully and closing the door behind him. He turned to Mary. 'Good morning, Miss Pollard.'

'Good morning, Mr Astin.' Mary's voice shook, and her eyes darted to him and back to her work.

'Miss Forrester tells me your work has been exemplary this past month, I thank you.'

Violet smiled at Mary who looked thrilled and terrified in equal measure as if she might faint any moment. Mary glanced at Violet, then at Julius, and back to her work saying in a low whisper, 'Thank you, Sir, it has been my pleasure.'

Violet returned her attention to Julius. 'Mr Astin, thank you for the courtesy, but you do not need to make an appointment to speak with me, it is your business after all.'

'I appreciate that Miss Forrester, but I am sure like me, your day is planned and you allocate time to your projects. I would hate to intrude on that.'

'That is very thoughtful, thank you.' She invited Julius to follow her to the staff room, not closing the door even though they were to talk about matters of business. They sat far enough away from the doorway for the conversation to remain private.

'Can I offer you a cup of tea and a slice of Mrs Dodd's cake, Mr Astin?' she asked before sitting which meant Julius continued to stand.

'Thank you, but I have had both in equal measure already today. Mrs Dodds does not like us to go unrefreshed,' he joked and Violet laughed, sitting, allowing Julius to do the same; he sat opposite. She ensured her chair was a little back so they did not touch under the table by accident.

'May I ask, purely out of curiosity, how Mrs Dobbs came to be in your employ? We are most happily spoilt by her.' She studied him as much as she dared – the set of his jaw, the hollow lines of his cheeks, his ample dark hair, and deep brown eyes – unlike his sibling who both had blue eyes. She wondered, was it his mother or father who had brown eyes like himself?

Julius appeared to relax in the conversation. 'Mrs Dobbs is a kindly woman who approached us to run our kitchen after we had the honour of burying her husband. A week after the funeral she came in to settle the account and when we asked if she was satisfied, she said, "Mostly!"'

'My goodness!' Violet bit her lip, restraining a smile.

'You can imagine my shock,' Julius said in jest, sitting back and offering Violet another of his rare smiles. 'There I was, running the funeral events through my mind, thinking of all the things we did not do to scratch, and then Mrs Dobbs said she was not offered a cup of tea.'

'Heaven forbid! How could you not?' Violet played along, looking appalled and placing her hand on her heart.

'I shudder to think on it now,' Julius agreed, making them both grin and hold their gaze a little longer than professional. Julius cleared his throat, glanced away and then back when he continued, saying, 'Mrs Dobbs said a cup of tea will solve anything and provide comfort, thus she offered to manage our kitchen and I must say, it has been a godsend. The customers do appear to appreciate it.'

'I imagine so. The offering of tea says you are not in a hurry. Do not rush, we are here to support your journey not to snatch your business,' Violet said and saw Julius cock his head to the side.

'Yes, I imagine it does. Perhaps I'd best give Mrs Dobbs a pay rise.'

Violet laughed. 'Speaking of business, forgive me, I am delaying you with my curiosity.' She nodded to the accounts in front of him.

'Not at all,' he said. 'I am not all about work, Miss Forrester.'

'Are you not? I am pleased you have other pursuits.' She felt herself colour as she spoke and wished she had not started down this path. She hurriedly added, 'I am guilty of not having enough interests but I am fortunate to have my brother home every evening telling me of his day. He is truly loving his work, I thank you.'

'I have little to do with it and I believe Lucian is most pleased with his efforts; Tom is a fast learner. I must call in on him at work soon and see how he fares.' Julian glanced at the papers in his hands. 'Speaking of work, the first month has been a great success. My bookkeeper tells me you have exceeded his first-month projections and the next few months are looking very promising. Thank you, Miss Forrester.'

'That is a wonderful outcome,' Violet said and exhaled, her shoulders slumping slightly as she relaxed at the news. Not that she doubted it. The orders had been forthcoming and the clothes they premade for fitting as needed, were walking off the hanger rack. 'Mourning never seems to go out of style.'

'Death is a constant,' Julius agreed. 'I would like to set up a bonus system for you and the ladies.'

'It is not necessary, I assure you; we are paid generously and need no incentive to work better or harder,' Violet retorted.

'I did not mean to imply that,' Julius added hastily looking a little affronted. 'All our staff and suppliers have bonus plans in place.'

'Oh, I thought—' she stammered, a little taken aback by his reply and realising she had sounded harsh. 'Forgive me, Mr Astin. I am not ungrateful, but may I make a suggestion?'

Julius nodded and she noted his eyes were studying her warily as if she were a cornered cat likely to strike out with a paw and scratch him.

'Allow us to work our roles until the end of the year, six months ahead, and if you are still as satisfied, perhaps provide a Christmas bonus. That will be helpful to the ladies and their families, and if you are not happy, then you need not do anything more than pay our wages. I shall not mention it to them so there will be no anticipation.'

Julius said nothing for a moment and Violet feared she had offended him. He was impossible to read other than his jaw seemed to have tightened and his eyes narrowed a little as he studied her.

'May I speak directly, Miss Forrester?'

'We do seem to do so, even if it is accidental in nature,' she said, offering him a small smile which he reciprocated to her relief.

'I feel you are untrusting of me. That you regard me as having ulterior motives. I assure you of my best intentions.'

She sat back as far as her chair would allow; his observation did throw her somewhat off guard even though she invited his frankness. Violet swallowed and hesitated.

He quickly added, perhaps recognising the position of power he was in, 'I beg your pardon, Miss Forrester, you need not respond to that. I accept your plan if that is what you wish.'

Impulsively, her hand shot across the table to rest on top of his. 'I trust you implicitly, Mr Astin.' Then realising she was touching him withdrew her hand just as quickly. 'I like to earn my way and I want my ladies to give their best, as they are currently doing, without needing to meet a bonus system. It creates unnecessary pressure. I hope you understand.'

She saw his eyes follow her movements as her hand withdrew; he clenched the hand she'd touched.

'I had never thought of it like that, of it adding undue pressure,' Julius said. 'I shall speak with my bookkeeper. Perhaps you are right and we should not have bonuses but rather season-related gifts.'

'Goodness, please do not let me be the cause of others in your employ losing their bonuses, they will come after me.'

Julius smiled. 'Fear not, I realise the difference,' he said as if it all now made perfect sense. 'This is a different industry to those who must meet deadlines for delivery of coffins or wagons or timber or to have our grave sites prepared on time. The bonus ensures they prioritise our work above all other orders. But I believe, the more I think about it, that you are right. The bonus does not apply to your industry as we are not asking for a certain number of garments to be made by any particular date. Thank you, Miss Forrester, for enlightening me and I apologise for any offence given.'

'My pleasure, Mr Astin and I assure you, an employer wishing to pay his staff more could hardly offend.' She sighed. 'My brother tells me I am never short of an opinion.'

'My sister and brother would say the same of me. Between the two of us then, we should have most topics covered,' Julius teased, and Violet laughed, realising they had much in common and she really did want the attention of Mr Julius Astin more than she cared to admit.

Chapter 6

B ENNET MARTIN HAD BEEN inundated with requests for his private investigator services, or rather his clerk, Daniel Dutton, had been, since closing their last case and finding the whereabouts of a missing family. With the enormous exposure received from Miss Lewis's newspaper and the formal thank you letter to the newspaper from the family expressly mentioning him as their private investigator, there was to be no peace now. He dabbed away at the canvas, staying as best he could with his morning routine of painting before he descended to the office below where Daniel and housekeeper, Mrs Clarke, would have the day well under way.

It had also increased the pressure on him from his father in England – a detective with Scotland Yard – who believed Bennet should now return home and take up a role with the local police constabulary. Bennet could think of nothing worse. His private investigator work was only meant to fill a few idle hours a day and provide a sound income until he could live off the proceeds from his art. The river scene he was painting had been commissioned by an attractive widow whom he suspected was more interested in an acquaintance than his art.

His brown eyes looked to the distance, to the very river he was painting and back to his canvas; he was pleased with the work and another few days would see it completed. But it wasn't his favourite subject. On easels and against the wall sat a collection of paintings of Miss Phoebe Astin in all her beauty. Truth be known he was feeling sulky as he had no excuse to visit her at the business, *The Economic Undertaker*. Julius was his closest friend since arriving in Australia the Autumn of the year prior, but he saw him last evening and could think of no reason to visit him at work. Unfortunately, Julius did not reside with his family since buying his own home so there was no point calling on him there. No, the time had come, Bennet had to declare his interest and ask to court Phoebe. He had to own his feelings.

With a sigh, he declared the morning session over and washed his brushes. Dressing in preparation for the office, Bennet arrived downstairs twenty minutes later.

'That's a nice shade of blue,' Daniel said admiring the streak in Bennet's blond hair.

'Ah, I've done it again.' Bennet sighed. His habit of running his hand through his hair while dabbing brushes in paint saw him sporting various colours. He thanked Mrs Clarke as she presented him with a cup of tea and went upstairs to straighten his rooms.

'I have some news that will cheer you up,' Daniel said, pushing his steel-rimmed glasses further up his nose and looking pleased with himself.

'Who says I need cheering up?'

'I am well versed with your moods and you are feeling low after the highs of such a successful case. What to choose next is rather daunting.' Daniel nodded at the pile of letters and requests in front of him. 'I am working through them and will reject those that I am sure will not interest you.'

Bennet made a disinterested huffing sound and sipped his tea. 'What is your good news then?'

Daniel removed his glasses and sat back in his chair. 'This morning while collecting the mail I ran into Mr Randolph Astin doing the same.'

'Oh, did you?' Bennet's eyes lit up at the mention of the Astin name and Daniel laughed. 'And how is Mr Astin senior?' he asked trying to sound nonchalant.

'He was rushing as he had to return for a meeting with a client. When I asked after Miss Astin, Mr Astin said she was busy as they had Mrs Tochborn in-house.' Daniel made the announcement as if it were the most fascinating news ever and he expected the appropriate reaction.

Bennet frowned. He had not long been on Australian shores and the name was not familiar to him. 'Tochborn? Should that mean something to me?'

Daniel rolled his eyes and briefly told him the story of the mother looking for her son and the two claimants. On concluding, Bennet gave a small shrug.

'A tragedy indeed, but I am still waiting for the good news element.'

Daniel lifted a letter from one of the two piles on his desk. 'I received this request in today's mail.' He waved the letter. 'It is from a relation of Mrs Tochborn. After your success with the Beaming case, they would like to hire your services to work with their solicitor in disproving the claimants are related to Mrs Tochborn, in particular the gentleman she was willing to endorse.'

Bennet sat upright. 'That is good news.'

'Indeed.' Daniel replied with a smirk. 'Shall I reply you are interested and request a meeting post-haste? I believe you will also need to call on Miss Astin and ask for her insights. She may have spoken with the family directly.'

Bennet shot to his feet. 'Daniel, you are a genius.'

'I believe so.' Daniel grinned. 'Shall I read their letter to you?'

'Yes, quickly.'

Daniel read the family's request and what information they hoped to glean. 'I shall set up the meeting.'

'And I shall go immediately to see Miss Astin.' Bennet grabbed his notebook and hat and halted as Daniel called him back.

'What is it?' he asked impatiently.

'Perhaps remove the blue from your hair first,' Daniel suggested.

'Oh, yes.' He ran back up the stairs, dismissing Mrs Clarke to his study while he underwent his grooming. The day was looking considerably brighter.

Phoebe could hear a familiar voice upstairs and soon enough Lilly Lewis began her descent to Phoebe's workroom, holding her skirt as she navigated the stairs.

'Phoebe, hello. Is my presence a disruption?' Lilly glanced around to see who might be lying on the worktable this morning.

'Only a welcome one,' Phoebe assured her as the two ladies embraced. They were contrasting in appearance, Lilly looking more like the dressmaker, Miss Violet Forrester, with her brunette hair and blue eyes, while Phoebe had hair of gold. But the two founding members of the *Vexed Vixens* social group of four firm friends had much in common with their careers in male dominions.

'I am desperate,' Lilly wailed.

'Good Lord, what has happened?' Phoebe untied the large apron she wore over her long black skirt and white shirt and put it aside. 'Do you need tea?'

'Thank you, no. But I do need to find a story and I have one day to find it.'

Phoebe exhaled and smiled. 'Is that all? I thought you were destitute or dying.' She started breathing normally again and gave her friend a wry look.

'Phoebe, this is worse than being destitute or dying,' Lilly insisted. 'If Fergus and I do not discover a good story to put to Mr Cowan by tomorrow morning's meeting, I will be back on the *Births, Marriages and Deaths* column and Fergus on the *Shipping News*. Disaster!'

While they spoke, Phoebe moved to the table to cover the face of a young man she was preparing for a viewing.

'My, he is handsome.' Lilly followed and admired the deceased.

'It is a great shame.' Phoebe hovered with the covering to admire the man who was of the same age as Ambrose or thereabouts. 'A railway accident, his injuries were quite severe.'

'It is such a waste when we need all the handsome men we can find.' Lilly sighed.

Hearing footsteps on the stairs, both ladies spun around in alarm for fear they had been caught talking of the need for handsome men, but the visitor appeared to have not heard the conversation or had the good grace to pretend otherwise. Detective Harland Stone arrived at the bottom of the stairs and greeted them with a smile on his face. He did look particularly handsome in a dark grey suit, his hat in his hands.

'May I enter? Your grandfather said you were available, Miss Astin?'

'Of course, Detective,' Phoebe said and turned long enough to cover the young man on her table. She did not see how he hid his disappointment at not finding her alone and the chance to get to know each other a little better, while not forgetting his acquaintance, Bennet, had intentions for Miss Astin.

'Miss Lewis, we meet again.'

'Yes, and thank you, Detective, for not saying my name with the edge of ice reserved for most police staff.' Lilly gave him a smile and a small bow.

Harland laughed. 'Well, our last experience was very amiable and I thank you for painting me in such a good light.'

'No more than what you deserved,' Phoebe contributed. 'Now, as you are both here, I must say your timing is excellent. I was to tell my family of a suspicious crime on the hour and it is nearly that. Are you interested Detective or do you have enough on your hands?'

Lilly gasped and clapped her hands together. 'You might just save me, Phoebe.'

Phoebe laughed and said to Harland, 'Do not fear, Detective, Lilly does not require rescuing. She is visiting all her sources looking for her next story.'

'It is my job,' she confirmed, 'and I've started here, Fergus is at the docks.'

'Yes, best you keep away from that rough place,' Harland said and smiled at the grimace Lilly gave him. He turned to Phoebe. 'Miss Astin, I am most interested in your suspicious crime, however, my priority and the reason for my visit is to view Mrs Henriette Tochborn. I believe she is in your care?'

'Yes, Detective, and by coincidence, my suspicious crime and your mission are one and the same.'

'Well, that is fortunate, perhaps,' he added and Phoebe's smiled appeared at his caution.

Before they could begin, the clock struck the hour and Phoebe could hear footsteps on the timber floor above. Moments later Julius and Ambrose made their way down the stairs.

Lilly took a sharp breath and stiffened beside Phoebe; her gaze went straight to Julius while Phoebe noted Julius seemed somewhat oblivious, but a glance at Ambrose told a different story. It was true, like her family had said, Ambrose was smitten with her dearest friend, Lilly, who was equally as fascinated but with the wrong brother. Oh, dear. She would think about it later.

Greetings were offered and the young people looked most social in a room where the dead lay waiting to be prepared for viewing.

'You look no worse for wear,' Julius said studying Harland.

'I feel it. But I hear thanks are in order for your vote of confidence.' Harland shifted as he explained to the ladies, 'I did a few rounds last night – a boxing bout.'

'He was enormous your opponent.' Ambrose clamped Harland's shoulder making him wince.

Phoebe gasped. 'Are you bruised and battered?'

'Yes, but not on my face fortunately or I would have to answer for it to my superior.'

'Goodness, you are lucky, I wish I could fight,' Lilly said and they all looked at her in astonishment as she presented in the palest of lemon dresses looking very much the lady. 'I have five brothers and how I would love to put on the gloves and box their ears, not to mention several of my male work colleagues as well. It must be a wonderful release.'

'That is exactly what it is, Miss Lewis,' Harland said surprised by her insight. 'If you give me a list of people you would like to see worked over, I will see what I can do,' he teased her and Phoebe noticed Ambrose did not look at all pleased by their flirtatious banter and the laughter that ensued.

'To business,' Phoebe suggested and then halted as her grandfather called down the stairwell.

'One more to come if there is room down there,' Randolph said with a chuckle in his voice and Bennet Martin appeared on the stairs arriving moments later.

'Goodness, it's the old team!' Bennet exclaimed looking at all the faces and greeting everyone in turn.

'It is good to see you, Mr Martin,' Phoebe said, 'but I am just about to brief the detective on a matter of business...' She feared holding Harland up further.

'My visit is business as well,' Bennet hurriedly assured her. 'I've been asked by the family of Mrs Tochborn to investigate the claimant. A previous investigator has done some work but the family is not satisfied.'

'Goodness, we are all here for the same cause then,' Phoebe said.

'The trial for the two claimants to prove themselves starts in a matter of weeks. They have given you little time,' Harland addressed Bennet.

'I know, I hope they are not expecting miracles,' Bennet said aware of the pressure of his deadline. 'I am to meet with them next and I understand the lady is in your hands, Miss Astin?'

The group exclaimed at the coincidence and Harland looked less than pleased but had the good grace to roll his eyes and make light of it.

'Am I never to investigate a case without a collaboration of private investigators, reporters and funeral directors?' he said with a weary shake of the head.

'It is your good fortune indeed,' Julius said in jest and Phoebe laughed at Harland's grimace.

'I am familiar with this story,' Lilly said, 'but perhaps there is a new angle?' she enquired of Phoebe.

'Perhaps,' Phoebe said not making any promises and unsure what everyone knew from their own recollection of Mrs Tochborn's story. 'I know you are all busy,' she started. 'But may I say that I have come by this information in the... um, unconventional way, do you wish me to proceed?'

Harland studied her for a brief moment and nodded. 'I am quite open-minded, Miss Astin and your information was correct and most useful in the last case. I shall try not to mix it with fact however until I can prove it.'

'Of course, Detective. And you Mr Martin?'

'I too accept your source of information and will be discreet.' Bennet glanced around the room. 'Do we have company?'

'Yes.' Only Phoebe could see and hear Mrs Tochborn, although Phoebe suspected Julius could as well. Uncle Reggie – a regular visitor to her rooms in his spirit form – claimed Julius could see him but a glance at Julius's countenance gave nothing away to confirm it. Phoebe gave Bennet a small reassuring smile. She accepted he might be willing to hear her observations but she sensed he was fearful of the other side, the company she kept, and she understood that. 'A reminder if I may? Believe or disbelieve as you see fit, but please do not share this information or attribute it to me for my family's sake.'

All parties agreed and Julius moved to stand beside her in a show of support as they grouped around the body of Mrs Tochborn laid out on the table. Harland and Bennet positioned themselves at the heads of the table and Lilly stood beside Ambrose on the opposite side of Phoebe and Julius.

'This is the lady you are seeking, Detective and Mr Martin,' she said and pulled back the shroud to show the deceased lady.

'She looks troubled,' Ambrose observed.

Phoebe grimaced. 'Yes, I thought the same, and I am not sure I can do much to improve Mrs Tochborn's countenance. But she assures me her family know her no other way.'

Harland stepped forward studying Mrs Tochborn's face, her colour, and her scent. 'I see no evidence of poisoning, but I am still inclined to ask for an autopsy.'

Lilly leaned forward eagerly. 'You believe her to be murdered, Detective?'

Harland stopped and straightened. 'Have we the same arrangement as last time, Miss Lewis? If I keep you abreast of my investigation you will seek advice on what can and can't be printed and show discretion?'

'On my word, Detective,' Lilly said.

He nodded. 'I have no evidence to say she may have been murdered, but I am inclined to check. I want to ensure the accusation doesn't arise when it is too late and Mrs Tochborn is buried.'

'Preferable and cheaper than digging up the body,' Ambrose agreed.

'Would you like us to return the body to Tavish?' Julius asked referring to the coroner, Dr McGregor at the morgue.

Phoebe answered before Harland had a chance. 'Detective, by all means, do the autopsy if you wish but Mrs Tochborn tells me she does not believe she was murdered.'

Ambrose glanced around. 'Is it Mrs Tochborn that is with us now?'

Phoebe looked to the chair below the high ceiling window and smiled at the demure lady who looked older than her years from the toll life had taken on her.

'Yes, Mrs Tochborn is here and pleased to be at rest. As you no doubt know, Detective, she was ill for a brief time and succumb to her illness. She says only her doctor and her companion were with her in the last few days before death.'

'Ah,' Lilly said as if enlightened and with a glance to the corner where Phoebe was looking. 'This is Mrs Tochborn whose son—'

'Yes,' Phoebe said in a low voice. 'The ransom was paid and James, aged ten at the time, was never returned.'

'Is that not an old case though?' Ambrose asked and offered his apologies in the general area he believed Mrs Tochborn was sitting. 'Or are the police reinvestigating it?'

Harland shook his head in the negative. 'No, just reviewing it in the light of the claimants.'

'Why do you believe Mrs Tochborn was murdered, Harland?' Julius asked and Phoebe saw Mrs Tochborn lean forward, keen to hear the detective's answer.

'I thought it a possibility given that from what I have read in the newspaper and my files, Mrs Tochborn was about to accept one of the two claimants as her son,' Harland said. 'He would inherit a considerable estate if proven to be so.'

'But… if Mrs Tochborn died and the matter did not get to court or he lost his supporter – that being Mrs Tochborn – then the case has less chance of winning,' Lilly finished.

'Precisely so,' Harland agreed, 'and that is a strong motive for murder.'

Phoebe looked to Mrs Tochborn and back to the party before her. 'Mrs Tochborn says again she was not murdered.' She saw the look of frustration on Harland's face as he moved back a step and appeared to be considering how to manage the situation.

'But for your records, it is probably best you undertake the autopsy, Harland,' Julius said with an apologetic glance at Phoebe. 'At least if the matter is raised down the track, you have cold, hard facts and we will not need to resurrect the body. We will deliver Mrs Tochborn to Tavish this afternoon.'

'Thank you, that is for the best,' Harland said and he exhaled, relieved for the support. 'Forgive me, Miss Astin.'

'I understand completely, Detective, no apology is necessary. We both have our jobs to do.' She did not turn to look at Mrs Tochborn who gave a frustrated sigh that her body would be subjected to the procedure.

'So, were you to find Mrs Tochborn wasn't poisoned to stop the claimants, is that the end of your case, Detective?' Lilly asked, discouraged at seeing the story slipping through her fingers.

'There is still a case for fraud and false identity, is there not?' Ambrose asked Harland. 'I imagine the claimants will be charged if they do not win their case, but that will not need your involvement, Harland, surely?'

'No, my role is only in the death of Mrs Tochborn if murder is proven and the family is under suspicion. Then, by default, the claimants may both be at risk as their death will put an end to any claim,' Harland responded. 'But, in the spirit of disclosure as Mrs Tochborn is present, my brief is ambiguous at best, so I am open to anything that may close the old case and contribute to the current case with the claimants.'

'What is the family seeking from you, Bennet?' Julius asked.

'I am yet to meet them but the letter wishes me to investigate both claimants and their authenticity. A butcher and an inmate at an asylum, I believe.'

Harland nodded that Bennet's facts were correct.

'We are forgetting our source of information who called this meeting, the link to the lady herself,' Ambrose said with a nod to Phoebe. 'What have you, Sister?'

'There is a bigger issue at play, I believe.' Phoebe looked at Mrs Tochborn. 'I do have your permission?'

The lady nodded and said, 'Yes, my dear. I value your help, thank you.' With that, she faded from sight.

Phoebe turned her focus onto Detective Harland Stone. 'Mrs Tochborn has left, I suspect she does not want to hear it spoken of again but I do not have all the answers. She says her son is on the other side, with her.'

Harland groaned, Bennet cheered that he now knew the claimants to be fake and he had but to prove it, and Lilly exclaimed, 'Oh my!' Julius and Ambrose exchanged looks. Phoebe's word was never in doubt.

'Then I believe it to be true,' Ambrose said, 'Phoebe is never wrong. But what do you do with that?' He looked from Harland to Lilly to Bennet.

'What indeed,' Harland said running a hand over his face.

'There is more,' Phoebe said and gave them an apologetic look. 'Mrs Tochborn said she never had a son. The child is a fake.'

Chapter 7

M r Alex Cowan, editor of *The Courier* was not a morning person, or an afternoon person for that matter, and having in front of him fresh-faced and enthusiastic, Lilly Lewis, looking pretty and eager, and Fergus Griffiths, a ruffled young man with his mop of brown hair, and intelligent dark eyes – both brimming with their youth and reminding him of himself as a younger journalist – did nothing for his cheery disposition.

At the mention of the name 'Tochborn', he waved a hand dismissively.

'I've already got a reporter covering the Tochborn case and a few other court matters. It is as dull as dishwater. What else have you got?'

Lilly's heart sank; it was not supposed to go like this, she needed to turn up the enthusiasm, she needed to sell the story like you would sell a newspaper. With a hasty breath, she added, 'Mr Cowan, the Tochborn case is about to blow wide open and Detective Harland Stone has agreed to allow us access to him to report on it. We will have the public snatching our copies from the hands of the paper boys!'

Mr Cowan looked doubtful but did not dismiss her out of hand. 'Blow wide open, hey? Righto, young lady. You've got five minutes to make your case and if you fail, you'd better have something good to back it up.' He sat back, webbed his fingers across his sizeable girth and glared at her.

Lilly could feel Fergus stiffening beside her. She could do this, she told herself and leaned forward, taking a quick breath and speaking rapidly, 'I only need one minute, Mr Cowan and picture this. Detective Stone has ordered an autopsy to see if the lady in question was murdered by the family who does not wish her to support a claimant; two claimants will be in danger if it is true she was murdered by the family, so that they may never see the inside of a courtroom; a trial where a madman and butcher must prove they are her son kidnapped at ten years of age; the family hiring a private investigator to derail the claimants and we have access to the private investigator on the job; and a rumour which we will investigate, that the child was a fake and either did not exist at all or was not a Tochborn by blood!'

'Bloody hell!' Mr Cowan leant forward slamming his hands on the table. 'It's a bloody vaudeville production in the making!'

Lilly looked to Fergus and her eyes relayed an apology. She was sure Mr Cowan would jump at it. Their other story choice was a possible smuggling ring operating on the docks which Fergus got a lead on, but witnesses willing to speak were light on the ground.

'Brilliant! Do it.'

Lilly snapped, gaping at Mr Cowan and just as quickly hid her surprised look replacing it with one of confidence so he did not change his mind.

'Check and double-check your facts, both of you,' he barked. 'The Tochborn family has money and I don't want them on my back. Keep the stories coming and if it starts to build, you'll get top billing. Use our court illustrator as needed.'

Lilly could have kissed him with joy but refrained, rising, and sporting a grin she could not hide.

'Thank you, Mr Cowan, we won't let you down,' Fergus said and jumped to his feet beside her.

'When will I get my first story?' Mr Cowan asked.

'Today, Sir,' Lilly assured him. 'We'll do the set-up story today and promise to keep the public abreast of it as it unfolds.'

'We will immediately establish ourselves as the best source for information on this story and keep it coming,' Fergus said.

'Make sure you do,' Mr Cowan muttered. 'I'll let the court reporter know he can drop it from his list as you two will cover it. Get to it then,' he demanded and Lilly needed no further invitation to make herself scarce. There was work to do and no one stayed longer than necessary in the editor's office.

Detective Harland Stone was no stranger to asylums. Over the years, several of his cases had led him inside their walls, and as a young police officer, several of his arrests found their way there. His young partner, Detective Gilbert Payne, was not as relaxed. They entered the foreboding gates of the Woogaroo Lunatic Asylum with its austere façade and cheerless interior and made their way to the attendant who would lead them to the claimant – the man now aged 30 who believed himself to be James Tochborn.

'Do not worry, Gilbert, they will not mix up us with the inmates,' Harland assured him and Gilbert smiled.

'I hope not, Sir, although I did see the surgeon-superintendent's report in the newspaper just recently, and there are 861 patients in residence of which 493 are men and 368 females, and only four discharged this month. So, it is not easy to get out.'

Harland smiled at his fact-gathering protégé. 'I shall vouch for you if you vouch for me.'

'They can be convincing, Sir. I have read that some patients believe they are still in employment and present as doctors or businessmen and are very respectable. One would not guess they are residents.'

'Interesting,' Harland said. 'Perhaps that goes some way to explaining why the patient we seek believes himself to be James Tochborn, although I suspect someone has put that idea in his head.'

'This way please, gentlemen,' the guard said and led them to a room where they were to wait for the inmate and his representative. The two men were not there five minutes before three men entered and introduced themselves as the man in question – William Varsewell – and his two brothers, Edgar and Duncan. The men shook hands and Harland surmised Edgar was the eldest and very much in charge. Duncan looked to him often, and William looked at neither of them nor did he speak.

'Oh my, there is a resemblance,' Gilbert announced to Harland's frustration.

'I'm telling you our brother is James Tochborn,' Edgar said and sat, crossing his arms across his chest and looking defensive before Harland had even begun his questioning. The two brothers were big men, labourers of sorts, with thinning hair and skin roughened and aged by the sun. Their relation, William, looked nothing like them. He had the doe-eyed look of a man haunted, his face gaunt, and his body slim, his colouring completely different – he did very much look like the young James Tochborn with his large brown eyes and thin lips. Harland would not have been surprised if William was an artist or poet. He addresses his query to William directly who looked him in the eye; Harland was not expecting that.

'Mr Varsewell, why are you in here?' He kept his voice low and calm so it did not sound accusatory but simply curious.

Duncan spoke before his brother could answer. 'You can call him William, he prefers that. But my brother does not speak.'

Harland kept his attention on William trying to read the man who was his age but looked a decade older; the facial hair and full beard ageing him. This time, Harland hoped Gilbert would speak up with one of his facts, and he was not disappointed.

'I fear how the judge might consider the case if one of the major claimants cannot speak for himself,' Gilbert said and Harland gave a subtle nod.

'He can speak,' Edgar said and gave his brother permission.

William swallowed, started, and stopped again as if testing his voice. He then spoke in a manner that indicated an educated man. 'I was brought here a few years back after I was found drunk and wandering, speaking in French. My brothers came to claim me, but I couldn't remember who I was, I was violent the authorities told me. I have been here ever since.'

'Do you recognise your brothers now?' Harland asked and saw them both bristle beside William. He would prefer to interview the claimant alone but persisted for now.

'Yes.'

'Of course, he knows us,' Edgar retorted. 'Dad and Mum brought William home one day, said he was our new brother and we were to treat him as such. They had collected him from the orphanage. We never asked any questions.'

'I was ten,' William said. 'I don't remember where I had been before that.'

'See?' Duncan said, gloating. 'Before that, he was a Tochborn and I suspect he lost his memory when kidnapped. The shock and all that. Mum and Dad probably thought they were doing the right thing looking out for him.'

'He has the same scar as James Tochborn had above his eyebrow,' Edgar pointed to it, 'and James Tochborn was tutored in French, he was fluent, like our William here.' He nodded to the quiet man before them.

While the men spoke, William stared at Harland, his expression unreadable. Perhaps he was insane, Harland mused, or perhaps he does not care what becomes of him. He could imagine how William Varsewell got that scar and it was likely at the hands of his "brothers". What would this man in an asylum do with the Tochborn fortune?

'If you have no objections, Detective Stone,' Gilbert leaned in and spoke to the brothers, 'perhaps Edgar and Duncan can show me how William lives now?' he asked. 'You will both have to accompany me as I need to ask some more personal questions that might distress your brother. He is safe with Detective Stone.'

The two men looked at each and given it was a police request, agreed with reluctance. Harland gave Gilbert a grateful look but was concerned and surprised by the young man attaching himself to two men of their ilk. Most brave, or foolish perhaps.

After they left the room, Harland studied the man who claimed to be James Tochborn.

'Is there nothing you can remember of your first ten years, William?'

The potential claimant frowned but remained perfectly still and calm. 'I can remember nothing from last week.'

'Is it because you don't wish to or because of medication?'

William considered the question. 'I have had no reason to remember before. This is my home now.'

'Do you recognise those men as your brothers?'

'I could not say.'

Harland refrained from sighing. 'William, do you want to be recognised as James Tochborn? What would you do as the heir to the Tochborn fortune?'

'My name may be James Tochborn, and I may have relatives who own me like Edgar and Duncan, but no one has come to claim me before, in the years I have been here. I need no fortune; this is my home.'

'So, your brothers only arrived recently?'

'Yes.'

'Do you recall going to live with them when you were collected from an orphanage or did they tell you that?'

'I have no memory of being in an orphanage but they seem familiar. It is not a good memory though, they were not kind.'

Harland nodded, waited for a beat and tried again. 'You have been very forthcoming, William, thank you. One more question, thinking back on your early childhood, do you have any memories of your mother, your family or your childhood home?'

William smiled. 'Yes. Some days I remember things.'

Harland waited patiently and was rewarded when William continued.

'When the warm bread is delivered here in the morning, I can remember being in the kitchen and being given a generous serving with lashings of butter. I can remember a song, a tune that a woman would sing while I was with her in the kitchen.'

'Who was the woman?' Harland asked gently not wishing to derail their discussion now.

William placed his hand on his heart. 'I believe she was my mother. I like to believe that.'

Harland gave him a reassuring smile as if he would not steal his happy memory. 'I would love to know what was the song. Will you tell me?'

In a very low voice, William Varsewell began to sing a nursery rhyme: '*Rock-a-bye baby, in the treetop, when the wind blows, the cradle will rock, when the bough breaks, the cradle will fall but Mumma will catch you, cradle and all.*'

Harland frowned; he was sure that was not the original lyrics but across from him William gave a laugh. Then he said nothing more until the brothers and Gilbert re-joined them.

After bidding the men farewell, Harland waited to discuss the visit until they were clear of the premises and breathing the fresh air of the free. He turned to his partner, not adverse to giving praise when praise was due unlike some of the seniors in the police force. 'Thank you, Gilbert, well done, although I did fear for your safety going off with those two men.'

Gilbert chuckled. 'As did I, but I saw guards on every corner so I was not too worried. They did not provide much that was useful. Both brothers said again how William came home one day with their parents and stayed. That even then he was quiet and not all there... as the eldest expressed it. William's room in the asylum had nothing sentimental in it and no portraits or mementos.'

'Interesting.'

They walked a distance to the entrance gate and awaited a hansom cab, one appearing minutes later. Once settled and en route to meet with the butcher who also claimed to be James Tochborn, Gilbert said, 'I did find out that the family had a connection with the Tochborns.' The comment grabbed his superior's immediate attention.

'Well done, Gilbert, in what capacity?'

'They claimed an uncle – their father's brother – was a stable hand and his wife worked in the kitchen at the Tochborn estate.'

'Hmm, that is interesting. They are domineering brothers,' Harland said with a sigh. 'I worry regarding the motives of the family and who might be looking after William's best interests.'

'Then he might be in the best place, Sir,' Gilbert suggested.

'Perhaps you are right. His memories were few... the smell of baking bread, eating in the kitchen and a woman he believed to be his mother singing the nursery rhyme *Rock-A-Bye-Baby* to him.'

Gilbert looked surprised. 'That is a troubling rhyme.'

'It is? Why so, Gilbert?' Harland indulged the young man.

'Well, Sir, I read a book about the story behind some nursery rhymes, they are rather nasty.'

Harland thought on it for a moment. 'That is true. Humpty Dumpty falls off a wall, Jack and Jill went up the hill but Jack fell down it, if memory serves me, and those three poor blind mice never had a chance.'

Gilbert chuckled. 'Right you are, Sir. But *Rock-A-Bye-Baby* is about an illegitimate child.'

Harland, alert with interest, looked at his partner. 'Go on.'

'It's a reference to an illegitimate baby boy who was smuggled into the birthing room of the Queen, so that King James and the Queen had an heir, a Catholic heir. The wind mentioned in the rhyme is when the Protestants blew them all away – when the cradle rocks, the bough breaks, and down they all came, the fall of the monarchy.'

'The child is a fake,' Harland almost whispered.

'Sir?'

Harland was not ready to tell Gilbert of Miss Astin's discussions with the spirit world, and he cleared his throat and added. 'You did very well today, Gilbert, very well, thank you. I fear we have more to prove than two false claimants.'

Chapter 8

I t was Phoebe's turn to host *The Vexed Vixens* and
they gathered at Phoebe's family home, all three guests
arriving in a timely manner. Her grandparents – Randolph
and Maria – were heading out to the theatre and Phoebe had
the residence to herself for several hours.

'Welcome ladies,' Randolph said as he appeared resplendent
in black tie with Mrs Astin dressed glamorously beside him
with her evening jewellery glittering.

Kate, Lilly and Emily greeted Phoebe's grandparents and
spoke with her grandmother as Randolph fetched a hansom
cab. The gracious senior lady enquired after each of them.

'Miss Kirby, your lovely red hair reminds me of my
grandmother.' Maria Astin sighed placing a hand on her heart.
'The Scottish-Irish side of the family that is, we don't talk

of the other side... black sheep all of them. But I believe my grandmother had a fiery temper to match the colour of her hair.'

Kate thanked her. 'Fortunately, I am not quick to temper but what I would give not to have the skin that freckles. I am not made for this climate.'

'Luckily your business keeps you indoors then,' Emily offered, whose complexion, by comparison, was more tolerant of the sun, and her appearance quite the opposite of Kate as she was tall and slim, with dark hair and dark eyes. Some might say exotic.

'And you are looking resplendent, Miss Yalden. Pray tell, how is your School of Deportment faring?' Mrs Astin asked.

'Thank you for asking, Mrs Astin. I am fortunate to have plenty of young women attending, and some of them will graduate as young ladies.'

Mrs Astin laughed and looked remarkably like Phoebe when she did so. She continued, offering a kind word to Lilly next, 'And you Miss Lewis, a famous reporter!'

Lilly laughed. 'That is my desire, Mrs Astin, but one story does not a reporter make or so my editor likes to remind me. I now must keep it up.'

Randolph re-entered the room. 'We are ready my dear,' he said to his wife and then turned to the ladies. 'I hope you have an enjoyable night, ladies, and you will not be disturbed. Ambrose is rumoured to still live here but we rarely see him.'

Phoebe laughed and kissed them as they departed. 'Rest assured; I shall send him off if he dares intrude on the *Vexed Vixens*.'

As they seated themselves at the table to partake in the light supper Phoebe had organised, Kate said in a low voice, 'I would be most happy to see your handsome brother, Ambrose. Or Julius for that matter.'

'I don't know where Ambrose is this evening; he was still at the office when I departed. Grandpa is right though. I am sure Ambrose thinks this is a hotel.' Phoebe smiled and passed the dishes around the table to her guests.

'He did not wish to move in with Julius?' Emily asked, helping herself to a large serving of shepherd's pie. 'My favourite,' she said by way of explanation and then added, 'the pie, not your brother, but I am sure Mr Astin is held in equally high regard.'

The ladies laughed.

'Julius likes his privacy,' Phoebe said answering Emily's question. 'But if Ambrose wants to find his own residence, Julius has offered to assist when he is ready to make the move from home. Ambrose did look at taking rooms in a boarding house but Grandma would not hear of it and believes that none of us need move out until we are to marry.'

'I love being out of home,' Emily said. 'My mother keeps adding to my trousseau, as if it will attract a man on its own if I don't.' She laughed at the thought.

'I escape to my photographic studio daily so being at home each evening is not so bad,' Kate said with a small shrug, 'especially now that father has decided I can keep myself if need be. Prior to that, he was obsessed with the idea he and Mum would die and I'd be left alone with the inheritance of their property and every man out to marry me for my fortune.'

'I am sure you could sift through them,' Phoebe said kindly.

'I am not so sure,' Emily teased Kate. 'You are such a romantic, you will be swept up by the first man to whisper a sonnet to you!'

Kate laughed. 'Perhaps you are right, Emily. I would so love to hear a sonnet on the lips of a handsome man looking in my direction.'

'Well, three of my five brothers are still living at home, so there is never a dull moment,' Lilly said and all four ladies turned to look at the door as it banged open and two very loud young men entered laughing.

Ambrose and his cousin, Lucian, stopped immediately, seeing the four ladies staring at them.

'Oh, my apologies,' Ambrose said with a small bow. 'You did not tell me you were having a tea party, Phoebe.'

'If you refer to the gathering of the *Vexed Vixens* as a tea party again, Ambrose, you will understand the true purpose of our meeting and how we can live up to our name,' she threatened with an amused look. 'Ladies, you remember my brother, Ambrose, and this is my cousin, Mr Lucian Astin. May I present, Miss Emily Yalden, Miss Kate Kirby and Miss Lilly Lewis?'

Lucian, who looked so much like Ambrose that he could have been his brother rather than cousin, gave the ladies a respectful bow.

'Forgive the intrusion,' Ambrose said. 'Rest assured we are passing through. I just need to quickly change.'

'We shall entertain Lucian in your absence,' Phoebe said and indicated a chair for him. She saw the envious look on Ambrose's face as the chair was beside Miss Lilly Lewis. He asked to be excused and hurried up the stairs taking them two at a time.

'Thank you, but I shall stand,' Lucian said. 'The scene is too pretty to interrupt.'

Kate battered her eyelashes happily, Emily did her best not to snort at his flattery as ladies of good deportment do not snort as she regularly told her pupils, and Lilly gave him a wide grin, happy to take the compliment.

'And where are you off to then, Mr Astin?' Lilly asked.

'We are meeting Julius and Bennet at—' he stopped and amended his answer, 'catching up with friends.'

'Ah somewhere sinful then,' Lilly said interpreting his reticence.

'Never,' he said looking shocked and playing along, earning himself a laugh from the ladies.

'You look like you could be brothers, yourself and Mr Astin,' Emily, ever frank, said.

'They do,' Phoebe agreed. 'Julius takes after our father, while Ambrose and I, and cousin, Lucian, take after my mother and the fairer side of the family.'

'Lucky us,' Lucian joked and regarded Phoebe. 'I thought to find Miss Forrester in your company. Her brother Tom is fitting in very well and enjoying his apprenticeship.'

Phoebe looked surprised. 'I am so pleased. And as for Miss Forrester, you are a mind reader, Lucian. I was going to suggest to my friends this very evening that we issue Miss Forrester an invitation to the *Vexed Vixens*.' She turned to them. 'A recent acquaintance whom I believe would welcome the friendship and contribute a great deal. She is the manageress of our new dress store and most talented.'

'Ah, the lady that Julius admires,' Lilly said indiscreetly.

'Does he now?' Lucian said looking as if he would store that information away for use at a later date. Phoebe gave him a warning glance and he winked at her.

'Let us go, then,' Ambrose said rushing back down the stairs and having changed from his sober black work suit to something not much different. 'Ladies, our apologies for interrupting the *Vexed Vixens*. I hope we have not vexed you too much.'

'No more than usual,' Phoebe assured him and she saw he only had eyes for Lilly as he bid them goodnight and the two men departed.

As the door closed behind them, Lilly placed her cutlery down. 'This will not do.'

'What?' Phoebe said alarmed. 'Is something not to your liking?'

'Oh, the meal is lovely, thank you, Phoebe,' Lilly hurriedly added, 'but can we not somehow organise to get all of the handsome men in our lives into one place so we can share? I have five brothers, four of whom are still single. Phoebe, you have two extremely handsome and single brothers – Julius and Ambrose – and is Mr Lucian Astin a single man?'

'He is and yes, I guess he is handsome and eligible.'

'He's lovely,' Emily said most out of character and they all turned to look at her; she offered a shrug. 'I have a cousin to contribute,' she added. 'He is a solicitor, nearing thirty and therefore should be in search of a wife.'

'I have only two single sisters of age and no men to contribute as my brothers are both betrothed,' Kate pouted.

'But that is perfect, we need ladies as well,' Lilly said. 'We should ask friends such as Detective Harland Stone and Mr Bennet Martin, and I believe the coroner is single, Dr Tavish McGuire.'

'He is single, and keen on you, Lilly,' Kate said. 'But how do we bring everyone together?'

'A dance, or a ball,' Emily said thinking about it.

'One of Grandma's charity balls,' Phoebe said brightening. 'There is a Hospital Ball she has been speaking of for some time – Grandma is on the committee for the ball, and as we do very well with our share of the hospital's deceased, we do try to support it.'

'That is clever of your grandmother to work on committees that align with your business,' Kate said impressed.

'Exactly so,' Phoebe agreed. 'She does not like the death industry nor wishes to work in it, but she does considerable work crusading our business behind the scenes.'

'It is coming together nicely,' Lilly said. 'A gathering for socialising and we can perhaps take a table to support the cause if the tickets are not too expensive. We will need equal ladies, so there are the four of us, your two sisters, Kate, if they will come, Miss Violet Forrester might join us...'

'This is turning out to be a brilliant idea, Lilly,' Kate exclaimed.

'I do have them,' Lilly agreed and laughed at their reaction, adding, 'Sometimes.'

'I shall consult with Grandma and come back to you all post-haste,' Phoebe said smiling enthusiastically. 'Imagine if we were all related through our brothers, sisters or cousins!'

'We will be friends for life then, for sure,' Kate agreed and beamed.

'There is a bigger issue at play,' Lilly said and looked at each of them as she took a bite of her bread roll. The three ladies frowned in her direction.

'I can't imagine, what is it,' Phoebe said. 'We will all be together and it will be most proper.'

'Well, I for one believe we should declare where our interests lie so that we don't step on each other's toes or break hearts,' Lilly said.

Emily gasped. 'We can't do that, Lilly, because the decision may not be in our hands. For example, what if you were to say that you were in love with one of Phoebe's brothers but then he decided to turn his attention to Kate? Is she to turn him down for fear of offending you or losing your friendship, when they might be very happy together?'

Lilly frowned. 'I see your point, Emily. Yes, you are quite correct. Then do we declare whom we don't have an interest in so that we all know the gentleman is available even if he is making advances?'

Phoebe, Kate and Emily looked at each other.

'I cannot see a problem with that,' Phoebe said, 'as long as we keep this conversation strictly between us.'

'I think that should be fine,' Kate agreed. 'But it is our prerogative to change our minds should we find ourselves charmed and our first impressions wrong.'

All the ladies nodded their agreement most heartily.

'You do recall one of our rules when we founded the *Vexed Vixens* was to not spend our nights speaking of men,' Emily reminded them.

'Very true,' Phoebe agreed, 'and as the hostess, I shall take responsibility for this wayward conversation. So let us say we were led astray by my brother's homecoming, but as it is now related to a charity ball, we will hurriedly finish our discussion so we may move on to more important matters.'

'There is a dress fabric sale at Edwards and Chapman's in Queen Street, and bonnets and hats are nearly half price!' Kate said wide-eyed remembering she was intent on telling the group earlier.

'Well, yes, discussions as such,' Phoebe said with a small laugh. 'So, shall we do as Lilly suggests and advise whom we are not interested in a suit from? Unless we change our minds. It is rather fraught, isn't it?'

'Yes, but it does seem sensible to be honest about our feelings so that we do not miss out on an opportunity by believing we are being loyal to each other when we have no interest in the gentlemen in question,' Kate said.

Lilly looked pleased that her idea was accepted. 'I shall begin then.' She leaned forward as if delivering a piece of news of great interest. 'I admire but have no interest in pursuing cordial relations with Dr Tavish McGregor, so please feel free to lose your heart to him, ladies.'

Phoebe was quite sure she saw a pleased look on Kate's face. Dr McGregor and Kate had crossed paths when, on the odd occasion, Kate was called on to photograph a death scene. Most interesting, Phoebe thought.

'Noted,' Emily said officially. 'But that is a shame given he is a man with a learned profession. I know very few of the gentlemen we speak of, so I cannot rule anyone out, but I am open to love.'

Phoebe spoke up but not first without a glance around and lowering her voice. 'I very much admire and enjoy the friendship of Mr Bennet Martin, but do not wish to pursue a matter of the heart.'

Lilly gasped. 'He is strikingly handsome.'

Phoebe gave a small smile. 'Yes, I believe he is. But Mr Martin is not for me.'

'And I am not interested in Detective Harland Stone,' Kate announced unceremoniously.

All three ladies looked at her in shock.

'I saw his portrait in Lilly's newspaper, he is quite striking and obviously a clever man,' Emily stated as if Kate were mad.

'He is very amiable,' Lilly agreed.

'And very manly,' Phoebe added.

Kate shrugged. 'He returned the photo of the Beaming family to me after he solved the crime, and while he was quite the gentleman, he reminds me too much of my eldest brother.'

'He does look a little like him, and his mannerisms are not dissimilar,' Phoebe agreed having met Kate's family on several occasions.

'Yes. That will never do,' Kate said wrinkling her nose, 'especially in the boudoir.'

The ladies smiled and exchanged looks at Kate's boldness.

'Well, that is sorted, ladies,' Lilly pronounced. 'Now Phoebe dearest, find us an occasion to come together, be it the Hospital Ball or something similar.'

'I shall make it my priority,' Phoebe declared and was personally very happy that one of her dearest girlfriends had no interest in Detective Harland Stone at all.

Lucian grinned at Ambrose and clasped his shoulder as they walked to their local meet-up with Julius and Bennet.

'So that is the lovely Miss Lilly Lewis that you are swooning over,' he teased.

'Hardly swooning,' Ambrose said trying to gain the upper hand. 'She is a wonderful reporter.

'And quite a beauty with those blue eyes and lovely chestnut locks. She has a teasing manner about her also.'

'Yes, that she does,' Ambrose agreed thinking of her and smiling a little. He turned to see Lucian grinning at him and rolled his eyes. 'She is not interested in me; all she can see is Julius.'

Lucian shook his head. 'As much as I love my cousin, what is it that the ladies find so appealing that they must throw themselves at him?'

Ambrose shook his head with bewilderment. 'I suspect they think he needs caring for and to be cheered up. They all want to save him. Heaven help us.'

Lucian thought on the subject for a brief moment and then added, 'Well, feelings of affection are not mutual between your Miss Lewis and Julius, and sadly, Miss Lewis is only too aware. She will be pining soon and looking for love elsewhere and there will be your opportunity to win her hand.'

Ambrose glared at him. 'And how do you know all this?'

'Because Julius likes Miss Forrester whose brother I apprentice. Miss Lewis said so,' Lucian said looking smug at being the fountain of all knowledge.

'I suspected as much but have not had it confirmed; Julius has been very coy about his newest staff member. So, Miss Lewis said that, did she? Tell me everything word for word,' Ambrose insisted slowing his pace so they did not arrive at the club before he had heard the whole story.

Now it was Lucian's turn to roll his eyes. 'We are gossiping like the ladies.'

'Do not stall, Lucian, tell me.'

Lucian gave a small chuckle and matching his cousin's pace, relayed the few comments said of Julius and Miss Forrester.

Ambrose thought for a moment. 'Then I must find a way to get Julius and Miss Forrester together sooner rather than later and remove Julius from the eligible gentlemen list. The more I think on it, I believe Miss Lewis is correct; Julius is quite affected by Miss Forrester even if he has not progressed with his feeling or intent since she started working next door.'

'Moving Julius along is one way,' Lucian agreed and then clicked his fingers as if he had just had a brilliant idea. 'I have it, Ambrose!'

'Have what? What is it?'

'You are too interested in Miss Lewis. I am sure she can tell. You look like a keen lap dog in her company.'

'I do not!' Ambrose proclaimed appalled.

Lucian raised an eyebrow while Ambrose grumbled some more.

'So, get to it, what is your great solution.'

'Well,' Lucian said, 'when you are next in Miss Lewis's company you must appear more like Julius... aloof, distracted, grumpy even. Perhaps look at another lady or give her some special attention. If Miss Lewis feels your light has been removed from her, she may miss it.'

Ambrose exhaled. 'It all sounds rather exhausting and how long do I pretend to be my brother?'

'Do you want her or not?'

'Fine then. I shall think on it,' Ambrose said as they arrived at the club.

'Do not think too long,' Lucian warned. 'She is quite a catch and I would ask her out.'

Ambrose turned on him to find his cousin grinning and giving Ambrose a wink, Lucian dodged past him into the club, and an unamused and sober Ambrose followed... very much of similar nature to his brother Julius at that particular moment.

Chapter 9

P HOEBE ASTIN DID NOT have time to read the newspaper before work; of course, if she rose at the hour her grandparents did there would be time, but then the newspaper would need to be divided three ways, so it was a practical decision she told herself. Ambrose never rose any earlier than was necessary, arriving at work right on the hour most days to Julius's constant consternation. Today, however, Phoebe was most keen to see the paper and gratefully accepted it from her grandfather on arrival at work – her grandfather arriving some twenty minutes earlier.

'It is there, page four, my dear,' he said of Miss Lilly Lewis's article.

Phoebe thanked him, greeted Mrs Dobbs, and tucking the paper under her arm, hurried down the stairs to her workroom. She spread out the news sheet feeling a terrible responsibility to Mrs Tochborn. If the story was misreported or the detectives did not do her clients justice, Phoebe felt accountable, as if it was her fault that she had not conveyed the fears and wishes of clients adequately. She found the story immediately and read Lilly's introduction piece to a familiar crime.

MRS LEO TOCHBORN DIES
MELODRAMA NOT OVER – CLAIMANTS TO FIGHT FOR RIGHTS

By reporters, Lilly Lewis and Fergus Griffiths.

Mrs Henriette Tochborn, widow of the late Leo Tochborn Esq., expired suddenly in Brisbane on Saturday morning May 31st from a short illness. She had conversed with her housekeeper on some commonplace topics for a few minutes while her breakfast was delivered in bed, and when the housekeeper returned, Mrs Tochborn was dead. In Mrs Tochborn's hand was a newspaper featuring the story of her belief that the butcher, Arthur Horton, was her kidnapped son, James Tochborn taken twenty years prior aged ten.

Without an heir, Mrs Tochborn's fortune will be divided among her relatives. The man she was intending to claim as her lost long son, the butcher, Arthur Horton – who fervently believes he is James Tochborn, the last claimant of the Tochborn estates – intends to now prosecute his cause in the courts. The second claimant, Woogaroo Lunatic Asylum inmate, William Varsewell's family intends to do the same.

Detectives Harland Stone and Gilbert Payne have requested an autopsy on the body of Mrs Tochborn to ensure she died of her illness and remove any potential speculation of misadventure.

The family of the deceased Mrs Tochborn has dismissed their previous private investigator and hired Mr Bennet Martin based on his success with the recent Beaming case, to determine the backgrounds of Arthur Horton and William Varsewell.

The Courier will offer exclusive insights and reporting on the findings of the autopsy and the claimants' legal proceedings.

Phoebe breathed again, there was nothing untoward in Lilly's story thus far. She closed the paper and looked up to see her great uncle in spirit nearby.

'Uncle Reggie!'

'Good morning, my favourite niece.' Her grandfather's younger brother often came to visit. The brothers had been close but death took Reggie at age 40 in a horse accident. Phoebe had not asked why he continued to return, he would say when he was ready, she had learnt that from her other visitors. She often wondered if her brother, Ambrose, would be like Reggie when he was 40 – they were of such similar light-hearted nature and infectious personalities. 'Is all well in the world, dear Phoebe?'

'All is well, Uncle Reggie, although I am hoping Mrs Tochborn returns.'

'She's gone to the morgue, has she not?'

'Yes, and her story is unfinished. She did not say what happened with her son – the son who she claimed was with her on the other side but a fake in this life. At least now we know the men claiming to be her son are not.' Phoebe shook her head. 'It is so odd. She was about to accept one of their claims before she departed this earth. I am worried I won't see her again and her story will remain unresolved.'

Reggie gave Phoebe a sympathetic look. 'You are a tender-hearted one, my dear. Let me share a secret with you.'

Phoebe brightened. 'You know something?'

'No, not about Mrs Tochborn,' he said dismissively, sitting on the chaise lounge, and crossing his legs with confidence, his hands draped along the top of the chair. 'But here is the thing, my girl... when you are dead, none of those earthly things matter. Mrs Tochborn won't care who gets her fortune, she is at peace now.'

Phoebe frowned. 'I guess so, but it would still be nice if justice was done. If I died tomorrow and I thought my family were left uncared for or someone was cheating me, I would be most cranky.'

'You could come back and haunt them as I do.'

She laughed at the suggestion and then paused, tilting her head to the side to study him. Here was her chance to ask as Uncle Reggie had introduced the topic. Did he want revenge for something? Was that why he was still with them? Was he really haunting someone? She could not believe it of her uncle. Phoebe was just about to ask a question of him when a visitor could be heard on the stairs behind her.

'Good morning, Phoebe.' Julius entered and came to join her, looking at the newspaper laid before her. She noticed he ignored Uncle Reggie, if he could see him. Nor did he ask whom she was speaking with if he had heard her conversing. Curiosity would demand it, surely. Most puzzling.

'Ah my most handsome, ambitious, and clever Great Nephew, good day to you,' Reggie said and faded from sight.

'Good morning, Julius. Did you have a pleasant night out with the boys? I believe Ambrose and Lucian were joining you after they interrupted our *Vexed Vixens* gathering.'

'Shame on them,' Julius played along. 'And yes, a good night and none of us is the worse for wear.' He did not elaborate which was true to form. 'Nothing untoward in the article?'

'No, it is very good. Do you know when we might get Mrs Tochborn back?'

'It depends on Tavish's workload at the morgue, but he thought midweek all going well.'

She did not speak for a moment to let Julius finish reading the article, his concern being any mention of *The Economic Undertaker* business attached to the Tochborn crime, or Phoebe's visions discussed, and he appeared pleased to find neither. Phoebe tried to gauge his mood but Julius showed so little light and dark shade that she could not, and decided now was as good a time as any to put him on the spot.

'I have something I wish to discuss with you.'

He looked at her surprised. 'Go ahead then.'

'The Hospital Ball is on next week and Grandma says tickets are still available.'

'Right,' he said, his eyes narrowing. 'We always donate to help with the running of it; they are a good client for us. Plus, Grandma gives her time freely.'

'I know all this, you are generous.'

He scoffed. 'Thank you, but I was not seeking praise.'

'I know that too, but you are generous.'

Julius gave her a suspicious look. 'Did you have something you wanted to discuss with me about the ball?' he cut to the chase, not comfortable with commendation.

'Yes. I thought this year, perhaps we could attend. The business need not pay for it if you have already donated, but a night of dancing and socialising could be good for all of us.'

Julius grimaced. 'I will happily buy you a number of ball tickets, Phoebe, if you will represent *The Economic Undertaker*. How many do you want? Will you take your lady friends?'

She noticed he was backing away toward the stairs as if ready to bolt should she commit him to attend.

'I am not trying to matchmake you, do relax, Julius' she retorted and his look of disbelief made her laugh. 'Okay, maybe a little, but—'

'I can't think of anything I would like to do less, than have to dance with numerous young ladies pushed my way by mothers keen to see them settled, and you plying your girlfriends on me as well. Take Ambrose and Lucian as your guests, they will love being the centre of attention.' His tone brooked no further discussion but Phoebe was nothing if not persistent.

'I wish for all of us to go. Last night, the ladies of the *Vexed Vixens* met...'

'Ah, I see,' he said to her annoyance. 'You four ambitious ladies decided to get ambitious about finding husbands?'

Phoebe was getting annoyed by Julius denying the importance of romance and dancing around the subject.

'Julius, you are right. It is foolish of us to wish for happiness. Forgive me for wasting your time, brother, please return to your matters of business.' She turned her back to him and organised her make-up for today's work. She waited, knowing her words would pain him and she heard Julius sigh, as expected. He was never one to fire back with a hasty reply he might regret. He once was, but the controlled Julius these days would not. He moved to her side so he was in his sister's line of vision.

'Forgive me, Phoebe. I would love to see you happy and I am a miserable sod.'

Phoebe looked up at him and grinned, a smile twitching at his lips.

'You are not a miserable sod, dear brother, but will you hear me out?'

He gave a small bow. 'You have the floor.'

'Excellent. Last evening, the *Vexed Vixens* determined we have many single friends and family members in our mutual acquaintance and we should introduce them. I suggested a ball hence we could enjoy ourselves and support one of Grandma's causes.' She paused but Julius did not interrupt and he managed a neutral expression. Phoebe continued, 'We also thought it might be good for some of our friendships to be expanded and also to be introduced to respectable members of the opposite sex.'

'I see,' he said and waited.

'So, we thought we could purchase tickets or two tables and invite yourself, Ambrose, Dr Tavish McGregor, your close friend Mr Bennet Martin, cousin Lucian, Detective Stone who is relatively new in town and may enjoy some new friendships, Emily has a gentleman solicitor cousin of age and Lilly has several single brothers of age. As for the ladies, it would be me, Kate, Emily, Lilly, Kate's two sisters, and of course there will be ladies outside of our circle in attendance. I thought I might ask Miss Forrester to join us.'

She kept the best for last, knowing that would be of interest to her brother and Phoebe was not disappointed as his expression betrayed him.

'That could be a good evening.'

'I believe so.' Phoebe grinned. 'But we all intend to pay our own way, there is no need for the business to step up, especially if you have already committed to a donation.'

'We have. But the business shall pay for the ladies' tickets. The men can purchase their own and make a donation as well, I will see to it amongst my circle. Harland, Lucian and Tavish can all well afford that.' He thought for a moment. 'Best to buy Ambrose's ticket when you purchase for the ladies, just in case.'

Phoebe laughed and clapped her hands together. 'Thank you, Julius, that is so exciting. I shall tell Grandma now and organise the allocation of tickets. Then I will let the girls know so we can all lock in the date and organise our gowns...' She stopped on seeing Julius smiling at her and gave a little shrug.

Phoebe was not normally caught up in matters of fashion or society.

'You are long overdue for some fun. Forgive my surliness earlier.'

'It is forgotten,' Phoebe assured him. 'Do you wish to invite your Miss Forrester personally?'

'No,' he said abruptly and then said in a more moderate voice, 'She is not my Miss Forrester' and added to Phoebe's surprise, 'although I would welcome that. But it should come in the hand of friendship from you. Don't you think?'

'I agree. But we will all be arriving with kin or friends; do you wish to offer to collect Miss Forrester and see her home safely?' She tried to make her suggestion sound as innocent and noble as possible but could tell Julius read her intentions. 'It would be the honourable thing to do,' she added and he nodded his agreement.

'If she wishes.'

'Thank you, Julius.' She brushed his cheek with a kiss and rushed past him up the stairs leaving Julius alone in her room and not seeing her uncle reappear or what came after.

Chapter 10

THE BUTCHER HURRIED THE two detectives into his small office at the back of the shopfront, leaving his workers to serve the customers.

'Sorry to delay your visit yesterday afternoon, gents, my aunt is not well and I am at her service,' Arthur Horton, claimant of the Tochborn inheritance said. He was a man of ruddy appearance and rough mannerisms but had a jovial face and from the reaction of his customers, appeared to be well-liked.

'Apology accepted, Mr Horton,' Gilbert spoke up when Harland didn't. 'I am often at the beck and call of my mother who believes her nerves are more important than police duty.'

Arthur Horton laughed a hearty laugh and even Harland smiled at his protégé. Once the three men were seated, Harland studied the claimant. Having seen Mrs Tochborn and a portrait of her husband, he could not see how this man could be her son, nor did he bear the resemblance to the 10-year-old missing boy like William Varsewell at the asylum bore.

'I know you are busy, please ask me what you need to and I'll answer honestly and openly.'

Harland nodded his thanks. 'Despite the passing of Mrs Tochborn, you intend to pursue your claim without her support?'

'Yes. I have the support of several of the extended Tochborn family members who believe me to be, well who I am, James Tochborn. It is also documented that Mrs Tochborn was to favour me as her claimant.'

'Her death was untimely,' Gilbert added.

'Not just from the perspective of being acknowledged,' Arthur Horton said and adopted a sad countenance, 'but after two decades, I believed I had been reunited with my mother and had found a home.'

Harland nodded. 'I am sorry for your reunion being short-lived.' It was as much as he could say without looking to support the claimant but not dismissing the death of Mrs Tochborn. 'We met with the other claimant, Mr William Varsewell, and he has the appearance of young James and speaks French. I understand you do not?'

'Ah, yes, the asylum inmate, a most curious thing.' Arthur thought for a moment on what matter Harland could not assume, and then said, 'I did speak French when I was younger, or rather James did if you wish to see us as separate entities, but I recall little of my French lessons these days. Do you recall the lessons learnt when you were a youth?'

'Yes,' Harland answered frankly. 'They were drummed into me with a cane to assist.'

Arthur laughed. 'Yes, I confess I remember those too, but language is different. You must practice it to retain it.'

'Like the piano,' Gilbert added then challenged himself, 'although you can always play but maybe not quite as well without practice, but you say you have lost the French words?'

Arthur Horton shrugged and smiled. 'Oh, I remember several of course – bonjour, adieu, merci, fille, garçon...'

He said the words with a harshness, and Harland surmised he had taken some quick lessons rather than studied the language.

Arthur Horton hurried on, 'As for looking similar to the only existing portrait of James Tochborn, then a man carrying my weight cannot create a fair comparison.' He touched his girth and smiled.

'Do you recall your tenth year, Mr Horton?' Harland asked, unmoved by the man's story.

Arthur Horton adopted a serious countenance. 'I have little memory of being snatched away from the breast of my family, Detectives, but I know that I was sent to sea, working as a ship-boy. Perhaps the kidnappers did that once they received the large payment so that I would never be found or be able to identify them. The ship I was on as a youth, *Bella*, sank and I was taken in by a family in the country. The head of the family was a butcher, hence my trade. They were good hardworking people.'

'And if we spoke to them, they would attest to taking you in?' Gilbert asked.

'Sadly, they have passed. I do have something that proves my identity.'

'Do tell,' Harland encouraged him.

'It is a delicate matter.' Arthur Horton cleared his throat. 'I have a genital malformation. My mother, pardon me, Mrs Tochborn, knew of it in her son and my doctor confirmed I have the same.'

'I see, thank you for your candour, Mr Horton,' Harland said.

They spoke for a while longer and then Harland realised what was happening. Mr Arthur Horton was cordial. People liked him, he had charmed Mrs Tochborn who wanted to believe he was her son. He would not charm Harland as he was seasoned, but he looked to his protégé to see if he was taken in. He was curious to find out and would question Gilbert about his impressions on the way back to the station.

The detectives thanked Mr Horton and exited via the front of the shop, encountering Miss Lilly Lewis arriving – young, pretty, flushed with the excitement of her story, and wearing a fetching shade of pale green.

'Detective and Detective!' she said as they stopped by her hansom cab to greet her. 'Here to stock up for the policeman's cook-up?'

'Very amusing, Miss Lewis,' Harland said giving her a grin and Gilbert laughed.

'I suspect the cuts are good given the patronage the shop is receiving,' Gilbert said and looked as if he might just go in and select an order for his mother.

'Have you met with the asylum inmate as yet?' Harland returned to matters of business.

'No, Fergus is on his way there now to cover that angle.'

'Good,' Harland said, 'not a place for a lady.'

'But by the looks of the housewives here, I shall be perfectly at home?' she mocked him and Harland glanced behind to the store and back at her.

'I believe you will stand out anywhere you go, Miss Lewis,' he said and surprised her with a compliment.

'Well thank you, Detective. Can I have a quote for my story since you are here and our meeting is opportune?'

He sighed and nodded, allowing her to ask a few questions while Gilbert reserved Miss Lewis's hansom for their departure.

On their way moments later, Harland turned to his protégé. 'Tell me your thoughts on the claimant Mr Arthur Horton, Gilbert. There is no right or wrong answer, I am just seeking any observations you might have made.'

Gilbert nodded and settled back in his seat opposite his superior. He thought for a moment and Harland allowed him the time to gather his thoughts. Gilbert normally said what was on his mind immediately, and Harland was pleased he was formulating a response and not being impulsive. What he said next made Harland realise Gilbert had great potential indeed.

'Sir,' the young man cleared his throat, 'I am sure you know the famous saying that some people attribute to St. Ignatius Loyola, and others attribute to the philosopher, Aristotle. It says, "Give me a child until he is seven and I will show you the man." Be that true, then Mr Arthur Horton is no James Tochborn.'

Mrs Dobbs had been worked off her feet this morning with the comings and goings at *The Economic Undertaker.*

'Do take a break, Mrs Dobbs, you must be exhausted,' Randolph said after seeing several more customers out the door.

'Deary me, no, but thank you, Mr Astin. Our generation is not afraid of a little hard work, are we? At one stage in my younger years, I had a large brood of children, plus a husband, and parents all in one small house, and I am sure I never left the stove. But thank you for your kindness.'

'Not at all. You are right, we are hard workers from hardworking stock but I'm slowing down,' he joked. 'I wish not as many people decided to up and die in June.' He sighed as they took a moment to sit at the table in the kitchen and enjoy a quiet cup of tea, the pot still warm from the last clients. 'Really, Spring is a lovely season to depart.'

Mrs Dobbs laughed with restraint; it was a funeral home after all. Randolph was about to speak but paused hearing footsteps hurrying up the steps from Phoebe's room. He glanced at Mrs Dobbs, eyebrows raised, waiting. Moments later, Phoebe raced into the tea room looking flushed and happy.

'Well, my dear?'

'He thought it was a good idea, Grandpa, and said the company is to pay for the ladies and Ambrose and to secure the tickets now.'

Mrs Dobbs clapped her hands together, pleased.

'You were right, Mrs Dobbs,' Phoebe grinned, keeping her voice low less Julius should appear, 'he did see the merit of the ball once I mentioned inviting a certain lady.'

Mrs Dobbs gave Phoebe a wink. 'I thought he might.'

'I shall go and see Grandma immediately if nothing is pressing?' Phoebe asked.

'Nothing more important than that, my dear,' Randolph said encouraging her and Phoebe gave a light laugh and departed with a wave.

'Ah, to be young again.' Mrs Dobbs sighed.

'I am not so sure I want to go another round of youth. But as to the Hospital Ball, Mrs Astin and I will be attending, would you like to attend, Mrs Dobbs?' Randolph asked. 'Bring a friend and enjoy some dancing and socialising!'

She looked at him surprised and then smiled. 'You know, I think I might enjoy that, Mr Astin.'

'I shall secure you two complimentary tickets; Mrs Astin is on the committee,' he said tapping his nose. 'Now, if you will excuse me?' he asked looking bemused. 'I have not heard Julius come up from Phoebe's office and I'm curious as to what he is doing down there. Please finish your tea and enjoy the brief break while we have it.'

'By all means, Mr Astin, and thank you sincerely, my friend and I shall look forward to the ball immensely.'

Randolph departed and slowed his steps as he approached the stairwell. It was not that he wished to spy on Julius, it was just that his eldest grandson had always been a bit of a mystery to him. The lad had been the happiest of boys until his parents were taken from him and then he had never been the same. His boyhood was stolen and once he was back on track – after a brief rebellious period – Julius took his responsibilities too seriously and all attempts by his grandparents to invite him to enjoy his childhood were ignored. Ambrose and Phoebe were young enough to find happiness in day-to-day activities and not worry about where their next meal was coming from, but not Julius. He worked a paper run, secured himself a school scholarship, and took responsibility for his siblings. He had stepped up, contributed to the family and now, looked after them all. He was the grandchild Randolph most wanted to see happy.

From the top of the stairs, Randolph could not see Julius but he could hear the timbre of his voice, speaking quietly, calmly, but to whom? Was Ambrose downstairs now? Randolph was sure he had not heard his other grandson enter. He took a few steps down the stairs, silently, curiously. His grandson stood by the wall, looking out of the high window with a view to the stables that Julius was tall enough to see through. His hands were clasped behind his back and he was listening. He nodded and said something.

Then Julius wheeled around on sensing someone nearby, and Randolph casually continued down the stairs, noting Julius's momentary look of alarm before he schooled his features to give away nothing.

'I am sorry to interrupt. Who were you talking with, lad?' Randolph asked with a glance around the room.

'No one, Grandpa, myself,' he said and moved to the stairs. 'Did Phoebe see you?'

'She did. She's very excited.'

'Good,' Julius said with a smile, and passed Randolph on the stairs, heading upwards. Within seconds, he was gone.

Randolph waited, he could sense nothing, see no one. But he said in a low voice, 'I wish I could see you, Reggie, if it is you. I miss you.' He waited a moment, turned and departed.

Chapter 11

BENNET MARTIN STRODE UP the hallway of the Roma Street Police Station, looking like a man who came from money, which he did. His polished shoes announced his every step on the tiles and his suits would cost more than a constable earned in a year. Seeing the desk sergeant was on the phone, he indicated his visit was to Detective Harland Stone and was waved permission. He was a familiar face now after the last case he had been hired to solve and had worked closely with the two detectives.

Bennet entered the room to find the young detective, Gilbert Payne, writing notes on the chalk board and Detective Stone pacing, looking deep in thought. He could have sworn he heard Detective Stone muttering the word "fake".

'Ah, Bennet, how is your case progressing?' Harland asked looking up at the man intruding on his thoughts.

'Good day, Harland and Detective Payne, I have made a good start. I hoped we could compare our notes if you were willing?' Bennet removed his hat and coat as if it were a foregone conclusion.

Harland nodded and indicated a seat in front of his desk for Bennet to sit, as he lowered himself behind his desk and both men faced Gilbert at the board.

'Shall I begin?' Bennet offered in a show of good faith.

'Please.' Harland nodded.

'I have met with the family who requested my services. The brother of Mrs Tochborn, Mr Lionel Ferris, who is an uncle to the missing boy, and Mr Joseph Ferris, a cousin on Mrs Tochborn's side. Both are adamant that neither claimant is legitimate and wish me to seek proof to prove that is the case.'

'Do you believe their intentions are honourable in protecting the estate or is it self-interest?' Harland asked.

'They admitted up front they would both be entitled to a share of the estate, but they claim their desire to see justice done outweighs that. I am inclined to believe them as both men seem to be independently wealthy and as the senior man, Lionel Ferris put it, they "don't want a scoundrel in the family" and they would rather see the money go to the church than an imposter.'

Gilbert wrote the men's names on the side of the board with Mrs Tochborn's details. He turned and addressed the two men sitting opposite, 'I would likely do the same. If I thought my sister was forming an attachment with an imposter or they were lining up to deceive her, I would want the claimants investigated. It is a matter of honour.'

'Indeed, if you had the means to challenge them,' Harland agreed and turned to Bennet. 'Did they offer any insights as to the men who claim to be James Tochborn?'

'Yes, and the notes from the private investigator they dismissed are quite thorough. The first claimant, Arthur Horton, paid a visit to try and curry favour with the men. Mr Horton has been very clever and has visited the family estates and met various people who knew Mrs Tochborn when she was a younger woman with a young son – himself, as he would have you believe.'

'He is gathering allies,' Harland said.

'And according to the Ferris gentlemen who have employed me, he has managed to acquire quite a few, including Mrs Tochborn's solicitor.'

'That is a powerful man to have on his side,' Gilbert agreed. 'Mr Varsewell in the asylum cannot do the same and visit for the purposes of supporting his claim, but I suppose his brothers could.'

'Very true, Gilbert. But I doubt the brothers have the skills or charm to edge their way into someone's favour like Mr Horton does,' Harland said. 'Do go on, Bennet.'

'The Ferris men tell me that by the time Mr Horton finished his tour, as they called it, he had convinced Mrs Tochborn that she had found her son again. Brace yourself,' he warned and Harland grimaced. 'Mrs Tochborn set Mr Arthur Horton up with a very generous allowance of one thousand pounds per year—' Bennet halted waiting for their shocked reactions and was not disappointed. He continued, 'And she gave him considerable additional funds prior to that which the Ferris gentlemen say he has used to research his namesake, James Tochborn.'

Harland inhaled sharply; his eyes narrowed as he thought. 'Thank you, Bennet, that is very useful.' He preceded to share their experience of visiting both claimants – the asylum inmate and the butcher – and invited Gilbert's contributions.

'And now,' Harland said in conclusion, 'we have a few new pieces of information from the birth records.' He nodded to Gilbert who fished for a piece of paper on his desk.

'Yes, Sir, there is no registration of a birth for a James Tochborn in 1860 or any years before or after,' Gilbert said. 'I have telegraphed Miss Lewis and asked her to see if there was any notice in the newspaper files of the announcement of his birth.'

'Was he born here?' Bennet asked. 'Not in England perhaps and they came here later?'

'No. It is recorded in the original police files at the time of the kidnapping that Mr Leo Tochborn claimed his son was born here,' Harland confirmed.

'Most odd,' Bennet agreed. 'I would understand if a family of poor means might not have registered the child but they are a well-to-do family.'

'And Mr Tochborn would have heralded an heir and announced it widely, I imagine,' Harland agreed.

'Unless there was no birth to announce and the kidnapped child was a fake,' Bennet said and then glanced to Gilbert realising he might not be privy to Miss Astin's other worldly insights.

'Fake? I have heard you say that a few times too, Sir,' Gilbert said looking from Bennet to Harland. 'Have I missed something?'

Harland grimaced and Bennet gave him an apologetic look, and turned his attention to his notes, leaving the situation to Harland to explain.

But before he was required to do so, Gilbert spoke up. 'You know, Miss Astin said Mrs Tochborn mentioned the child was a fake. A most intriguing statement,' Gilbert said and rubbed his chin in thought.

Harland's expression relayed his surprise. 'Miss Astin told you of her vision?'

'Yes, I was passing by after securing the appointments with the claimants and thought I would drop into *The Economic Undertaker* to offer you a lift back to the station, but you had left. Miss Astin generously asked if would I like to see Mrs Tochborn, and gave me a briefing that she said you would elaborate on when appropriate.'

'I see,' Harland said wondering how Gilbert reacted to Miss Astin's obscure discussions with the dead.

'It was in strict confidence, of course, Sir,' Gilbert assured him, thinking that was what his superior was concerned about. 'She said you and Mr Martin were in that confidence or I would not have mentioned it.' Gilbert looked stricken. 'Should I have whispered it then?'

Harland relaxed and chuckled. 'No. I confess Gilbert I debated whether to tell you as I was keeping Miss Astin's confidence, and I assumed a man with your penchant for facts would lean more to science than the spirit world.'

'There is a lot of speculation in science, Sir. I believe Galileo and even Charles Darwin were regarded with much suspicion until their ideas were proven.'

Bennet grinned. 'You are an intriguing young man, Detective Payne.'

Gilbert smiled. 'Also, my grandmother used to regularly see her soothsayer and my sister thinks she can read tea leaves. As Shakespeare wrote, "There are more things in heaven and earth, Horatio, than are dreamt of in your philosophy." I believe Miss Astin to be most sincere.'

'Thank you, Hamlet, as do I,' Harland teased his protégé and got a laugh from the young man. 'Back to business. This fake child... we need to know more. I am off to see Tavish at the morgue to see if he has a result from Mrs Tochborn's autopsy. Gilbert, will you see if the detective on the case twenty years ago is still alive and could make time to see us about the missing boy?'

Bennet laid his plans on the table. 'I am off to find as much background information on the two claimants as possible in the limited time I have. I must determine if Arthur Horton was indeed a ship-boy on the *Bella*, if his parents are really deceased, and how William Varsewell came to be adopted if he was indeed James Tochborn.'

'That will save us time if you can continue to share?' Harland asked.

'Of course,' Bennet agreed. 'Although the responses I receive might be different if it were the police asking the questions.'

'We will cross-check, I assure you,' Harland said. 'I would like to speak to your clients, the two Ferris gentlemen if you will leave their contact details. I also want to find out who worked for the Tochborns twenty years ago when James was kidnapped, and to speak with any staff who is still available. I want to know who saw that child and if he really did exist.'

Bennet leaned forward and taking the offered writing implements, hurriedly wrote the details for the Ferris men. 'I shall call in on Miss Lewis and chase up the newspaper birth announcement if one exists.'

'Thank you,' Harland said rising. 'Bennet, we shall speak again soon.'

Julius Astin looked up at the fine blue sky and saw everything a little brighter and a little crisper on this most lovely of winter days. He also appreciated the temperature more suited to his occupation when dressed in a dark suit and working outdoors for a portion of the day. Nevertheless, he could think of somewhere he would rather be and that was most unusual for the owner of *The Economic Undertaker*.

'Some days are too nice to be burying the dead and be clad in black,' he said with a small smile. He breathed in the crisp air.

Alarmed, Ambrose hurriedly asked, 'Is everything alright, Julius?'

'Yes, why wouldn't it be?'

Ambrose gave a huff of amazement. 'I have never heard you express that sentiment before in the years we have worked side by side. One might think you were in love.'

Julius groaned. 'It did not take you long to get there. Is this ball idea some concoction of yours and Phoebe's?'

Ambrose grinned. 'Do not flatter yourself, brother, I too have just heard of it, but I am very much looking forward to it. Besides, you would not have attended even if Phoebe and I did organise such an event. Now, you have a worm on the hook.'

Julius glanced over at Ambrose and grimaced before turning his attention back to the street and guiding their horses and hearse to the stables at the back of the business.

'A most unpoetic turn of phrase.'

'Forgive me. Shall I quote you a sonnet then? Now you are thinking of Miss Forrester and comparing her to a summer's day, or in this case, a winter's day?' Ambrose began to recite it: "Shall I compare thee to a summer's day? Thou art more lovely and more temperate". Ah, she is indeed.' He gave a small shrug. 'Unfortunately, that is all I can recall of the verse.'

'Just enough to hook the ladies then, and impress them with your poetic prowess?' Julius asked shooting his brother a grin as he pulled up in the yard. He handed the reins to the stable lad with thanks and jumped down from the hearse.

'Yes, but if the occasion calls for it, I'll bother to learn more. Fortunately or unfortunately, it hasn't to date.'

Julius shook his head at his little brother and was about to follow him inside when the back door of the dressmaking shop next door opened and the lady herself, Miss Violet Forrester emerged carrying a leaflet and accompanied by her senior dressmaker, Mrs Nellie Shaw – a woman in her forties and most efficient of nature. The brothers hesitated.

'I am sure they wish to speak with you,' Ambrose said.

'Stay,' Julius requested. He did not like being outnumbered and Ambrose could be charming when it was needed, a skill he believed himself to lack.

'As you wish,' Ambrose said with a small smile, keen to witness his brother and Miss Forrester in each other's awkward company for no other reason than to tease Julius later.

'Miss Forrester, Mrs Shaw, a beautiful day,' he said by way of introduction.

'Oh, it is, Mr Astin,' Nellie agreed. 'You wouldn't be dead for quids.'

'Which is not good for business,' Violet added and Julius laughed, which he noted made the ladies study him and smile as if they had sighted the rare plume of a strange creature.

'Fortunately, people do tend to turn up their toes more in the winter months than warmer months,' Ambrose informed the ladies earning another round of chuckles.

'May we have a moment of your time?' Violet requested.

'Of course,' Julius said. 'Do you want to step into the office or yours?' He noted neither lady was wearing a hat, no doubt having just stepped away from their machines on hearing the horses arrive back.

'No, we are happy in the fresh air, if you are?' Violet said and Julius gave a nod, not taking his eyes from her.

'Is something amiss?'

'On the contrary,' Violet said. 'Mrs Shaw's brother is exhibiting his saddles at the Brisbane Trade Exhibition in a few months and when Mrs Shaw showed me the leaflet, I wondered if a small stand promoting our mourning wear might bring in business and help spread the word of our services.' She handed it to Julius, their fingers touching momentarily and it took him several moments to focus on the leaflet after feeling her skin against his own. Ambrose leaned over his shoulder to read it.

'Have you exhibited before, Mr Astin?' Mrs Shaw asked.

Julius was pleased Ambrose answered as he was only just reading the leaflet now.

'No, Mrs Shaw, but I think it is a fine idea,' Ambrose said. 'We had considered it in the past, isn't that so, brother?'

'Yes,' Julius said. 'But we decided we might not claim to be economic if we were seen to be promoting. Hence the importance of our hearses being seen.'

'Ah, that makes good sense,' Mrs Shaw agreed.

Julius looked at Violet. 'But the mourning dress wear is a very different business and I believe these trade shows draw quite a crowd.'

Violet beamed up at him, pleased he did not dismiss the idea out of hand. 'We too believe it would help as we are relying on recommendations and passing trade at the moment. As we are starting to get orders from people planning for the departure of their loved ones, I believe this will be our biggest market.'

'Could you handle more capacity if business increased? I am also thinking we could offer a family discount for household mourning whether the family is large or small. What do you think?' Julius asked.

'Oh, that would be a great consolation to families in need,' Violet said looking to Mrs Shaw who nodded her agreement. 'And yes, we can always put on resources as demand grows, can we not?'

'As long as you can all fit into the office space,' Ambrose said. 'We could extend.'

'We can always convert the lunchroom to a workroom, Mr Astin,' Mrs Shaw said, ever practical. 'We can come next door for lunch.' She gave Julius a wink which he wasn't quite sure how to interpret but Violet stepped in and hastily added, 'I believe Mrs Shaw and Mary would welcome more of Mrs Dobb's sweets.'

'Ah,' Julius said and nodded, not having anything to add to that and giving silent thanks that Ambrose was beside him to make a similar jest about also enjoying his and grandpa's company. Julius re-joined the conversation asking, 'Shall I ask the lads in the stable to prepare the trap for you both so you may visit the organisers to enquire about a site and price?'

It was an enormous leap of faith to leave this in their hands for a man so controlling of his business and Ambrose's surprised expression reflected that.

'Oh no, Mr Astin, thank you,' Mrs Shaw said before Violet could get a word out. 'That is nothing to do with me, I was just supplying the leaflet, and I have a lot of work to do. Perhaps Violet is best to inspect the site with you, Mr Astin, as you will have a better idea of the business and budget.'

'Yes, that makes good sense,' Ambrose offered and nudged his brother, giving Mrs Shaw a conspiratorial smile.

Violet flushed slightly at the obviousness of Mrs Shaw's suggestion, but Julius looked as if that was the best idea he had heard that week, and Ambrose smirked happily beside him.

Julius nodded. 'I shall check my appointments and if you could do the same Miss Forrester, then we can confirm a day and time. Maybe tomorrow all going well?'

'Happily, Mr Astin,' she said with a nod and a small bow, and then the ladies retreated hurriedly back inside, while Julius stood watching Violet depart. He turned to see Ambrose watching him, rolled his eyes and headed inside, his brother laughing behind him.

Chapter 12

THE ASYLUM WAS A hive of industry in the morning. The patients had their assigned chores to do, that is, those who were of sound mind to undertake activities. Phoebe Astin chose today to visit. She did not tell her family where she was going, but merely said she had a chore to run. They would assume it was concerning the coming ball and some frippery like obtaining gloves or having a fitting. But it was not.

The deceased Mrs Tochborn had said the oddest thing to Phoebe before being returned to the morgue, and Phoebe had not shared it with the detectives or Mr Bennet Martin because she was not sure of the meaning herself. It was a message and she had promised to deliver it. She would take the opportunity to study the recipient and his reaction before reporting it to Detective Stone, if it were at all relevant to his case.

Phoebe felt no apprehension about entering the asylum; if she did not fear the dead visiting, she certainly did not fear the living. Fortunately, visitors were welcome and some poor residents never received any, she wondered if William Varsewell, the second Tochborn claimant was one of them. Phoebe did not know what to expect – Lilly's story today in the newspaper had said Mr Varsewell was a gentle soul with ambitious brothers. Phoebe hoped to have a moment alone with him.

She came dressed demurely which did not raise any eyebrows in the office of *The Economic Undertaker* this morning as her family had long given up on guessing what Phoebe might wear. Today, it was a straight long dark skirt, a matching fitted jacket, a white shirt underneath, and a straw boater hat trimmed with a red ribbon to add a little splash of colour to her outfit.

'William Varsewell is in our low-security wing, Miss, so you will not be in any danger,' the attendant said with a smile. 'At this time of the day, he's assigned to the carpentry rooms.'

'Ah, he has a trade.' Phoebe smiled pleased and noted the attendant was most happy to attend to her. That bodes well for gaining information.

'As such. He is not the faster nor the slowest of the workers, but his work is of quality.' The attendant laughed and added,

'He says that his hands understand what the timber wants to become – a drawer, a table, or a desk.'

'What a lovely thought,' Phoebe said with a smile as she walked beside the sizeable man towards the carpentry room. Several other visitors were in the garden and common rooms.

The attendant continued, 'But his favourite piece to make is a cradle, and I must say, he is very good at it.'

'A baby's cradle?' Phoebe's tone expressed her surprise.

'Yes. Initially, we left him to his own devices with the wood and took kit, and he produced a cradle that was a lovely piece of work. Let's just say his talent was recognised for commercial gain.' He gave Phoebe a wink as if it was a great secret that the asylum was as self-sufficient as possible and that they sold their goods. She was well aware that another asylum out west of Brisbane made coffins for local funeral parlours at a negotiated price.

'Are you related to William?' the attendant asked.

'No, I am not. I am bringing a message to him from an old friend, a lady who had just passed.'

'Is it likely to upset him?' The attendant frowned.

'No, it is a kindly message, I believe. But I will desist if I believe he is agitated.'

'Alright. Just call for help if you need it, Miss. There are several attendants on duty in the workshop.'

'Thank you, Sir, that is appreciated.'

They walked across a green lawn to a building with plenty of natural light on the lower floors where the workshop was located.

'So, William works on cradles that are sold to the outside world where real babies lay in them, loved by real parents? I wonder if that reminds him of his family or makes him sad,' she said to herself, not expecting a response, but the attendant had an opinion.

'Hard to say, Miss, but there would be a lot of men here who were never loved or wanted, I'd say. And the same goes for the women next door,' he said with a nod in the direction of another large building behind a stone wall.

The attendant led her into the room where she drew curious glances but offered a kind smile to all who glanced her way.

'William, you have a visitor,' the attendant said, stopping in front of a man with shoulder-length hair, a light beard, hollow cheeks, and large brown eyes that gave him a haunted look.

'Remember, Miss, if you need help,' the attendant said and indicated one of the staff in the corner. Phoebe nodded and thanked him again.

'You are a visitor for me?' William asked in a low voice and remembered his manners enough to rise.

'Yes, hello Mr Varsewell, my name is Miss Phoebe Astin. May I sit with you for a while?'

William glanced around. Phoebe had heard from Detective Payne of the domineering brothers and wondered if William was confused as to whether he was allowed to speak with her or not. Moments later he appeared to come to the conclusion that he could and invited Phoebe to sit. She thanked him, giving him a kindly smile, which appeared to relax William. Phoebe sat not too close nor presumed to touch the timber he was working on. She understood from her own trade how each person had their routine and manner of doing things.

'Did my brothers send you?' he asked.

'No, I am not acquainted with your brothers, and you and I have not met before either,' she said softly, 'but we both work in places that are quiet and away from people.'

'Do you work here too?' he asked with interest, resuming his work as they spoke, his hands gently chiselling the timber with a small carving knife that was too dull to do any harm to Phoebe but still allowed him to ply his trade.

'No. I work in a funeral parlour.'

William smiled with delight, making him look younger, although he was only a man of thirty. 'Do you get lonely?'

'No. I like my own company and I have the company of the deceased some days.' She tested him for a reaction. He did not register surprise. 'My brothers work there too and my grandfather. I met a lady recently who mentioned you to me.'

He looked up surprised. 'Was she dead?'

'Quiet so. Does that concern you? I will not mention it again if you prefer.' Phoebe gave him the option.

'No. We will all die soon enough. Does she know me then?' He continued to work slowly but Phoebe felt as if he concentrated on her every word.

'I cannot say as I do not know what she might mean to you. Her name when living was Mrs Henriette Tochborn.'

He nodded and said nothing for a while and Phoebe waited, watching him work. Eventually, he asked, 'She had a message for me?'

'Yes. I don't understand it myself but I hope you might.'

He nodded. 'I will hear it then.'

'Mrs Tochborn said to remind you of a nursery rhyme and to tell you that the bough has broken.'

He smiled slowly as if the meaning was dawning on him gradually. 'Ah, she knows my brother. He is there on the other side.'

'May I ask, William, who is your brother?'

'Me,' he said and then began to sing a nursery rhyme to himself as if he did not know Phoebe was even there.

She whispered goodbye, rose, and looking back from the door thought it a most poignant sight – the man making cradles and humming *Rock-a-bye baby* to himself.

Phoebe was so deep in thought she almost missed the hansom cab as it dropped off a visitor at the asylum and was about to leave. Leaping to her feet, she waved and called, and the driver stopped.

'Want a ride, Miss?'

'Yes, my apologies, I was miles away. Thank you for stopping,' Phoebe said and accepted the driver's assistance into a seat. 'Would you please take me to the Roma Street Police Station?'

'Of course, Miss. Are you alright?' the elderly driver asked with genuine concern.

'Perfectly so, I thank you.' Phoebe smiled at him. 'A little distracted with thinking.'

'Ah, it happens to the best of us,' the driver said jovially and Phoebe laughed.

As the hansom began its journey, she sat back and enjoyed the ride into the city; it wasn't often she got out and about during the working day. The back roads to the asylum soon disappeared and the streets became busier as the centre of town approached. The hansom passed by all sorts of industry en route to the police station at the far edge of the city. When the driver pulled over, she alighted and paid him with thanks.

It was a little intimidating entering the police station with so many men in uniform and people coming and going. She was not social by nature and was happier in her own company. Her world had always been her family and the *Vexed Vixens*. Allowing her eyes to adjust for a moment from the beautiful day outside to the darker interior, she spotted a counter with an older uniformed officer behind it.

'How might I help you, Miss?' he asked.

'Good morning. Would Detective Harland Stone be in, please? My name is Miss Phoebe Astin and I just need a minute of his time.'

'Miss Astin, I'm afraid he is out. But his partner, Detective Payne is in. Could he be of assistance?'

'He could indeed, thank you.'

She followed the detective down the hall and entered as he announced her.

Gilbert jumped to his feet. 'Miss Astin. Please come in, will you take a seat?'

'Thank you, Detective,' Phoebe said and moved to sit in front of his desk. Gilbert resumed his seat.

'I hoped to have a few moments of your time if now is convenient? I know Detective Stone is out but I wanted to share a small piece of information that may be useful or it might be nothing.' She gave a small apologetic smile.

'Oh, Miss Astin, you would be amazed how many times the smallest clue or link can crack a case wide open.' Gilbert reddened. 'That's not from personal experience, I've only been a detective for a short while, but I've read a lot of case files.'

The pair smiled at each other as they both sat. They were of the same age and both conservative by nature; Phoebe began to relax opposite the earnest young detective. She noted his suit was not as well cut as Detective Stone's – reflective of his pay grade – but Gilbert was neat and shiny and groomed to within an inch of his life.

'I wanted to discuss with you something that relates to my messages with the spirit world...' She contemplated him with trepidation.

'Please proceed, I am most interested,' Gilbert said coming into his own as the most senior detective in the room.

Phoebe nodded, took a deep breath, and continued, 'Mrs Tochborn gave me a message for Mr William Varsewell, the claimant in the asylum. I did not mention this to Detective Stone as it seemed unimportant at the time, but now I am not so sure. Mrs Tochborn asked me to remind Mr Varsewell of the nursery rhyme, *Rock-A-Bye-Baby*, and to tell him that the bough had broken.'

Gilbert leaned forward. 'That's very significant, Miss Astin.'

'It is?' she asked wide-eyed. 'I am sorry I did not say something sooner.'

'Actually, it might be for the best that you didn't. We would not have realised the significance until we spoke with Mr Varsewell ourselves,' Gilbert assured her. 'He recalled that very nursery rhyme when we asked him to think back on his childhood.'

'Is that so? Well, I am pleased if it means something to you.'

'Pray tell, what exactly did Mr Varsewell say when you gave him the message from Mrs Tochborn if you can recall?'

'Well,' Phoebe pondered for a moment to ensure she was accurate in her retelling, 'Mr Varsewell smiled and said that the message was good news and that it meant his brother was with Mrs Tochborn. He seemed pleased to know that. I particularly noted this as the attendant was concerned my message might upset him.'

'Yes, I imagine so. His brother, you say?' Gilbert asked, and then decided to jot this development down. Looking up, he asked Phoebe to continue.

'Naturally, I asked who his brother was, thinking it might be James Tochborn, the missing boy.'

'Good thinking, Miss Astin, you have an excellent inquisitive mind,' Gilbert said with a smile which was reciprocated gratefully by Phoebe.

'Thank you, Detective Payne. However, his answer was most confusing. He responded that his brother was "Me", meaning himself, and then he spoke no more and started humming the nursery rhyme. What do you make of all that, Detective?'

Gilbert breathed out, webbed his fingers and sat back. 'My goodness.'

Phoebe did not speak. She could almost hear Detective Payne's mind whirring, and did not want to interrupt his thoughts. Then, Gilbert seemed to remember she was there and leaned forward again. He spoke as if he was thinking aloud.

'According to Miss Lewis's story in the newspaper today, and from what Mr Varsewell told Detective Stone and me, he was collected from an orphanage by extended family who felt an obligation to home him.'

'And Lilly wrote that he can't remember anything of his first ten years,' Phoebe added.

'Yes, he told us the same except for a scene in a kitchen which Detective Stone did not offer to the press.'

'I imagine that is necessary with some details,' Phoebe said. 'From the portrait I saw in the newspaper, he does bear a resemblance to the young boy.'

'I said the very same thing on sighting him,' Gilbert agreed. 'Mr Varsewell told Detective Stone and me – the bit we withheld from the newspaper – that he remembered being in a kitchen, being happy, eating freshly baked bread, and hearing the lady with him singing "*Rock-A-Bye-Baby*". It is odd that before she died, Mrs Tochborn was about to claim Mr Arthur Horton as her son, and now on the other side, she wanted to give Mr Varsewell a message and not Mr Horton? Why?'

'Why indeed, when she told me her son was with her now in heaven, so neither claimant is the missing boy,' Phoebe said, equally as confused, the pair going around in circles.

'Her son whom she said was a fake, but then how could he be there?' Gilbert pondered. 'A boy who is not her son, but who is dead. A message for Mr Varsewell that reminded him of his brother. Is the son she does not have, Mr Varsewell's brother?'

'Is he a fake because he is adopted maybe?' Phoebe asked. 'After all, Mr Varsewell was taken from the orphanage. Could the brothers have been separated at birth and Mrs Tochborn adopted James and poor William was sent to an orphanage and eventually adopted by the Varsewell family?'

'Yes, exactly where I was going with that thought,' Gilbert agreed and they smiled at each other, then sobered as Phoebe added, 'But the brother is "Me". That's what he said.'

'And the nursery rhyme, "*Rock-A-Bye-Baby*" is about a child replaced at birth,' Gilbert said rising now and coming around to Phoebe's side to pace. 'Could both of the boys – James and William – be her sons?' Gilbert shook his head and sighed. 'But if so, why were they separated and the Tochborns claim to have only the one child?'

'Unless,' Phoebe added, 'they did have two but one child was born with a deformity and banished to an orphanage or a lunatic asylum. That is not uncommon.'

'Good gracious it is frustrating. In effect, we have a child who is said to be a fake, a son that is not a son, a man in an asylum who believes his brother is in heaven with Mrs Tochborn but claims to be that brother, and a nursery rhyme that speaks of a child being replaced and a bough that has broken.'

Phoebe frowned. 'Goodness. But William Varsewell is in an asylum... might he be truly insane?'

'Quite possibly,' Gilbert said, stopping and rubbing a hand over his face as he thought. 'If my brother was me... if I were my brother, what would I be?'

'A twin?' Phoebe offered and Gilbert turned to look at her and smiled.

'A twin. It is possible, very, very possible, Miss Astin. Then I must go to the asylum and ask Mr Varsewell if he was a twin, or find his real name and check birth records, and find Mrs Tochborn's staff from twenty years ago and see if anyone can remember twin boys...' he stopped abruptly. 'But first I must tell all of this to Detective Stone and allow him to determine our way forward.'

'I have done my part and must return to work,' Phoebe said rising. 'I thank you for your consideration and shall leave you to your duties, Detective Payne.'

'Thank you, Miss Astin.' Gilbert bowed over her hand in a quaint gesture. 'Your contribution has been most enlightening.'

Phoebe smiled. 'My pleasure, Detective.'

Gilbert grabbed for his hat and a notepad. 'I shall see you into a hansom, Miss Astin, and I will walk to the morgue where Detective Stone is currently in attendance.'

The young people hurried on to their next round of duties.

Chapter 13

'OH, MY HEART, MY beating heart,' Dr Tavish McGregor said in his lovely Scottish accent, placing his palm on his heart and sighing. 'If it isn't the lovely Miss Lilly Lewis, famous reporter and the intrepid Detective Gilbert Payne!'

Lilly laughed. 'Thank you, Dr McGregor, that is a better welcome than I receive in most places.' She gave Detective Stone a teasing look and greeted him.

'Miss Lewis,' Harland said with a smile, returning the greeting less exuberantly than his friend, Tavish.

'Gilbert and Sullivan,' Gilbert proclaimed as if the thought had just come to him.

'Indeed, my learned young detective friend,' Tavish said, slapping Gilbert on the back. 'The line comes from *HMS Pinafore*. I saw the production earlier this year.'

'As did I. It was excellent in my humble opinion,' Gilbert said.

'Gilbert, what has brought you and Miss Lewis here?' Harland asked cutting to the chase and surprised to see his young protégé, whom he had left office-bound, now at the morgue.

'We did not come together but met by coincide, Sir. But there is a riddle, some new information, and the need to clarify what direction you would like to take next as I believe we may be derailed.'

'This does sound serious,' Tavish sobered.

'The source of this new information?' Harland asked before asking for the information itself.

'Miss Phoebe Astin, Sir. She dropped in to see you but spoke with me in your absence.' Gilbert noted his superior stood to attention now as if the information had more credibility which was odd given the source could not be proven. He also detected a hint of disappointment from Detective Stone that he had missed Miss Astin's visit. It was a flinch of his eyes that would have gone unnoticed by most, but Gilbert had been reading books on interpreting body language and expression, which he assumed would be most useful for his occupation.

Tavish McGregor added, 'I have a result that will cause you some consternation, too.'

Lilly gasped. 'Mrs Tochborn was poisoned, wasn't she? Goodness, what to report first? This case is getting more and more mysterious.'

'Yes and no,' Harland confirmed. 'Tavish has just confirmed Mrs Tochborn's system contains carbolic acid.'

'Why yes and no? Was she poisoned or not?' Lilly asked confused.

Tavish explained, 'Carbolic acid can be used as an antiseptic; it will kill germs when applied. Mrs Tochborn had a small bottle on her dresser as she had fallen a few weeks back and cut her leg. According to her doctor, it was a wound not healing well.' He went towards several boxes on a metal shelf, found the one marked 'Tochborn' and pulled out several bottles. 'This is the bottle of carbolic acid. Unfortunately, this is her medication.' He pulled out another bottle that looked just like it.

'I see. So Mrs Tochborn may have been poisoned but it may have been an accidental mix-up,' Gilbert surmised.

'Exactly,' Harland said and added, 'The initial police report, before we were handed the case, cited that Mrs Tochborn saw no one in her last couple days while on her deathbed, except the doctor and her trusted companion whom I believe started as her maid. Her death was not suspicious due to her illness, and it begs the question why would anyone kill a dying woman?'

'And what would the maid or doctor gain from doing so?' Gilbert added.

'Nevertheless, we shall speak to both to ensure they have no ties to the claimants or her extended family,' Harland said to Gilbert who nodded and made a quick note in his pad. 'Best we leave Tavish to his work and you can tell me elsewhere what you learnt this morning.'

'There's no need to depart; I am due a break,' Tavish said. 'Let us all sit and allow me to enjoy some living company for a brief while. This case does have me intrigued.'

'As you wish,' Harland said and they moved outside of his workroom to a small office next door and sat around his table. Gilbert began the story abstaining from mentioning in the company of Tavish, that Miss Astin's source was a ghost.

Gilbert could not see, nor could any of the party, Mrs Tochborn's spirit nearby as she listened to their tale. But today she would be returned to *The Economic Undertaker* and Phoebe's care.

Some days, Ambrose Astin was particularly pleased to work in the family business and to not have the wrath of an employer or clients to deal with should he appear at work a little worse for wear. Yes, his brother and grandfather set high standards but he was family and that came with some leniency. After all, he was a young man, and this was the time of his life when he should be enjoying himself while he had little responsibility. Oddly, he was coming to the realisation that he would happily give up a bachelor's lifestyle in a heartbeat for the chance of winning Miss Lilly Lewis's hand.

On this afternoon, he had found himself at a loss. His grandfather was in the meeting room with clients, Julius was consulting his business manager, Phoebe was in a terrible hurry catching up on whatever she had to do given she had spent the morning out and about, and Mrs Dobbs was preparing refreshments for his grandfather's meeting. For a short while, he visited the lads in the stable but got bored. He thought about going next door and stirring up the ladies in the dressmaking business but knew they too were busy, and he did not want Miss Mary Pollard to think he was interested. Good Lord, she swooned anytime he passed the window. He did not have time to visit Lucian at the carpentry business given Julius would need him in an hour or so, thus he determined he had little choice but to use the time wisely and nap, catching up on the sleep he did not get the night prior.

Ambrose entered the family showroom and knowing the coffins were for display only and he was at no risk of being sold and buried, he chose one in the far corner of the room that could not be seen from the doorway. It was set on a bench a few feet off the ground and comfortable to climb into. His grandfather had already brought the clients in to choose one suited to their budget, but should they return, he determined he could hurriedly close the lid or jump out and pretend to be dusting the timber.

Ambrose vowed to congratulate cousin Lucian as the top-of-the-line coffins were most comfortable but after his late night prior and the promise of another, he was asleep in no time. Ambrose's slumber was short-lived when a noise startled him awake. He realised he was not alone and a glance to the doorway was cause for alarm. A young girl was looking at the coffins nearest the window. She was dressed in black, her fair hair plaited on either side of her head and she looked to be not yet ten. He recognised her as the young girl who had been in the meeting with her parents and his grandfather; she must have been permitted to wander.

What to do?

His heartbeat went up a notch. If he rose, he would terrify her and the prank might lose them the family's business. Julius and his grandfather would see he was buried for that – a little extreme perhaps he thought, but he would certainly face their wrath. She drew nearer.

Good God, think, think.

Ambrose decided his only choice was to lay as still as possible and continue looking like a wax shop display mannequin so as not to frighten her. He subtly crossed his hands over his chest and affected his best dead expression – eyes closed, minimal breathing, alert and listening, not that the dead did the latter from his experience in the job.

He could sense and smell her coming nearer; he recognised the scent of the black dye colouring coming from her dress. Poverty, no doubt, dictated that her dress be dyed black for mourning, or the death came as a surprise and the family did not have mourning clothes prepared.

Blast, this was a nuisance.

The girl must have spotted him, he was not brave enough to hazard a look, but she had stopped nearby and was not moving. Then he heard the front door open and the small bell over the door ring. He almost sighed with relief. Hopefully, her family was departing and they would call for her now to follow.

Instead, he heard the footsteps of a man and then Julius's voice greeting Mrs Dobbs in the kitchen. His meeting was over and Julius was back early.

Good God no, could anything else not go my way today?

Moments later before the child could resume her investigation, the footsteps came to the door of the coffin display room; Julius must have seen the young girl in attendance. This will test his charm, Ambrose thought and almost smiled.

'Hello young lady,' he said.

'Hello, Sir.'

'Have you a favourite?' he asked and Ambrose almost chuckled. That was a good question to ask a child. Well done, Julius, he mused.

'I like the white one.'

'When I was your age and visited a funeral parlour, I liked the white one best too. But now that I'm older, I think I like the dark one the best.'

'My grandfather died. Mama said he was sick and old. Do not worry, he was older than you.'

'Thank you,' Julius said with a slight laugh in his voice. 'I hope to be around for some time yet.'

'What's your name?' the girl asked.

'Julius. Mr Julius Astin. And your name, Miss?'

'Clara.'

'Well Miss Clara, I am sorry that your grandfather has passed away. Would you like to ride up front with my brother and me at the funeral? You could help us with the horses.'

'Yes please, I would love that.' Her voice went up a few notches with excitement. 'I want a horse but Mama said we can't afford one.'

'They are expensive to keep. They'll eat more than you do.'

She laughed. 'That's not much. But if they eat more than my brother, we could sell my brother and keep my horse.'

This time Julius laughed and Ambrose marvelled at his skills for talking with this child. Sometimes, Julius surprised him. Then, his heartbeat raced, he heard Julius move further into the room and he knew he had been spotted... Julius's breath hitched, and then he lightly cleared his throat.

'Have you seen our wax mannequin in the coffin? It shows you how comfortable they are and that they are a good size.'

He wouldn't, would he?

'I did,' she answered and her voice dropped as if she were to make a confession. 'He looks very real; I was too scared to go near him.'

'Yes, he does look real but they have not made him as handsome as me,' Julius agreed and the little girl laughed again. 'But you can touch him. I'll give him a poke and show you.'

Julius, you are a hunted man! Just wait.

He felt the two of them bearing in on him and the next minute, Julius gave Ambrose a good poking in the stomach and arm.

'See, dead as a doornail.'

Ambrose tried not to react even though it was ticklish.

What the hell was Julius doing? Did he want to scare this child half to death and lose the family's business? But then again, Julius had just told her that she could ride with them and the girl would recognise him on the day. Would she believe a mannequin was modelled in his likeness? Most likely.

He wanted to hiss 'go away', but he couldn't and had to keep up the front now that Julius had declared him a mannequin of all things.

'Wait a moment,' Julius said, dragging out his words. 'You know, Miss Clara, this looks like my little brother, Ambrose.'

'I told you he was lifelike,' she said.

'I think you are right, and he is sleeping on the job!'

'Will he get sacked?'

'Mm, he probably should be, but maybe we can get him to clean up the horse manure in the stables instead.'

She laughed again but with a thrill to her laugh as if the child thought it was a good idea. *The cheek!*

'I think we should tickle him awake and get him back to work,' she suggested.

'Excellent idea,' Julius agreed with too much enthusiasm for Ambrose's liking and moments later he felt hands set upon him until he could not hold his countenance any longer and sat up laughing and fighting them off. The child squealed with delight; at least it was not a squeal of terror resulting in her running from the room.

'Ah, you were right, Miss Clara, he's not a waxed mannequin after all, he just looked like one.' Julius narrowed his eyes at Ambrose who at least looked contrite. Ambrose stretched and faked a large yawn and then looked surprised to see the young lady. Getting Julius to help him down, he gave her a bow.

'Ambrose Astin at your service, Miss.'

She laughed and curtseyed. 'You two are funny.'

At last, a door was heard to open and a woman called the child's name. If only it had been before Julius returned, Ambrose fumed anticipating a lecture.

'Come then, Miss Clara, I shall see you out,' Julius said without a look back.

'Don't forget you promised I could ride with you,' he heard the young girl saying.

Ambrose repaired his appearance and once he heard the front door close, he raced out to reception only to find his brother, halfway towards the back door.

'I am just going to let the stable boys know you want to do the rake out tonight,' Julius said with a gleam of humour in his eyes.

'I cannot believe you poked me when I was clearly trying to not cause alarm.' Ambrose's tone was most indignant.

'I can't believe you were asleep in one of our coffins!'

'If I get you, I will poke you into next week,' Ambrose said starting for his brother who grinning, took off at a great pace out the back.

He heard his grandfather asking with laughter in his voice, 'What on earth is going on in here of late?'

Mrs Dobbs added as Ambrose ran past, 'I don't know, but I hope it continues.'

The two men sobered as the morgue's wagon pulled into their yard, bringing Mrs Tochborn back for Phoebe to prepare.

Chapter 14

'THANK YOU, DEAR, I believe that is close to my natural colour.' Mrs Tochborn studied the face of the body lying on the table. The small woman smiled, pleased with the result even though her face looked unrestful.

'It is my favourite colour, Mrs Tochborn, and most becoming. I feel it gives the subject a glow.' Phoebe looked from the lady on the table to the spirit nearby. 'I am pleased you have returned to us.'

'Thank you, dear Miss Astin, I am pleased to be back. Not for long though I imagine.'

'No. I believe your relatives have requested a showing tomorrow for mourning and your funeral is the day after.'

Mrs Tochborn made a scoffing sound. 'I suspect no one is truly mourning me. Rachel, my maid companion will be the only one to miss me, I imagine. She is a good soul.'

'I have not heard of a maid companion before.'

'When we were married, my husband hired Rachel as a lady's maid for me. He was never one for having much staff on hand, he liked his privacy. In time, Rachel became one of my friends and confidants and when he died, she became more of a companion than a maid.' Mrs Tochborn smiled. 'She gave herself the title maid companion.'

'She sounds loyal and lovely. At least there are people to stand up for you at your funeral. Sometimes my brothers are the only ones in attendance along with the priest. That is sad at the end of a life, isn't it?'

'It is, but it can be deceptive. I've known friends who outlived everyone in their family and circle of acquaintance. It is no reflection on their good hearts that no one is there to see them off.'

'My grandfather made the same observation, Mrs Tochborn. Goodness. I hope I don't outlive everyone! Although I imagine it is an honour to be able to stand up for others.'

They continued in silence for a short while, both in hushed contemplation, until Mrs Tochborn spoke. 'At the morgue, I heard the detectives and the lady reporter speaking with the coroner of me and my missing son.' She sighed. 'I never wanted to be in the public eye and yet I have spent my life in it in a manner that nobody would ever desire.'

'Oh Mrs Tochborn, I cannot fathom what you have been through.' Phoebe's hand went to her heart. 'I would not have the strength or conviction to cope with it.'

'I suspect you would, Miss Astin. You are compassionate, a fighter for justice as proven by your willingness to crusade on my behalf, and you clearly have a mind of your own, I can tell from the manner of your dress which is courageous with all the opinionated ladies out there. But it is the suspicion and uncertainty that wore me down. Some people even accused my husband and me of killing James. Can you imagine such a thing?'

Phoebe shook her head. 'People are odd, Mrs Tochborn.'

The lady in spirit form laughed. 'They are indeed.'

Phoebe did not press Mrs Tochborn to tell her more about the son she claimed was fake, even though she was desperate to do so. She had found in the past that her clients said what they needed to say at the end of their lives in their own good time, and she would not force them. What would be the purpose of that? It might serve to drive them away. Eventually, Phoebe's patience paid off.

'I wish to unburden my soul. I know you are not a priest, but I would feel better for it.'

'Of course, Mrs Tochborn. I believe I am a capable listener.'

Mrs Tochborn said nothing for a while as she gathered her thoughts and Phoebe put the finishing touches on the body, working methodically and with a sense of calmness about her.

'I never had a son, Miss Astin,' she said, and Phoebe did not react. She knew her role was to listen, so she gave a small nod and an encouraging look of interest.

'I pray when your time comes, should you wish to have children, you are blessed with them, but I was not. Oh, and the good Lord knows how desperately Leo and I both wanted a child. Yet, around us, children were born in and out of wedlock and to those who did not want or deserve them.'

'I have seen that too, Mrs Tochborn, there is no justice in it. Did you decide to give an abandoned child a home then?' she asked now that the subject was raised, she was invited to speak of it.

'No. I wanted to adopt a child but my husband would not hear of it. Leo said we don't know what the child's pedigree is or their background. They might be from unbalanced parents or ignorant stock.' She sighed.

Phoebe smiled. 'Mr Tochborn was not convinced by the argument of nurture over nature?'

'Oh no, dear, and I tried to convince him. I brought the reverend in to speak at length about how our lives are moulded in the wider community and how the church and family can help in forming a young person's mind. But it was to no avail.'

'So, may I ask, where did your son come from?'

'It began because we had to have an heir, and Leo could not bear the thought of any of his relatives, whom he had colourful names for, inheriting everything from his hard labour and that of his father before him. So, he believed if he could create a fake heir, it would give us time to be in the family way or to find a worthy recipient. The fake heir could then meet with an accident in time, having the second child or our first-born step up to be the heir.'

'I see. He must have been under great pressure to create such a rouse.'

'My husband was not a well man and he feared dying before having his estate in order.'

'But you could have inherited if that was the case. Would he not accept that?'

Mrs Tochborn smiled. 'He would if I promised to never remarry. He could not bear the thought of fortune hunters seeking me out and marrying me to claim our fortune. He had little faith in me to tell the difference between love and flattery.'

'I'm sorry, how frustrating for you. But maybe he didn't like the idea of another man being with you.'

'Oh indeed, he was a possessive man. But I went along with his grand plans because I did hope to be in the family way, and when we were so often invited places and featured in news stories, Leo wanted to mention his wife and son. I felt incredible guilt and pressure to produce an heir.'

Phoebe gave Mrs Tochborn a heartfelt look of sympathy. 'Which a lady trying to have a family does not need. It must have affected your health?'

'It did. Fortunately for Leo, our cook and the stable manager became entangled and married. They stayed on with us and had two beautiful little boys, golden-haired angels, twins. They would sit in the kitchen while their mother cooked and learn their lessons. They were never any problem. As they got older, they would work with their father in the stables but continue their lessons for several hours a day. It was the deal my husband struck.'

'Oh dear,' Phoebe said. 'So, am I to understand that one of the boys pretended to be your son as needed in return for both boys being educated?'

'You have surmised correctly, my dear. The boys were taught the French language and instructed in reading, writing, arithmetic, history, geography and grammar.'

Phoebe immediately thought of Mr William Varsewell at the asylum speaking fluent French or so Lilly claimed in her newspaper article.

'The boys were three when we did the first official family portrait with one of them, little James. If anyone visited or asked, one of the boys was momentarily seen with us before the cook, pretending to be their nanny, took them off. But that was a rarity as we did not socialise at home where avoidable.'

'Was it believed?'

'Of course. Who would question Leo Tochborn? And it was not hard for me to have remained out of the public eye for some time on the pretence of needing rest during my confinement.'

'I saw the portrait of three-year-old, James and again when he was ten. Was that really his name?'

'Yes, we thought it best so as not to risk him saying out loud a different name in company. Imagine if we were having the portrait taken and he proclaimed otherwise!'

'Hmm, that would have been difficult to explain,' Phoebe agreed. 'And your husband continued the deception for all those years?'

'It did not take a great deal of work. A few portraits, a few throw-away lines that his wife and son were well but I was not of a mind to socialise, or we were away on the Continent, or the boy was at boarding school – whatever excuse he needed to make for James not being seen too often. But the reality was there was no child, no son, and no heir coming any time soon.'

Phoebe sighed, reciting a line from the poet, Sir Walter Scott, whose work she most admired. 'What a tangled web we weave, when first we practice to deceive.'

'Oh, so true, my dear, so true,' Mrs Tochborn agreed. 'And then our act of selfishness brought tragedy to James's family. He was kidnapped for ransom.'

After their brief meeting with Detective Stone, intrepid reporter Miss Lilly Lewis had so many leads to follow that on occasion, she was stunned into standing absolutely still to decide what to do next. Lilly and Fergus had met with both claimants; Lilly found Mr Arthur Horton to be amicable, and Fergus declared Mr William Varsewell most interesting, but now the nursery rhyme and the claim of the fake son had captured her imagination. Lilly had been given her boundaries by Detective Stone and would abide by them; he was an ally she wished to keep on side.

It took some determination to find and gain access to some of Mrs Tochborn's original staff. The lady who was both companion and maid would say nothing of her employer, claiming to be too distraught to speak. Lilly was not giving up on her; she would approach the middle-aged woman several days after Mrs Tochborn's funeral.

The link that Detective Gilbert Payne had uncovered courtesy of the inmate, Mr Varsewell's brothers claiming to have an uncle and aunt who worked with Mrs Tochborn was more revealing, but yet everywhere they went, they met with closed doors. Lilly fervently hoped Detectives Stone and Payne had more luck and could get the information by nature of their office. She felt frustrated, desperately wanting to uncover her own lead and bring something new to the story. But how, when the case was so old and the claimants seemed so rehearsed in their convictions?

For now, tomorrow's deadline was pressing and in agreement with their editor, Mr Cowan, they began to build the scene for the pending court case which was but a week away when both claimants would attempt to convince a judge and jury that they were the missing heir, James Tochborn. Unless of course the detectives could crack the case wide open before then and find what happened to the real James Tochborn... the fake boy and prove he was a fake. Lilly sighed, the odds of them doing so in such a tight time frame were not good.

'At least we have the latest news and we are the first newspaper to have it,' she said to Fergus as he wrote his part of the story. He looked up confused and she added, 'The poisoning, even it is most likely accidental. I shall lead with it.'

'I have found the advertisement Mrs Tochborn placed in the newspaper seeking information about the missing boy, now a man. I shall include that,' Fergus said with a grin, pushing his mop of brown hair off his face.

Lilly's eyes widened and she leaned in closer to Fergus, lowering her voice so the rest of the newsroom did not overhear them. 'Why would she run that notice looking for the boy if he was a fake? It makes no sense.'

Fergus shrugged. 'But we don't know what she meant by fake yet,' he whispered. 'Maybe she meant he was adopted, or the boy was her son but not Mr Tochborn's son. It could be scandalous!' He gave her a dramatic look and Lilly laughed at his antics. She was so pleased to be partnered with Fergus. He was calm when she was over-excited, focused when she was distracted, and supportive when the men in the newsroom made lewd remarks her way. As he was married with a child, it also put an end to any speculation of a liaison and kept their partnership purely professional.

'Notwithstanding,' Fergus continued, 'the boy existed and he was kidnapped according to those original police reports. She still needed an heir and wanted him back I suspect, regardless of who he was, hence the advertisement. That is just my guess; the poor little lad.'

'She was opening herself up to much aggravation,' Lilly said with a shake of her head. 'Can I see the ad?'

He pushed it to her and she marvelled at the words and the desperation as she read:

PUBLIC NOTICE:

A HANDSOME REWARD is offered to any person who can furnish such information that will discover the fate of JAMES TOCHBORN who was stolen from a private garden in Brisbane, Australia, twenty years ago on 1 January 1870 and has not been seen since.

James would be at this present time 30 years of age, of delicate constitution, fair hair and blue eyes. James is the son of Leo Tochborn (now deceased) and heir to all his estates. A most liberal reward will be given for any information that may point out his fate.

All replies to Mr Cubbit at the Missing Friends Office, Eagle Street, Brisbane.

'I am surprised there have only been two claimants,' Lilly said pushing the advertisement back to Fergus.

'I thought about it, but I am too young,' he said and gave her a cheeky grin before they both returned to their writing and pending deadline.

Chapter 15

Detective Harland Stone was not one for relying on those who claimed to speak with the dead, nevertheless, he was secretly hoping that the return of Mrs Tochborn's body to Miss Astin, would result in more information. He trusted Miss Astin and on his last case, she had proven to be correct with her information. Harland also never turned down any help that could lead to a conviction or a case being closed.

'I would hate to be the judge having to decide which claimant was the correct one, if indeed there was a true son between them,' Gilbert said as they walked briskly up the long driveway to the Tochborn estate.

'As would I,' Harland agreed with his young partner. 'On face value, Mr Arthur Horton could persuade you to believe his claim, especially with his so-called deformity, but Mr Varsewell is similar in face and feature to the young boy, and speaking fluent French is an interesting connection.'

'But you do not think either of them is James Tochborn?' Gilbert pressed his superior.

Harland grimaced. 'My gut instinct says no. But if I had to pick one under torture,' he gave his partner a grin, 'I would choose Mr Varsewell over Mr Horton.'

'So would I, Sir,' Gilbert exclaimed pleased they were thinking alike.

Harland tried not to smile at his protégé's enthusiasm; one would think that sharing a similar thought for Gilbert was a rare occurrence. But the young man was coming into his own, time would tell.

'Did you find out anything interesting about the estate?' Harland asked having left Gilbert earlier to do some research while he updated his superior.

'Nothing of note. It is being managed by Mrs Tochborn's solicitor and several staff members remain on-site ensuring the properties upkeep until they receive information about their futures. That includes the gardener, Mr Wicks, and Miss Temple, the maid companion. Both are expecting us. The solicitor told me their services will be terminated after the house has sold, or they will receive orders from the new owner – whoever inherits the estate.'

'I imagine they are expecting to be dismissed,' Harland said. He glanced around at the enormity of the property; it was certainly an impressive estate to leave behind and someone would inherit it or benefit from its sale. But today, Detective Stone wanted to come away with more answers than questions and he hoped Miss Temple and Mr Wicks might assist. They had both been with the household since the beginning, over thirty years ago.

The detectives were shown into the drawing-room by Miss Rachel Temple herself, who organised the cook to bring them tea; Harland took the opportunity to study her. She was similar in age to her former employer, Mrs Tochborn, and he studied the companion to see the woman she would have been thirty years ago. Today, she was small and thin, almost frail. Her hair was a mix of grey and brown, tied neatly back in a bun affixed at her neck, and her clothing was understated – black for mourning, no jewellery.

'Thank you for seeing us, Miss Temple. I understand this is a distressing time for you,' Harland started.

She nodded her thanks. 'It was not a surprise though, detectives. Mrs Tochborn had been declining for some time. Some might even say it was a blessing.'

'Would you?'

'With all that came before, yes, I would.'

'Miss Temple, what was the household like when you joined three decades ago?' Gilbert asked.

'As quiet as a tomb,' she said. 'It was a big estate with no children then. The newlywed Mrs Tochborn was not a confident creature. She appeared almost grateful to have been wed so late.'

'She was one year shy of thirty, was she not?' Harland asked.

'Yes, and Mr Tochborn was six years her senior. He married young and his first wife died, they were childless. She told me in time, that he did not wish to bother with romance, and as Mrs Tochborn came from money, it was arranged by her family, a fortuitous marriage for both parties. But Mr Tochborn wanted an heir and wanted it immediately.'

'Perhaps he was the one to bear the responsibility of not being able to produce a child,' Gilbert suggested.

'It would appear that way after two wives,' Miss Temple concurred.

'But then they had a son, James,' Harland stated studying the woman carefully for her reaction, and to his frustration, the cook entered with the tea tray. He saw the looks they exchanged as the cook had obviously heard the question. Miss Temple thanked her and said she would pour.

'We were speaking of James,' Harland prompted her.

'Mrs Tochborn and I were sent away briefly when James was kidnapped, so I cannot speak on the subject to any great depth.'

Harland nodded, understanding it was more likely that she did not want to speak of it, but he expected she knew quite a lot. She had sidestepped conversing on the birth of James with the ease of one experienced in doing so.

'It must have put terrible pressure on you and the household over many years,' Gilbert added sympathetically and she turned and smiled at him.

'Thank you, Detective, yes it did. It made Mr Tochborn more adamant about privacy and security. Some days, I felt like we were living in a prison.'

'But you didn't leave?' Harland asked.

'I could not leave Mrs Tochborn. I came to care for her and she seemed so very alone.' She took a sip of tea and added, 'Besides, Mr Tochborn paid handsomely for loyalty and I had parents and siblings to support. I was one of ten children, the eldest. I sent most of my wages home as I had board and keep.'

Picking up on that angle, Harland asked of the other staff, 'And what of your happiness, Miss Temple? Was there no one on staff that you might find happiness with?'

She flushed at the direct question.

'There was a man many years ago before the boy went missing. But after the tragedy, Mr Tochborn halved the staff,

and the man I loved was dismissed. I did not leave with him.'
She rose and both men hurried to their feet. 'I am afraid I
cannot say anymore, detectives, I find myself feeling quite
weak.'

'Of course, Miss Temple. Perhaps we can continue this
another time,' Harland said, knowing she would be unlikely to
give them an audience unless forced to by law, but her silence
spoke loudly. She knew more than she was saying and surely
twenty years passed would have cooled the passion. Why could
she not speak easily of the staff of yesteryear? Bidding Miss
Temple goodbye, Harland was satisfied he had a better picture
of the household and the pressure at the time. More to think
about later.

The detectives did their best to keep on the paths, but
finding the gardener in the furthest corner of the estate
trimming a hedge, they strode across the lawn.

Harland noted the older man looked as if he had worked
outside for twice that many years. He was short and solid, grey
hair peaked out from under a large hat and his skin was tanned
and leathery. After introductions, the men moved to sit on a
lower stone wall in the dapple warmth of the sun filtered by a
large gum tree.

'Mrs Tochborn liked the native trees. Once Mr Tochborn
died, she had me plant plenty,' the gardener said, looking up.
'She was right too. They brought in the birds, and sitting out

here with her book under the tree and hearing the birds was one of her favourite things to do.'

'You remember Mrs Tochborn coming here as a young bride?' Harland asked.

'I do, but she wasn't a young bride, she was past her prime, in her late twenties when they wed, if I remember correctly. Probably accounts for the lack of children.'

Harland studied the man. 'No children?'

Mr Wicks shuffled uncomfortably. He was the type of man, Harland mused, who was not given to assumption and gossip. He squinted at the gardener and said in a kindly voice, 'They are all dead now, Mr Wicks, your discretion is admirable, but your loyalty has served its time.'

'I imagine you are right, Detective,' he said and sighed. 'There was the boy, James, of course. The agony that kidnapping caused.'

Both detectives waited but Mr Wicks did not elaborate or fill the silence as many did when faced with it.

'Terrible affair,' Gilbert agreed eventually speaking up. 'Mr Wicks, I met with Mr Varsewell at the asylum and with his adopted brothers.'

Harland noticed the sour look that crossed Mr Wicks's face.

'Be careful of those brothers. Not men of honour, I'd say.'

'Why would you say so?' Gilbert asked. 'Although I had the same impression.'

'They'd sell their grannie for a pound, the pair of them. That poor inmate being saddled with them. They didn't care enough to get him out before, only when they thought there was a pound or two to be made from him.'

A light breeze brushed them, reminding them it was winter despite the blue-sky day.

Harland asked directly, 'So, you don't believe the inmate to be James Tochborn?'

Mr Wicks gave a small shrug. 'I could not say.'

'Could you say if you met him?' Harland pushed.

Mr Wicks looked up at the lead detective and Harland could feel the man assessing him.

'Why do you ask? Do you believe him to be the kidnapped boy?' the gardener retorted.

'I could not say either, Mr Wicks. Tell me if you will, who worked here thirty years ago when you were here? Specifically, what children were on the estate be it James, or children of the staff, or Tochborn relatives?'

Mr Wicks nodded. 'I knew it was only a matter of time until you asked me that question. That's going back a bit then, but it is not a hard question to answer.' He looked toward the house and tipped his hat back off his forehead. 'You see, Mr Tochborn was fierce about his privacy. He paid good money to keep staff loyal and not have a turnover. He never socialised here and he was not close to any of his family. I felt sorry for Mrs Tochborn because she was quite isolated.' He gave another small shrug. 'She could go out, of course, she was not a prisoner, but it was a big house, with little spirit.'

'Was he always like that or just when it became clear they were not able to have a family?' Gilbert asked and Harland gave him an encouraging nod for a good question.

'Oh no, he was always like that. A bit of a cold fish was Mr Tochborn.'

'But there were children?' Gilbert pushed.

'For a while, yes,' Mr Wicks said. 'The stable manager, George Hickling and the cook, the lovely Frances, paired up and married. Mr Tochborn kept them on staff and gave them a small house on the property to live in. The rest of us had rooms in a quarter for staff. They were a lovely couple, the Hicklings, he was a good stick, George.'

'Gone now, dead?' Harland asked.

'Long gone. Frances outlived him but by only a couple of years.' He tapped his head. 'Went a little insane.'

'Why?' Gilbert jumped in sniffing a connection.

'She had twins and one went missing. The other left here not long after. Frances had a breakdown, got sick and weak.'

'And George Hickling?' Harland asked.

The gardener sighed. 'Poor George died of illness and the bottle. They left here not long after the boy went missing and took a small place on the outskirts of town. But George never got over the boy going missing and would always have a new idea of where he might be. He'd go off half-cocked to find him. Then he'd drink to compensate for the loss when there was no sign of the boy where he hoped. I saw him at the pub more times than I saw him working in those days.'

'One of the boys wouldn't be named James, by any chance?' Harland asked narrowing his eyes and knowing Mr Wicks knew exactly what he was asking.

'Yes, Detective. His name was James.'

'The brothers of William Varsewell in the asylum claimed that William was brought home to live with them from an orphanage. They also claimed a connection – an aunt and uncle who worked for the Tochborns for a period of time. Could that be George and Frances? Could their surviving son have been put in an orphanage when both parents died?' Harland asked.

'It is a reasonable theory, even if I don't like the brothers,' Mr Wicks said begrudgingly. 'But it doesn't make sense, does it?'

Gilbert looked a little confused and Harland shook his head.

'No, you are right, because then they had the perfect leftover heir,' Harland said and Gilbert clicked his fingers as he just caught on.

'Of course. If the boys were identical, they could have said James had been returned, substituted the brother for the heir who was lost to them, and no parents stood in the way as they were both deceased.'

'So, you'd be thinking, why did they not go collect the other lad from the orphanage?' Mr Wicks asked, 'Or why was he sent there in the first place when the Tochborns could have adopted him?'

'That is what I am thinking. Can you answer that riddle?' Harland asked drily and Mr Wicks laughed.

'I wish I knew. But I don't. In fact, I don't know what became of that boy.'

'What was the boy's name, the twin of James Hickling who was stolen?' Harland asked.

'William Hickling,' Mr Wicks said. 'His name was William, just like the man in the asylum.'

The day was drawing to a close; the light fading earlier in winter, and Bennet Martin and his clerk, Daniel Dutton, had been digging all day. Not the digging that the men from *The Economic Undertaker* paid workers to undertake, but digging for facts and details, and to look at them both, one would think they were quite pleased with themselves. Bennet in particular.

'It was not too hard to find that information,' Bennet said, tapping the pages of paper in front of him on the desk as he and

Daniel met to compare notes. 'I don't think the other private investigator was worth his salt.'

'In fairness,' Daniel started, 'the private detective who was dismissed did not have your funds to bribe informers, or a father working in Scotland Yard, nor did he have a police detective in his pocket.'

'Detectives Stone and Payne are hardly in my pocket and they would cut me off cold if they heard you say so. But it is nice to be able to mention their names if needed,' Bennet said with a satisfied smile.

Mrs Clarke hurried in with a tea tray and sandwiches. 'I bet neither of you men has had a bite all day. I know it is late, but I am sure you will manage to do short work of these. I am off for the day now and bid you good day.'

'Mrs Clarke, you are an angel, I am famished.' Bennet full of good humour, grabbed a large corn beef and pickles sandwich with lashings of butter and thick bread before the plate had hit the table.

She smiled pleased. 'I thought as much. You haven't been home all day, working so hard the pair of you. Come on then, Daniel, your mother will have me if you start looking any thinner.'

He thanked his aunt – Bennet's housekeeper – and wasted no time digging in as she poured them both a cup of tea and they proceeded to talk with their mouths full, not worried about manners in front of the familiar Mrs Clarke. She soon retreated with her tray and their thanks.

'You first then,' Daniel said even though Bennet was the boss. 'In case I have all the same information as you gained, but I suspect I have a lot less.'

'Goodo. As you know, I sent a telegram to my father at Scotland Yard to ask if there was any information or talk of the Tochborn case over there?' Bennet said, wiping his hands on a serviette and reaching for the first piece of paper on his pile.

'Were you expecting there to be so?' Daniel asked surprised.

'Indeed. I found in the previous investigator's files that Mrs Tochborn's husband, Leo, grew up in England and his father had considerable business interest there before Leo came of age and sailed to Australia, remaining here. I suspected there might be some talk of the case amongst his circle.'

'And your father graced you with a reply or did he summon you home?'

Bennet chuckled. 'Ah, yes, my father loves it when I am doing police work. He lives in the hope it will inspire me and I will drop everything, sail home and become a detective just like him... a chip off the old block.' Bennet rolled his eyes. 'Nevertheless, I received a wire from him to say that there had been some talk and an interesting story in the local paper not so long ago. It was in relation to the first claimant, Arthur Horton. His father, Mr Horton senior, was from the British town of Wapping, and took a long sea journey to Australia with his wife and young son, Arthur, in the hope of curing his nervous condition.'

'Don't tell me,' Daniel sat back with his tea cup in hand, 'they sailed over on a ship called *Bella*?'

'How did you know?' Bennet joked. 'Indeed, they did. Mr Arthur Horton was on that ship as a lad, that much is true of his claim. But he certainly wasn't a working ship-boy, nor was he alone or orphaned.'

'An interesting half-truth as his name will be on the ship's passenger record. It is a safe way to tell a lie, to keep the truth close by or so I've been told, especially when few are alive to challenge him.'

'Most astute observation, Daniel,' Bennet said, 'especially in our line of work. His family settled in Australia; the parents were alive according to a friend who said in the very same newspaper article that he corresponded with them for some time.'

'But according to Arthur Horton, they are dead now.' Daniel waved his notebook. 'I found that to be the truth and I found a burial record for them in the country town of Wagga Wagga. They died in this country and he was not an orphan at sea.'

Bennet grinned. 'Excellent. So that lie and history are debunked. But it will not be that easy to defame him.'

'Why not?

'Because we only have the word of a man in England who claimed to be a friend of the family against the word of Arthur Horton who was on the ship, as he said he was. Also, unless we can find the undertaker himself to attest to burying two bodies, Arthur Horton might say that he purchased two headstones for his parents to remember them by, without them having passed away here. Mind you, he does have that medical condition that the real James Tochborn supposedly had. And he has his supporters who believe him, some of them quite impressive.'

'Ridiculous, I bet he has offered them a payment should he inherit, a nice incentive,' Daniel said with a shake of his head. 'But at least your client will be happy to receive that information.'

'I will have to present it in court, I imagine. I have asked my father for the contact details of the English fellow so I can telegram him directly if needed. My father had the news article transcribed and telegraphed to me.'

'He's probably having your room readied as we speak,' Daniel teased. 'I have news on the other claimant but it was easily obtainable so I don't understand why it wasn't in your files from the previous private investigator.'

'I suspect the family had him focus on too many aspects of the case. Oddly, he seemed relieved to be removed from it when

I spoke with him,' Bennet mused. 'Go ahead then, tell me what you have.'

'I visited several orphanages that were in business twenty years ago at the time that James Tochborn went missing, and William Varsewell was saved from an orphanage by his extended family. I ran into Miss Lilly Lewis at one of them and we shared the journey for the remaining distance.'

'Did you, now? Well, we are on the right path then,' Bennet said looking smug. 'And?'

'There were no records for a William Varsewell at any of the orphanages twenty years ago, so that part of his story may be a fabrication. However, one of the orphanages had lost its records in a fire.'

Bennet leaned forward. 'How inconvenient. Nevertheless, this is promising,' he said keenly, finishing the last bite of his second round of sandwiches.

'That is what Miss Lewis said.' Daniel grinned.

Bennet sat back and groaned. 'My, what a twisted tale. The court case is going to be most complex.'

'They don't have to pick a claimant of course,' Daniel reminded him. 'The judge might declare no claimant is valid.'

'My clients tell me they will benefit if that is the case, along with the church to who Mrs Tochborn left a generous sum to, and oddly, an orphanage of her choosing.' He saw Daniel's expression. 'Don't get excited, it is one of the places you visited today so that clue runs cold.'

'Hmm. It's a grubby affair,' Daniel said shaking his head. 'Thank goodness I have no one in my family rich enough to leave me money.' He smiled at his own hypocrisy.

'Yes, lucky you indeed,' Bennet agreed, thinking of the inheritance that should come his way if his father softened before departing this earth. The thought of supporting Miss Phoebe Astin on it for the rest of her days when she agreed to do him the honour of becoming Mrs Bennet Martin made him extremely content.

Chapter 16

I T WAS A FINE morning for an outing, and Julius stood at the back of *The Economic Undertaker* business near the stables. He inspected the horse and small covered trap that the stable hands had prepared, ready to take himself and Miss Violet Forrester to make enquiries about a display area at the Exhibition. He spoke softly to the large chestnut horse, named Huck, brushing his hand down the horse's neck as the horse nuzzled into him. Julius felt ridiculously nervous – most out of sorts for a man not subject to emotional reactions. It did not help that Ambrose kept hovering around trying to be useful. The good wishes from his grandfather and sister were also rather extreme given he was only on a short business trip. He sighed. Would he never get any peace until he found himself a wife and made it official?

'Now, have you a clean handkerchief should Miss Forrester need it?' Ambrose teased.

Julius groaned. 'If you have nothing better to do than annoy me, brother, I can suggest several things that need doing including refreshing the hearse with supplies and seeing to our weekly advertisement in *The Courier.*'

'That all sounds rather dull though,' Ambrose said. 'Ah, here she is.'

Julius looked up to see Miss Forrester exiting the dress shop from the back steps and coming to meet them right at the hour of eleven. She wore a lilac dress that would pass for mourning wear after a period of time, which she had not yet observed; it looked most becoming on her. Her hair was neatly pinned up, and cream lace adorned her neckline and sleeves in a most feminine manner.

'Gentlemen, good morning, I hope I have not kept you waiting,' she said and smiled. 'Are we all going?'

'No,' Julius growled and then moderated his tone. 'Good morning, Miss Forrester. Ambrose is just leaving.' He glanced at his brother.

'I am,' he agreed and went to put out his hand to assist Violet into the trap but Julius shouldered him out of the way and assisted her. He did not see Ambrose's grin nor Violet trying to repress her smile.

'I best get back to work then, I'm very busy,' Ambrose said as Julius stepped up beside Violet and took the reins.

'That's a fine idea,' Julius agreed and gave his brother a wry look.

'Do not rush then, Julius, you are prone to forget it is not a racetrack and Huck likes a leisurely ride,' Ambrose said and stepped back out of their way.

'Huck?' Violet asked as they moved out of the yard.

'Yes, Ambrose named him after Huckleberry Finn. He was given the book, *'Tom Sawyer'* on his eleventh birthday and loved it. It does explain quite a bit about his unruly behaviour.'

Violet laughed softly beside him. 'Ah, brothers. They can be most annoying at times.' She added by way of clarification, 'Little brothers only, as I can't speak for big brothers not having one.'

'I believe my brother is a lot more annoying than yours,' Julius said. 'Tom is such a good lad, Ambrose's mission in life is to vex me.'

Violet smiled at him. 'He has great affection for you. You are such close brothers; it is lovely to see.'

They drove along in silence for a short while as Julius navigated them into the street to join the other moving vehicles. Because he was on this occasion nervous, and methodical by nature, Julius had prepared some topics to raise should the need arise. Normally he would not work that hard as most young ladies gushed and filled the silence allowing him to listen, nod and make the occasional comment with one eye on the exit. Miss Violet Forrester was not one of them and was of a more silent nature too. Nevertheless, he did not want her to think him dull, especially when Ambrose's light shone so brightly.

And then, they both spoke at the same time.

'Would Tom like to—'

'I wish to thank—' Violet laughed.

'Please, go ahead,' Julius said not taking his eyes from the road, but ever so conscious of Violet's proximity, the fabric of her skirt slightly pooling over his trouser leg, and the scent of jasmine or something similar that she wore.

Violet nodded. 'I wish to thank you for the company's invitation to attend the Hospital Ball, for the complimentary ticket, and the offer of transport. I know I should not be attending.'

'Why?' Julius glanced at Violet and back to the road. His thoughts whirled as he thought about why she might not wish to attend and he responded, 'Please do not feel pressured to attend if you don't wish to; it is not a company obligation. We like to support the hospital because they are a good client, and Phoebe was keen to get a large group of friends together for a night of dancing and socialising.'

'Oh no, I don't feel obliged,' she assured him hurriedly. 'I am very much looking forward to it. It is just that, well, I am in mourning.'

'Oh,' he said and relaxed again, his shoulders slumping slightly realising it was not another rejection or that he had somehow manipulated the manageress of his store into attending.

'I shouldn't even be wearing this lilac colour for at least another year,' she said looking down at the skirt of her dress.

'It's most becoming on you,' Julius added uncharacteristically. Except for his sister, Phoebe, the number of women to score a compliment from Mr Julius Astin that was not expected or that he had not been cornered into, could be counted on one hand.

'Thank you,' she said smiling at him and then releasing the material she had fisted, running her hands down the fabric of her skirt.

'But did you not promise your grandmother that you would not observe another year of mourning or wear black? I recall you saying so,' Julius reminded her of their discussion.

'I did, and I will abide by it, but I feel most improper. I am sure anyone in my or grandma's acquaintance – and she did have many lady clients – will stare at me at the dance as if I am quite scandalous.'

Julius looked over long enough to give her a sympathetic look.

'People,' he muttered.

'Yes,' she agreed and they smiled at each other.

'I'll see if Ambrose can organise some form of distraction or scandal so that anything else seems rather mundane,' he teased. 'I am sure he would enjoy the challenge.'

'Heavens no, do not do that! I would hate to bring shame to the family or lose business because I chose to be rebellious.'

'In that case, blame me,' Julius offered.

Violet looked toward him, a confused expression on her countenance.

'You can say your employer insisted that you attend and wear a dress that highlighted the skills of the store of which you are manageress.' He paused. 'Will you be wearing a dress you have made yourself?'

'I know no other sort, except for that which my grandmother made me, so yes, I shall be.'

'There you go then. They will hold you in great sympathy and scowl at me for being such an unobliging employer.'

'You would fall on your sword for me?' she teased. 'How very gallant. But no, I thank you. I will hold my head up high and say I am honouring my grandmother's wishes. Just don't let me have too good a time or smile too much. That might be taking matters a little too far.'

'Miss Forrester, if you allow me, I fully intend to ensure you have a wonderful evening as you deserve, and I hope you will keep several dances for me.'

'So, you do dance?'

'Not if I can help it,' Julius admitted and Violet laughed. She turned slightly to look at him and Julius, having no choice but to watch the road ahead, bore her inspection. He had been doing the same – subtly observing her as they spoke when the opportunity presented itself. 'But I will make an exception and take to the dance floor when the temptation is too great.'

And now she blushed and looked away. 'I shall not be dancing a great deal, I think that is best, but I welcome a turn around the floor. Is there a particular dance you prefer and I shall put your name in my dance card?'

Julius frowned as he thought; he knew exactly which dance he wanted with Miss Violet Forrester but would she be alarmed if he announced the waltz? It was the most intimate of dances. When he did not immediately answer she suggested a couple of dances.

'Not the quadrille then? Where we change partners regularly and do those small bouncy steps?' Violet smiled.

For a moment, he tried to read her enthusiasm for the quadrille before returning his attention to the road ahead.

'Is that your favourite dance?' he asked with trepidation.

'I enjoy the energy of it and it is a very good choice if you do not wish to get too close to your dance partner or be forced to make small talk. A respectable dance, one might say.'

Was she baiting him to say he was not interested in anything more with her than that which was respectable? He would not!

'Ah, well definitely not that then,' Julius said being most forward and making Violet laugh again but he was quite serious. It was his grandfather's advice, to get a hurry along, and it was best that he discovers – one way or the other – if he was wasting his time with Miss Forrester. The days in the office knowing they were one wall apart and his evenings at home alone imagining Miss Violet Forrester residing with him in the future, her brother Tom also in the household in their care, often ruffled his composure, but most agreeably.

'Hmm,' she continued and he could not help but smile a little at her teasing. 'A Scottish reel, perhaps? If you enjoy a fling.'

'Good Lord, no.' Julius looked horrified and turned to see the look of amusement on Violet's face. She was doing her best to stir him from his sober appearance as he enjoyed the journey beside her. If only she knew how he drew in slow deep breaths to calm his heartbeat. He could not help but stare at Violet's lips for just a moment as she tapped her bottom lip, thinking.

'I have it! A polka! Oh no, that will never do… it requires too much jumping and turning in circles.'

'No polka,' he agreed with a chuckle. 'May I request every waltz on your dance card?' Julius raised an eyebrow in her direction as if challenging Violet to deny him. 'I believe I am quite capable of waltzing.'

'All three?' she asked feigning shock.

'All three,' he insisted.

'Well, you best get practising because I have been told I am very good at the waltz, and if I am having all three with you, I will not have the opportunity to show off my waltzing skills to anyone else. Best you match my skills and appreciate them,' she issued the challenge.

'Very well,' he agreed with more confidence than he felt. 'I will come in fine form. I believe it requires me to hold you close, however, otherwise you might spin off as we glide through our turn.'

'If I spin off anywhere, Mr Astin, I will hold you personally responsible,' she said and they exchanged a laugh, and not a moment too soon – as they were both flustered – they arrived at the Exhibition and Julius drove them into the grounds, seeking the stalls and staff for their horse and trap.

Phoebe smiled as she thought pleasant thoughts about Julius and Miss Forrester who had just departed. Ambrose sighed as he leaned on his grandfather's reception desk, talking with the family.

'Well, we have done all we can for Julius, it is up to him to fly now,' he said.

Phoebe laughed. 'You have done nothing but annoy him, Ambrose. Poor Julius. I hope one day he gets to pay you back when you fall in love.'

'I take umbrage at that,' Ambrose said with false indignation. 'He asked me to stay the other day when Miss Forrester and Mrs Shaw approached.'

'But it is knowing when to leave that counts,' Randolph said tapping his nose as if he were in the know.

Ambrose laughed. 'Fine then, I may have been unwelcomed this morning, but Julius was genuinely unbalanced. It was quite endearing.'

'I want them to be in love,' Phoebe said. 'Wouldn't it be wonderful?'

'I want you all to be in love,' Randolph said looking at his two youngest grandchildren. 'So, get a move along, your grandmother and I are not getting any younger. Who are you both intending to pursue?'

Ambrose shuffled uncomfortably and Phoebe frowned.

'I have to see to that advertising for Julius,' Ambrose said suddenly becoming busy.

'And I have much to do too,' Phoebe headed towards the steps to her office.

'Well, I must remember that next time I want to clear the room I should talk of matters of the heart,' Randolph said with a satisfied smile. 'Off you go then, but that won't be the last of it.'

Phoebe laughed as she ran down the stairs, pleased to have escaped the inquisition. On arriving she saw her Uncle Reggie lounging in the corner.

'Have I kept you waiting?' she teased. He was dead after all and probably had very few pressing engagements.

'I am very busy and in demand my dear, but the small break has been welcome.' He rose and gave her a wink and a grin that reminded her of Ambrose. With a glance at the covered body in the corner, Reggie asked, 'Did Mrs Tochborn tell you the rest of her story?'

'Only as much as she knew,' Phobe said. 'A most tragic life she has had.'

'She is at rest now, and with everyone dear to her, so take comfort from that,' Reggie assured her.

'That is comforting.' Phoebe suddenly felt a shock of realisation. Surely not... 'You are not here to hurry Grandpa along to be with you, are you?'

Her uncle gave her a devilish look. 'Have you heard the saying we are "a long time dead", my dear niece? I would not suggest anyone rush to the other side unless they are in pain. No, dear Randolph has work to do.'

She breathed a sigh of relief. 'Thank goodness for that. I apologise, Uncle Reggie, for putting you on the spot.'

'Quite alright, Phoebe, I understand. So, Mrs Tochborn then, she has left for good?'

'You have not encountered her on the other side yet?' Phoebe asked and gave him a cheeky smile.

'There are a few here,' he conceded, 'but I like to know who to expect in your waiting room when I'm visiting you.'

'I guess it is a waiting room of sorts,' she agreed with a smile and glanced around her large work area. 'I believe Mrs Tochborn has departed. She told me all she knew but was very much in the dark after the kidnapping,' Phoebe said lowering her voice. 'Her husband sent her abroad for a period. He told everyone the shock of the kidnapping was too much for her, which it was, but it also looked very odd that the mother of the missing boy was not present.'

'Hence creating rumours that they were somehow implicit in his disappearance or death, not that a body was ever found.'

'True. If it were, that would put an end to the claimants' court case.'

'Was she not upset about the claimants now that she knows the boy is on the other side?' Reggie asked. 'You must forgive my curiosity but I listened in on all that was said to the detective and the private investigator who fancies you, and I must say, it is a most interesting case. Before my time though... I believe I was already dead when the boy went missing.'

'It is fascinating. I am hoping Lilly will have a spare media seat and let me come along with her to the trial at least on one of the days. But no, Mrs Tochborn did not seem to care that they claimed to be her fake sons, knowing that they weren't. I thought she might be more inclined toward Mr William Varsewell in the asylum since Mrs Tochborn just unburdened herself and told me he is the twin brother of the dead boy, James.' Phoebe had not yet had the opportunity to share that news with anyone and waited for her uncle's reaction.

'She knows that?' Reggie asked shocked.

'Yes, and she sent me with a message, a rather obscure one, that Mr Varsewell understood to mean that his brother – the kidnapped boy – was in heaven with Mrs Tochborn and not missing. Detective Payne and I thrashed it out as one of our theories, it was like doing a puzzle, most rewarding.'

'Is that so? He is the young detective, isn't he? The eager lad with the good heart?'

'Yes, I believe that describes him well.' Phoebe smiled thinking of the lovely Detective Payne, and then her thoughts quickly drifted to his superior, Detective Stone. Reggie's musing interrupted her thoughts.

'Interesting. I must say I am surprised the remaining twin was not recruited into the role. Mind you, if I was his parent, I would not allow it.'

'Nor I, but they died soon after. Still, he was not made a Tochborn.'

'And, despite receiving the message, Mr Varsewell will continue his claim that he is the missing boy?' Reggie strode around, his hands clasped behind him.

'I don't think he is of mind to do so, but his brothers, or should I say adopted brothers – they are most likely cousins now that I think on it – well, they will pursue it while there is a pound to be had.'

'Someone is coming,' Uncle Reggie said but did not disappear. There was no need, as few could see him. But it was not a person, a living person; Mrs Tochborn appeared beside him.

'You are back, Mrs Tochborn, hello,' Phoebe said surprised. 'We were just speaking of you.'

'Hello Miss Astin and who is this gentleman? Will you introduce us?' Mrs Tochborn requested.

Phoebe did the introductions and Reggie bowed to the lady two decades his senior.

'I heard a little of your discussion, it is hard to leave when my earthly body is still here.' She looked towards the table and the covered body in the corner.

'Only for a few more hours, Mrs Tochborn. Your family was pleased to spend time with you this morning. Were you present?'

She gave a nod. 'They seemed sincere.'

'You heard my question, perhaps?' Uncle Reggie asked. 'In relation to whether you are distressed knowing the two claimants are not the original boy and knowingly deceived you?'

'Yes. And I heard both of your thoughts. I believe you are correct; I think I should be upset,' she said to Phoebe's surprise. 'I would not be so distressed if Mr William Varsewell was declared to be my son, James. After all, it was his twin brother who was taken, and William lost everything he knew. But he has no use for the money, nor is he capable of managing it, I believe.'

'So, you asked me to deliver the message for his peace of mind?' Phoebe asked.

'Exactly so. He now knows his brother has passed, and that information will give him some rest within himself.'

'It will. Most thoughtful of you Mrs Tochborn,' Reggie said. 'But you were about to endorse the other claimant were you not?'

'I was indeed, Mr Astin. And now, on reflection, I am annoyed that he would win my confidence. It is not that I have a great love for the family left behind, but their sincerity seemed genuine this morning, respectful at least. And I would rather they, along with the church, received the benefits of the estate than a shyster.'

'Sadly, it is too late,' Reggie said. 'It happens when we leave this worldly place, most inconvenient.' He gave her a small smile and she laughed.

'I bet you were a charmer in your day, Mr Astin. But there is still a young lady with the right connections who can help right a wrong.' She looked to Phoebe.

Phoebe straightened. 'Of course, Mrs Tochborn. I am at your service, but it is easier said than done. I cannot just say that I have spoken with your spirit and expect to be believed.'

'They may even lock my dear niece away,' Reggie exclaimed in mock horror and both ladies laughed.

'I understand,' Mrs Tochborn said looking from Reggie to Phoebe with affection. 'I am grateful for anything you can do, Miss Astin, and I do have evidence.'

'You do?' Phoebe asked. 'That is just what the detective needs. Evidence of what, may I ask and where might I find it?'

'I have information from the young boy's parents who have also passed over, as to why the remaining twin boy, William, was not adopted and made to step in when James disappeared and they passed away.'

'We did wonder,' Reggie said in a low voice. 'It seemed like the perfect solution for your husband.'

Mrs Tochborn nodded and told Phoebe and Reggie what was needed to stop the estate from falling into the wrong hands and to set things right. Once again, Phoebe had news for the detectives and time was of the essence.

Chapter 17

L ILLY LEWIS SPENT THE night in her head, going over the Tochborn story, looking for a unique angle she could pursue. She was a reporter after all and did not want to just report stories as they happened. Lilly wanted to investigate, source stories, and have break-throughs. The thought excited her and she sighed thinking of her father's displeasure at her career. If she had been a boy, he would have loved the ambition ebbing from her every pore.

The next morning, Lilly was convinced she had to delve more into the nature of the claimant in the lunatic asylum – William Varsewell. He was the man unable to represent himself, or to charm and win over the relatives because of his confinement. But what if he was the real James Tochborn and Arthur Horton was stealing the show? There must be something she could dig up to help or hinder William Varsewell's cause. Maybe her writing partner, Fergus, did not ask all the right questions or maybe the inmate was not comfortable with a man. Lilly Lewis was going to find out.

Arriving at the office early, she glanced at Mr Cowan's office and saw him in a meeting.

'Thank goodness,' Lilly said slipping into the seat at her desk next to Fergus, who was also an early starter, most likely due to his young child at home. 'I am dashing to the asylum.'

'I knew this day would come,' Fergus joked and Lilly grinned.

'None of your cheek. I just want to explore that claimant more, if I can get a word out of him.'

'It is worth a try, Lilly,' Fergus agreed. 'He might be more inclined to talk with a lady than a man'

'Thank you for not saying I shouldn't go or need to be accompanied,' Lilly said sincerely.

'I am not that brave,' he said with a wink. 'I met late yesterday with a man who was apprenticed with Arthur Horton at his butchery and he said they had a little too much to drink one night and Horton spoke of his preparation for the trial.'

'Ooh, that is interesting, I wonder what lengths of research Arthur Horton has undertaken to become Mr James Tochborn.'

Fergus gasped. 'You don't believe he is the heir?'

Lilly grinned and played along. 'No more than you are, Fergus Griffiths, and don't tell me you believe him to be!'

'No, I think he is a vaudeville actor.'

'A good description. Your contact may find himself without a job after the interview.'

'He now runs his own store and seems to have no great loyalty to Horton despite starting his career with him. I am writing up that interview and then will check on telegrams. I'm expecting one from a Wagga Wagga funeral business in relation to our queries about Horton's real parents.'

'You have plenty to keep you busy.' She glanced again at Mr Cowan's office. 'I will leave now lest we get called in. Wish me luck.'

'Indeed,' Fergus said, as Lilly rose, grabbed her pad and headed off. She hailed a hansom out the front and requested the lunatic asylum.

'The Woogaroo Lunatic Asylum?'

'The very same, thank you, Sir.' She bore the looks of the driver who assessed her as if she might be a potential inmate.

'I assure you I am visiting, not checking in.'

The elderly driver chuckled and they were off. Given the journey took over an hour, Lilly had plenty of time to write and prepare some questions that she hoped might get Mr William Varsewell talking about his childhood. She dreaded what would happen if there were strict visiting hours or a restriction on the press, but she would face that hurdle when she got there, even if she had to embellish who she was and why she wanted to see William Varsewell.

The site of the foreboding building did not deter Lilly Lewis from her mission as she alighted on the front steps of the main entrance.

'Would you wait for me, please? I might be thirty minutes or so.'

'No problem, love,' the driver said pushing his cap back off his forehead. 'I'll water and rest the horses.'

'I am happy to share the ride back and split the fare, should you get a query,' Lilly said, mindful of Mr Cowan and his budget. 'Preferably not with an escaping patient.'

He chuckled. 'Right you are, Miss.'

Lilly need not have worried, visitors appeared to be welcome and her occupation was not enquired of – no one would have suspected the attractive young lady in the apricot dress to be a reporter. It was nearing 10am and Lilly was taken to William in the carpentry rooms. She spotted him easily from the description Fergus had written after his visit.

'William, you have a visitor this morning, a lovely lady,' the guard said leaving them alone but not before indicating where he would be standing should Lilly need him. She nodded her thanks.

William's eyes were wide and he smiled. 'Miss Toussaint! Bonjour,' he said in perfect French.

Miss Toussaint?

Play along, Lilly coached herself.

Her French lessons had been drilled into her but it was a good three years or more since she had spoken the language.

'Bonjour, William,' she said gently and continued in English hoping he would. 'It has been a long time.'

'I miss you.'

'I feel the same. Are you eating and sleeping well?' She didn't know what else to ask in her capacity of Miss Toussaint, but given William's wondrous look, Lilly assumed Miss Toussaint was liked and possibly loved, hence she would care for his welfare.

'Yes, but I am sorry, I have not kept up my French lessons.'

Lilly smiled. 'That is perfectly understandable, William,' she said, trying to speak with a light French lilt in the hope that was correct. 'I confess, I have let my lessons slip too.'

He smiled, studying her and added, 'but you are the teacher.'

Miss Toussaint – that is who you are, the French tutor!

'You were one of my favourite pupils,' she continued, not averse to playing a role to get more information. She was a reporter after all.

William laughed and looked much younger for doing so. 'No, my brother was your favourite. James was better at French than me.'

'Ah, James. He was a good student, but you tried hard,' Lilly kept going. 'Where is James?'

William looked like he had been slapped. His mouth dropped open and she hurriedly changed the subject, guessing his distress might see her early exit.

'Your mother liked that you both learnt French,' she said softly and smiled, watching as he processed her words and his countenance relaxed again.

William smiled. 'She liked that we were going to be men of the world, even if she could not practice with us.'

'No, but there were others who could,' Lilly fished, 'besides me of course.'

'Only Mrs Tochborn.'

Lilly's breath hitched and her heart leapt with excitement. The lady in question, and he had not called her mother. *Oh, my goodness, this was amazing.*

She scrambled to stay calm and respond. 'Yes, Mrs Tochborn was good at French.'

William started to whittle at the piece of timber in front of him as if he had just seen it, and began to hum, occasionally looking at her and smiling.

'I have missed you,' he said again, and then he added, 'and James.'

James, the brother, not James Tochborn the missing heir.

'What was James's surname, do you recall?' Lilly asked knowing it was a silly question since James was supposedly William's brother so it should be Varsewell. But Lilly hoped William might say a different name.

He said, 'the same as mine.'

'Of course, I am confused today. I shall see you again, William. Take care, won't you?'

'I will, Miss Toussaint.'

Lilly could not get back to her ride fast enough and thanking the guard, she rushed to tell the driver to take her straight to the Roma Street Police Station. A lady waited to share her lift and was returning to the city. They greeted each other and took their seats inside the hansom.

Lilly needed to tell Detective Stone that William Varsewell's mother was not Mrs Tochborn, and he was not the heir. No wonder the brothers did not want William to be left alone when interviewed, but no doubt the guards turned a blind eye to women in attendance. For once, being a lady on the job had worked to her advantage.

Detective Harland Stone closed the door to his office. Not because he was worried the discussion would be overheard, but because he did not want any more interruptions or anyone else to enter. It was just past midday and the private detective, Bennet Martin, was in attendance claiming to have news and appearing most enthusiastic. Miss Lilly Lewis also joined in with news to share and he sensed she was keeping something close to her chest. All the parties were gathered in one room.

Harland always had a sense when things were coming to a head and now, he felt there was something on the periphery of his mind, on the edge of the case out of reach. Something that would crack the case wide open. The frustration was boiling in his stomach.

'Perhaps Mr Martin might start, and time is of the essence,' Gilbert said and Harland looked to him, surprised. The boy was stepping up. He nodded and Bennet seemed happy to have the floor. But then Harland held up his hand.

'Miss Lewis,' he addressed Lilly as she sat, pen at the ready, looking like a deadline was pressing as it was every day.

She spoke before he had a chance. 'Detective, I will confer with you at the end of the meeting about what I can print, but I have my own lead from an interview this morning that

I intend to publish and share with you.' She gave him a smile bordering on a grimace of frustration.

'Thank you,' he said and nodded to Bennet to begin.

'You may know this but...' Bennet stood and spoke from his notes as if addressing parliament, covering the information that he and his clerk, Daniel Dutton, had uncovered. He spoke of his father at Scotland Yard transcribing the contents of a new clipping, and a Horton family friend from Wapping claiming Arthur Horton was not orphaned or a ship-boy but travelled to Australia with his parents. Lilly's pen flew furiously across her page, only matched by Gilbert taking notes for himself and Detective Stone.

Bennet continued, inviting Lilly to also include her information from visiting several orphanages with his clerk. He updated the detectives on finding no record of a William Varsewell at any orphanage. Bennet sat down looking smug.

Harland looked to Gilbert who said, 'We had secured that intelligence from our visit to the orphanage, but not the family friend information from Wapping.'

'Thank you, Bennet. Miss Lewis, would you like to share?' Harland asked.

'Indeed, I would,' Lilly said remaining seated. 'William Varsewell of the asylum inadvertently told me this morning that Mrs Tochborn was not his mother.'

'Good grief!' Bennet exclaimed.

'Do go on, Miss Lewis,' Harland invited, keen to hear more.

'Fortunately, his brothers were not present,' Lilly said and told of what happened. 'I wonder where Miss Toussaint is these days.'

Harland looked at her with admiration. 'Well done, Miss Lewis, a fine piece of investigative journalism. I believe it to be the truth.'

'As do I, Detective,' Lilly said delighted with his support.

'Our news complements what you have just discovered,' Harland said and the room buzzed with the developments rolling out.

Harland explained, 'Gilbert spoke with Miss Astin who had interesting information from the gentleman you just visited, William Varsewell of the asylum. Miss Astin visited him with a message from Mrs Tochborn. We also spoke with Mrs Tochborn's gardener of thirty years and learnt of twins.'

'Twins! Could it be William and James?' Lilly exclaimed and Bennet shot to his feet. They spoke over each other with questions for the detectives.

'You are saying the kidnapped child had a twin?'

'Where is he? What happened to him?'

'Were both boys kidnapped then?'

'No, no,' Harland said firmly and everyone stilled. 'Gilbert will explain.' Harland strode around the room, looking at his board and notes as Gilbert filled the small party in on what they had discovered.

'We believe the maid companion knows a great deal more,' Gilbert concluded, 'but the gardener was very helpful.'

'But why? Why would they not rescue the boy out of the orphanage and pass him off as their returned son and heir?' Lilly asked, her nose sensing the story immediately.

'Our thoughts exactly, Miss Lewis,' Harland said. 'Why indeed. But you cannot publish that yet, as we must explore it. If it gets out too early, we will derail the claimants' trial and I must have all my facts before I do that.'

Lilly nodded. 'I understand. But I will be publishing my conversation with Mr Varsewell, and you will give me your story first?'

Harland nodded in agreement. 'Bear in mind that the brothers will try and claim William wasn't of sound mind when he said that to you, or that you coerced it from him.'

'I suspect as much,' Lilly agreed.

'We have not found anything yet that is an irrefutable argument and established beyond the shadow of a doubt,' Harland said with a small sigh. 'A good legal team will contest everything we have to date.'

'Frustrating to say the least,' Gilbert added.

Harland closed the meeting. 'Thank you all for your contributions. Bennet, I believe you have clients to update;

and thank you, Miss Lewis. You have a meaty story to write for tomorrow after your interview at the asylum. I am also happy for you to write about the Wapping friend of the family and the challenge to Mr Arthur Horton if you find that suitable material for your issue?'

'Yes, thank you, Detective Stone. That will fire up Arthur Horton, and I will follow up with him for comment.'

Bennet offered Lilly a ride back to her place of work and the group dispersed. With the door now open for interruptions, several people neared but seeing Harland pacing, hands behind his back, and a frustrated look on his countenance, they moved on. Behind him, Gilbert organised his notes.

'You were not surprised by Mr William Varsewell's admission, Sir?' Gilbert asked his superior.

'No, I suspected he wasn't the missing boy. But why would they not take him and make him James Tochborn?'

'I'd understand if the parents were alive, they would not want to risk losing another son, but they were both dead not long after,' Gilbert mused. 'The Tochborns could have said the boy was found and in steps the other twin, William.'

'Yes. What was the obstacle to them doing so? I can't imagine it was Mrs Tochborn herself; I suspect she did what she was told. Leo Tochborn appeared desperate enough to clutch this opportunity. The twins' parents had been paid for letting James stand in as the fake son in the first instance so had little recourse. I imagine not many people knew of them or knew the boys well enough to come forward and challenge the Tochborns. They could have raised the remaining boy as their own and if Mr Tochborn did die, at least he could take comfort in keeping his estate between his wife and new son. He had the existing photo record of the boy growing up with them.' Harland shook his head and ran his hand over his face. 'It would have been so opportune.'

The desk sergeant knocked on the door and walked in, brandishing a piece of paper. 'A note from Miss Phoebe Astin for you, Detective.'

'Thank you.' Harland grabbed for it, desperate for any input, even from the spirit world and he was not disappointed. He read, *'Detective, I have vital new information. May I have an audience with you at your earliest convenience at my premises or yours, please? Yours Faithfully, Phoebe Astin.'*

This is what he wanted to hear.

'Gilbert, we are off to *The Economic Undertaker*.' He grabbed his hat, as Gilbert leapt from his seat and followed suit.

Chapter 18

JULIUS STRODE INTO THE office through the back door, and arriving at the front desk saw the hopeful faces of his grandfather and brother staring at him.

'It went well, we will hire space for the dress store to feature at the Exhibition. I have asked for the paperwork to be sent to you for signing, Grandpa,' he said, and then added on reading their expression, 'I have nothing else to add, so do not ask.'

'But you look happy, brother,' Ambrose teased. 'I have never seen you quite like this.'

'I am happy. Can we leave it at that?' He shifted uncomfortably and made a mental note to ask Phoebe to waltz with him a few times for practice. It had been a long time since he had taken to the dance floor and needed to refresh his skills.

'Are you both happy, you and Miss Forrester?' Ambrose asked and Julius sighed.

Randolph stepped in. 'A good day's work then, Julius, well done lad. Now, no more dallying, you two have Mrs Tochborn's funeral early this afternoon – Ambrose and I have placed the body in the hearse – and tomorrow will also be busy with two funerals.'

'Business is booming,' Ambrose exclaimed. 'Come on then, Julius, I know you are just back from your outing, but you can tell me all about it as we do our preparations.'

Julius grimaced and gave his grandfather a look that spoke of rescue but received nothing but a raised eyebrow and a pleased look. The front door opened and they all donned their respectful looks and then Julius's countenance changed to that of a hunted deer. Mrs Reed and her daughter, Hannah, entered and looked thrilled to finally have come at a time to find Julius in attendance. The elder of the ladies wore black in remembrance of a deceased husband who passed over eighteen months now and the youngest wore a dress of dark grey. The selection of a headstone had become an opportunity for husband-hunting and had dragged on needlessly. Julius did his best not to groan as the men offered the two ladies a greeting.

'You best get to it, lads,' Randolph said and turned to the ladies. 'Forgive them, Mrs Reed, Miss Reed, they are way behind schedule, but I am at your service.'

Mrs Reed would have none of it and addressed Julius directly. 'Mr Astin, I hear from the Hospital Ball committee that your business has taken a significant number of tickets. Will you both be attending?' she asked with great interest looking from Julius to Ambrose and back to Julius.

'We will be, Mrs Reed. Our sister has organised a small party and we like to support the hospital and our grandmother who is on the committee.'

Julius edged his way closer to the hallway to make his exit out the back where the hearse awaited.

'Well, that is delightful. My Hannah will be attending, as will I.' Mrs Reed clasped her hands in front of her as if expecting the young men to be most pleased by that news. 'Of course, I won't be dancing as I couldn't possibly do so with the memory of my husband so dear, but Hannah will be.' Beside her, Miss Hannah Reed nodded and smiled at Julius with a practised expression and the silence of expectation that followed. Julius felt Ambrose shift beside him as he restrained a laugh.

'I am sure the hospital very much appreciates your support, Mrs Reed,' he said. 'Please excuse us—'

'It might be an opportune moment to secure a dance.' The ambitious mother continued, 'You know how the dance cards fill up so quickly for the most beautiful and popular young ladies.' Mrs Reed smiled at her daughter.

A thousand excuses ran through Julius's head but none were quick enough to reach his mouth. Fortunately, Ambrose stepped forward.

'An excellent idea, Mrs Reed,' he said. 'I am not sure what time Julius will be in attendance, but Miss Reed, please do pencil me in for a dance early in the evening. I leave it to your discretion which one.'

She nodded and blushed prettily on cue, and without any hesitation, Julius wished them a good day and was gone before there was a chance to dance around the topic again. Ambrose caught him up at the backdoor.

'Thank you, Ambrose,' he said in a low tone.

'I believe you owe me now, brother. So, I look forward to hearing all about your business meeting with Miss Forrester, and not the boring business parts,' he said with a satisfied look and laughed at seeing his brother's cornered expression.

Detective Harland Stone was distracted on the hansom ride to the business place of *The Economic Undertaker*. He sat beside his protégé in silent contemplation while displaying evidence of frustration – moving forward in his seat, clasping his hands, rubbing his brow, and sitting back again in a repeated fashion.

On occasion, he said aloud what he was thinking or reacted to an observation by Gilbert.

Harland desperately hoped Miss Astin had something useful. The claimants' trial started the next day and he did not want one of them to win because he was unable to prove with facts why the two men were not the grown-up missing boy, James Tochborn, or if the boy might still be alive. Better still, he hoped to prove the boy was, in fact, dead, declare who took his life and where the body was buried. How satisfying that would be.

When he was given the case, the brief was quite ambiguous. His superior had simply said, 'Have a look at it, Detective Stone,' as if he fully expected Harland to find something that would lead to the truth despite the number of police and investigators that had studied the file over the years. But still, he felt there was something major he was missing or not privy to seeing.

'I feel we are right on the edge of it,' he said out of the blue.

Gilbert nodded, getting used to his superior's manner. On their first case together, Gilbert might have asked a thousand questions about that statement. Harland was pleased his young partner was learning that not every thought required a reply and that Harland liked to voice his thoughts aloud occasionally. Now, Harland looked to Gilbert which he read correctly as an invitation to speak.

'Sir, you are more optimistic than me. I cannot grasp any of the loose ends and I am trying to connect them.'

'That is an excellent description of my frustration, Gilbert, excellent. It is as if the police gave up on looking for the boy or his murderer; the real parents of James were silent or silenced; his brother was unjustly sent to an orphanage despite all that had befallen his family, and that boy has such confused memories which implies his health was not the best or he suffered some sort of psychosis. Add to this, Mrs Tochborn had poison in her system which may have come from an accidental dose, and Arthur Horton has no rights, in my opinion, to be making his claim.' He threw his hands up in the air as if all the balls were there waiting to be caught.

They sat in silence again for a while on the short journey that seemed to be taking an inordinate amount of time for Harland's liking.

'The twins,' he muttered randomly, running a hand over his lower face.

'Approximately one in a hundred women have twins,' Gilbert said.

'Interesting.' Harland glanced at Gilbert. *But not relevant*, he thought. Sifting through what Gilbert said that was relevant was one of his daily challenges, but a small price to pay when some observations were most useful. Then, Gilbert began humming a tune.

'What is that?' Harland asked.

'I too, am thinking over everything constantly and comparing it to what we know, as you are training me to do.'

'Good, and?' Harland hurried him along.

'The nursery rhyme gave us a hint that the baby was not the Tochborns, that it was a substitute.'

Gilbert began to sing the lyrics. 'Rock-a-bye-baby, in the treetop, when the wind blows, the cradle will rock.' He stopped.

'Nothing sinister there that I can think of related to this case,' Harland mused. 'Go on, next lines.'

Gilbert resumed his singing. 'When the bough breaks, the cradle will fall, and down will come baby, cradle and all.'

They sat for a moment thinking in silence until Harland said, 'As you informed me earlier, the nursery rhyme is believed to be about a baby substituted for the King and Queen, and the wind and cradle falling is their downfall at the hand of the Protestants.'

Gilbert nodded. 'That is one interpretation, Sir.'

'Let's look wider.' Harland's eye narrowed as he thought. 'What was it William Varsewell told me?' He clicked his fingers remembering. 'He said it was the cook singing the nursery rhyme to him while he sat in the kitchen eating warm bread.'

'Do you think the cook was planting a seed in the mind of the young boy that the ruse will soon be up and the Tochborns will fall from glory for their deception?' Gilbert asked.

'Or was she singing it for her own satisfaction perhaps and hoping that might happen?'

'Maybe. But did you not say that the lyrics William sang at the asylum were slightly different and you thought he got it wrong.'

'Yes! Well done, Gilbert, I did. But is that significant or has he just forgotten the lyrics and is mixed up, as we know him to be? I am more inclined to believe there is some significance to it.'

'I believe I wrote down what we learned at that visit when I returned to the office, Sir.'

Harland looked surprised, his brow furrowed as he considered this. 'Excellent. But did I tell you the last line William sang?' He waited impatiently as Gilbert flicked through the pages of his notebook, pleased for the young man's thoroughness as too much was left to memory by many detectives for his liking. He believed a good junior detective should fulfil that role.

'Here it is.' Gilbert looked to Harland with an apologetic look. 'You stated that William Varsewell said a woman in the kitchen sang the rhyme to him while he was enjoying the warm bread and that William sang the last line incorrectly... but you did not tell me the line.'

Harland sighed and rubbed his temples. 'It was something innocuous... just the last line that varied, and I surmised at the time that it was a line that any parent or nanny might sing so the child wasn't frightened by the nursery rhyme.'

'It is rather gruesome.'

'What was the line?' he muttered. 'It might be one more clue in the rhyme.'

'This might help, Sir,' Gilbert said looking at his notebook. 'You said William felt safe with the woman.'

'Yes! The line was something like "but Mother will catch you, cradle and all" or of that nature.'

'Oh my!' Gilbert said and snapped the notebook closed; his eyes were huge. 'Mother? That is significant. Was the mother singing the rhyme Mrs Tochborn? No, she wouldn't be in the kitchen. She would leave that to the staff.'

'Precisely, Gilbert. If only the inmate William could tell us who his mother was, but thanks to Miss Lewis, William has said to her it was not Mrs Tochborn. That will have to do us,' Harland said. 'If that woman in the kitchen is the cook, and that is a very likely scenario, then William's mother was the cook providing him bread, singing to him of her protection. If we can prove that is the case, then she is the mother of James as they were twins, and thus the boy they paraded as a Tochborn was definitely a fake. He was never a Tochborn, nor are the claimants.'

'But William and James's mother is dead, as is their father. So, if the cook is their mother, we cannot confirm it.'

'But we were looking for the birth records of James Tochborn and William Varsewell. Not the birth records of twin boys with the cook's surname. Hickling, was it not?'

'Yes,' Gilbert agreed with excitement. 'I wonder if there is a record for a William Hickling at the orphanage and his removal by the Varsewell family.'

'Yes, let's hope so,' Harland mused.

Gilbert continued. 'And if William Varsewell of the asylum would recognise his surname – Hickling.'

'I think we will put that to the test.'

The hansom arrived at *The Economic Undertaker* and the men alighted to hear what would be Miss Astin's most important clue yet.

The sound of boots on the staircase to her office told Phoebe that several gentlemen were on their way to see her. *The detectives,* she thought, and she was right as they came into sight.

'Good day, Miss Astin, is now convenient?' Harland asked, removing his hat and Gilbert followed, doing the same and patting down his hair. She saw the way Detective Stone's eyes softened at seeing her, the respect he afforded her. She could not deny her attraction, but did the detective feel the same? He had not given any indication that he had any thoughts of her that were not professional. Phoebe smiled a greeting.

'Detective Stone, Detective Payne, by all means. Please come in. Forgive me for summoning you but I have information that might be useful if proven.'

'We are happy for any information, Miss Astin,' Gilbert said before Harland could speak.

'Indeed,' he agreed. 'The trial is due to begin and I am feeling the clock ticking.'

For a man under pressure, Phoebe was surprised at how calm he appeared and she told him so. 'Perhaps you are a duck, Detective. Paddling furiously under the water and calm on the surface?'

He laughed, which she enjoyed and was pleased to provide a moment of relief in his day.

'Well, I've never been compared to a duck, have you, Gilbert?'

'Not this week, Sir,' Gilbert said joining in the light-hearted conversation.

'But I am definitely treading water,' he said and exhaled. Phoebe saw the tension and exhaustion in his countenance. When he met her gaze again, Phoebe had the overwhelming desire to reach for him and provide comfort. She cleared her mind of such a thought.

'Let me get to business as you are both under pressure,' she said and saw Uncle Reggie had arrived and sat on the lounge observing the discussion. 'Mrs Tochborn is not with us,' she said trusting the two men. 'She has gone to be buried.'

'Ah, of course,' Harland said. 'I hope there will be no incidents. But this information is from her?'

'It is.'

Both men accepted the seat Phoebe offered at a small table in her workroom. Harland's knees briefly touched Phoebe's as he sat, his long legs taking up considerable room under the small table.

'I beg your pardon,' he said and hurriedly pulled back as far as the wall behind him would allow.

Phoebe gave them a brief overview. 'Mrs Tochborn is upset that Mr Arthur Horton is proclaiming to be her son when the boy, James, has crossed to the same side as her. She has informed me that William Varsewell of the asylum was the brother of the missing boy, James, her fake child.'

Harland inhaled. 'So that is true. We spoke with the gardener who talked of the cook and stable manager having twin boys – James and William.'

'That is them and it is true.'

'We just have to prove it before the claimants make their case,' Gilbert said.

'But how do we prove it?' Harland's frown deepened. 'We can bring the gardener to the stand, but as Gilbert said, one woman in a hundred has twins, his mother could be anyone.' He glanced to Gilbert as if realising the fact was useful after all and continued, 'and who would believe that the esteemed Mr Tochborn would pass off a servant's child as his own? Our claim is no sounder than that of the claimants' unless William was to say he was William Hickling, but that does not discount Arthur Horton.' Harland's foot tapped impatiently and realising it, he stopped the action. 'My apologies, Miss Astin, I find myself most frustrated.'

'I cannot blame you for that, Detective Stone. I have more.'

He breathed a sigh of relief and leaned forward keenly.

'Mr Leo Tochborn tried to shield Mrs Tochborn from the ransom demands and the kidnapping stress, keeping her in the dark which she claimed made matters worse. She was terrified that young William would be asked to step in to replace his brother and could be kidnapped as well.'

'I can imagine his parents felt the same and were trapped by their initial agreement,' Gilbert said.

'Exactly so, Detective Payne,' Pheobe agreed. 'Mrs Tochborn said she learnt that her husband did, in fact, try to replace James with William and wanted to let the police know he had been returned after the ransom was paid. He threatened, coerced, and bribed the boys' parents who were on his staff, and he was a most influential man.'

'Mercenary.' Harland shook his head in disgust.

Phoebe hurried along. 'Mrs Tochborn said her husband offered to set the boy, William, up for life and officially make him the heir if they agreed to let him be a Tochborn, and he would put a private investigator on the case to find James when the police could not. Otherwise,' Phoebe lowered her voice as she delivered the ultimatum, 'they would all be turned out.'

'Shocking!' Gilbert exclaimed.

'How did they stand up to him?' Harland asked. 'We know William was never flouted as the Tochborn's son, so were the parents resolute in their decision? They must have feared for their safety and that of their remaining child.'

'Yes, I was told that they were terrified. But they had their own power.'

'How so?' Harland pushed and then just as quickly apologised. 'Miss Astin, I forget myself when caught up in an injustice. Please take your time.'

Phoebe appreciated his kind words and noticed he seemed a little off balance – perhaps it was the stress of the situation.

'No apology is necessary, Detective. I too forget myself when engrossed in my work. To continue, the Hicklings were stronger than Mr Tochborn gambled on.' She saw the keen interest on the detectives' faces. 'It happened because of a letter that was written by the parents, threatening to expose Leo Tochborn and how he bullied them into providing an illegitimate son.'

'That was a very dangerous and courageous thing to do,' Harland mused, listening attentively as if it were a radio play unfolding before them.

'This letter? Where is it?' Gilbert asked what Harland was prepared to wait for from Miss Astin.

'I'm sorry, but that is for you to determine,' Phoebe said with a small look of apology. 'Mrs Tochborn was not privy to that information and she did not know about the letter until a decade later on her husband's death. But someone in the Hicklings' circle of friends may still have that letter... someone that they could trust and who knew about the fake child – which narrows down your contenders. The Hicklings could not have risked giving the letter to anyone else for fear of it falling into the wrong hands. It could have been used for blackmail even after Mr Tochborn's death or given to the police. That is what Mrs Tochborn surmised.'

'I believe she is correct.' Harland sat back and closed his eyes, his fingers drumming on the table, going through all that was said. He muttered, 'threads not yet joined.' Phoebe did not speak and Gilbert made notes from their discussion. She studied the hollow planes of Detective Stone's face, where he was gaunt from not eating regularly or not sleeping or both. She studied his strong jaw, the dark lashes and then he opened his eyes and seemed to look right through her.

'Miss Astin, forgive me, I know I am taking up your time.' His voice was lower, gravelly and he cleared his throat.

'My time is yours Detective, for such an important matter.' For just a moment she forgot Gilbert Payne was nearby, like a chaperone, on what felt like a moment of intimacy with the detective. Wishful thinking, she knew.

He nodded his thanks. 'This letter, who told Mrs Tochborn about it after her husband's death?'

'Mrs Tochborn said that she heard of it directly from the remaining staff. They were loyal to her and trusted her, they understood her distress was for the Hickling family.'

Gilbert clarified, 'So, Mr Leo Tochborn was told of this letter and thus not knowing who had it for safekeeping, found himself at a disadvantage.'

'Precisely,' Phoebe confirmed. 'In anger, he turned them out but the Hicklings warned if anything nefarious was to happen to them or their remaining son, that letter existed and would be made public.'

Gilbert exhaled and shook his head at the drama of it.

Phoebe continued, 'Mrs Tochborn believed until her dying day that James might still be alive as his body was never found, thus the desperation to right a wrong and accept one of the claimants as James Tochborn. She thought she owed him that much.'

'Hence the newspaper advertisement and search for a missing "son",' Gilbert said.

'A noble gesture, be it late,' Harland agreed. 'We need that letter and the holder to step forward.'

'Mrs Tochborn is adamant that the letter still exists – a dangerous document that would not be discarded easily.' Phoebe ensured she had their attention and said, 'Detectives, now Mrs Tochborn wants it found so that Arthur Horton's claim can be dismissed and William Varsewell's cousins receive nothing.'

Harland's eyes widened as if a thought had just occurred to him.

'You know?' Phoebe said, her face lit with anticipation.

His smile appeared. 'Miss Astin, I believe I do. You mentioned blackmail earlier... given the letter did not see the light of day to shame Mrs Tochborn, I suspect the holder cares for her a great deal or did. If I am right, the letter is right under our noses.'

Chapter 19

MID-AFTERNOON, JULIUS RETURNED FROM the funeral of Mrs Henriette Tochborn and undertook his usual routine; he thoroughly washed his hands and face and brushed down his jacket and trousers. He always felt dusty after a funeral. As if the earth he had just buried their client in had touched him and had some claim on his person. Ambrose was quite the opposite. He shucked off his jacket – if no clients were in the office – and looked perfectly at ease being back amongst the living. Refreshed, Julius entered the kitchen to find his family in attendance and accepted, with thanks, the offered cup of tea from Mrs Dobbs.

'I am going over to see cousin, Lucian,' Ambrose said and took a large bite of one of Mrs Dobbs' peanut crunchie biscuits. He made an appreciative sound before adding between chews, 'He has several coffins ready for us to collect.'

'Excellent, thank you,' Julius said pleased to have Ambrose occupied and not have to attend to the collection himself.

'Was it a nice ceremony?' Phoebe asked, sipping her tea, and studying her brothers. 'Mrs Tochborn deserved that.'

'It was our top-shelf product,' Ambrose said as if that was answer enough. 'Although I don't know why with her fortune the family chose our business.'

'Because they are tight and don't wish to spend on the dead what might be coming their way, I'd suggest,' Randolph said. 'We have seen it before.'

'Disgraceful,' Mrs Dobbs said with a shake of her head but quickly added with a smile, 'but I for one am not outraged as it is good for business.'

The family smiled and Randolph agreed.

'I was concerned there might be trouble,' Julius admitted. 'Mr Arthur Horton insisted on attending and was putting on a performance of great emotion, wailing that he had lost his mother when he had only just found her again.'

Ambrose picked up the story. 'Not that anything was stopping him from contacting her before this, from what I understand.'

'What was the reaction of the family?' Randolph asked.

'The family members who believe his claim indulged him,' Julius answered, 'and those who did not, appeared most angry at him. Fortunately, there was a deep grave site between them.'

'I confess I am pleased to have Mrs Tochborn put to rest.' Phoebe lowered her voice as if it were a secret. 'She was a lovely lady but had quite a sad presence in my room.'

Ambrose chuckled. 'Are most of your dead visitors happy?'

Phoebe smiled at him, happy to be teased. 'Well, as a matter of fact, yes, they are, dear brother. Most are not begrudging the life they lived, they just need my help to finish off something important to them.'

'So, what is Uncle Reggie doing hanging around you then?' Ambrose asked.

'I am sure he will tell Phoebe in good time,' Julius added with a glance to his grandfather who said nothing. It was a sensitive subject for Randolph.

'When can I expect my next clients?' Phoebe asked her grandfather, changing the subject.

'There is a gentleman to collect from the hospital in the morning and the family would like an open casket if you can work your magic, Phoebe dear,' Randolph said. 'We have also been put on notice of an elderly lady rapidly declining whose family live across the southern border. They wish us to prepare her for burial when the time comes. She has been taken to the hospital and they will travel here on her death. I believe one of their party is on the way.'

'If we are lucky, she will turn up her toes overnight and we can pick the two of them up at the same time,' Ambrose said and the family hid their smiles at Ambrose's irreverence.

'Lord help us,' Julius said with a glint of amusement and a shake of his head. He turned to Phoebe. 'Why don't you take the remaining hours of the afternoon off and go shopping for the ball?' He encouraged her to take the time for herself, but Julius also had a matter he wanted to speak with Phoebe about privately, once Ambrose had gone and everyone returned to their duties. The matter of dance practice.

Phoebe grimaced. 'I suppose I should prepare for the ball.'

Mrs Dobbs laughed. 'Young ladies are supposed to find that most exciting. I know I did at your age.'

Phoebe gave Mrs Dobbs a sheepish look. 'Oh, I am looking forward to the ball very much, it is just the shopping that I don't enjoy. I have a dress that I am keen to wear... the one you and Grandma gave me last birthday, Grandpa, that I've only had one occasion to wear, but I do need new gloves and shoes.' She gasped remembering her pending appointment. 'Lilly has secured me a seat at the trial the day thereafter, just for the morning session. Fergus will be reporting outside the court. Can I be spared a few hours then rather than now?'

Ambrose's gaze met Phoebe's at the mention of Miss Lilly Lewis's name. 'You lucky thing,' he said.

'That is fine with me if your brother has no objections?' Randolph looked to Julius. 'There will only be one body to prepare, the other is not urgent as the family will take some days to travel here. Besides, she may not pass overnight despite the inconvenience to Ambrose.' He gave his youngest grandson a raised eyebrow and Ambrose grinned.

'I think we can spare you this afternoon and mid-week without you swapping one for the other,' Julius assured his sister. 'Bennet will be there at the trial too, with his clients. What did Mrs Tochborn wish the outcome to be?'

Phoebe gave a small sigh. 'In the end, I think she wanted Mr Arthur Horton's claim thrown out and the estate to go to her descendants and the church, as stated in her will. I believe she had great sympathy for Mr William Varsewell in the asylum, but her wealth is of little use to him. He does not want to live in the outside world, according to Detective Payne.'

Randolph shook his head. 'A strange and sad tale indeed.' He rose. 'Thank you, Mrs Dobbs. Nobody makes peanut crunchie biscuits like you. Please do not tell my wife I said that.'

'Your secret is safe with me, Mr Astin,' Mrs Dobb chortled with pleasure.

Ambrose rose to depart to collect the coffins, and Julius followed Phoebe down the stairs to her room.

'Might I have a moment?' he asked.

'Of course,' she said entering her now empty room and beginning to straighten and clean her tools and kit. 'Are you alright, Julius?'

'Yes, never better. Why?' he asked suspiciously.

Phoebe laughed. 'No reason, you look well. But what is on your mind, you are quite distracted of late.'

Julius took a breath and blurted out, 'I have written in Miss Forrester's dance card – three dances actually. The waltz.'

'My, have you?' Phoebe tried to restrain her delight knowing her brother would not be comfortable with it, but it was a battle to do so. 'All three waltzes? Well, that is wonderful.' She studied him. 'You are good at the waltz; I remember you dancing with Miss Hill at the ball several years back.'

'That is the problem, I have not danced since then. I need to practice, just a few turns of the floor. Will you—'

'Yes!' Phoebe cut him off. 'I would be delighted.' She clapped her hands together and looked around. 'Help me push these two tables to the edge of the room and we can take a spin. It will be good for me to have a little practice too.'

'Is there anyone in particular you wish to dance with?' Julius asked with a raised eyebrow and noticed his sister's expression change.

'I would welcome a dance with Detective Stone.'

'Really?' Julius asked surprised as he moved a heavy winged-back chair out of the way. 'Not Bennet? I know he has feelings for you, not that he has said as much but it is apparent. I keep expecting him to declare them.'

'No,' she said firmly and did not elaborate. 'Detective Stone.'

'I see,' Julius said. 'Well then, I hope he asks you. Would you like me to—'

'Definitely not, Julius. Promise me you will say nothing,' she demanded, her eyes huge.

He nodded. 'I will say nothing. As tempting as it may be,' he teased.

She smiled at him. 'Hmm, I trust you. If Detective Stone has any feelings for me, then I wish him to discover them without a prompt or friendly obligation to you.'

'I doubt I know him that well that he would feel obligated or loyal to me,' Julius said and stood in the middle of the room, ready to proceed. He smiled. 'I remember Miss Hill; she was good company. I wonder whatever became of her?'

'I believe she married a teacher and they moved out west.' Phoebe went to the sideboard and opened a small timber music box. She flicked a switch and a tune started that would be sufficient for them to keep the beat. Returning to Julius she raised her hands and he slipped an arm around her waist and took her offered hand.

They started and glided smoothly together. A handsome pair they made as siblings – Julius a head taller, dark and handsome, Phoebe slight, her hair golden and free, moving gracefully.

'Regarding Harland – Detective Stone – sometimes we men need a nudge in the right direction. I for one admit to being somewhat baffled by the female sex,' he said and Phoebe laughed.

'Well then, I shall die an old maid. I want a man who knows what he wants and comes to claim it.'

'I'll remember that lesson,' Julius said with a dip of his head. It was as his grandfather said, step up and make haste, lest someone else should steal Miss Forrester from under his nose.

They heard footfalls on the steps and waltzed past their grandfather as he descended laughing.

'What madness is this?' he asked grinning at them happily.

'A dancing lesson, a refresher,' Julius said passing again. 'Join us if you wish.'

'I shall,' he said departing back up the stairs.

Reggie sat in the corner smiling at his nephew and niece as they waltzed around the room and moments later Randolph reappeared with Mrs Dobbs.

'Oh my, I haven't waltzed since my dear husband died.'

'Then you are long overdue for a turn around the floor, Mrs Dobbs, and you would be doing me a favour as I am a bit out of practice,' Randolph said and gave a small bow before taking her hand and proceeding to join his grandchildren.

'I believe you will do just fine, brother,' Phoebe said.

'It is all coming back to me,' he agreed. 'Thank you, Phoebe.'

And the music played on.

Chapter 20

THE NEXT MORNING BRIGHT and early to beat the crowds, *The Courier*'s Miss Lilly Lewis and Mr Fergus Griffiths were seated with fellow journalists in the allocated rows for the first part of the court case – Mr Arthur Horton's claim that he was James Tochborn, only son of Leo and Henriette Tochborn and the missing heir to the Tochborn fortune. Lilly wore a dark-coloured skirt and crisp white shirt; a straw boater donned her head. Fergus was dressed in a similar conservative manner in a dark suit. After all, a court of law was not the place for frivolous dress. Her story of Mr William Varsewell's admission had caused a sensation – despite the Varsewell brothers' efforts to refute it – and Lilly hoped her final story for the case would come from Detective Stone and would be the truth of the matter.

'Mr Arthur Horton has brought his supporters with him,' Lilly whispered to Fergus as she studied the robust heir-to-be. He was acknowledging people in the seats below as if he were at the theatre recognising fellow guests in the stalls. 'He is well-liked.'

'He is well fed,' Fergus retorted and Lilly laughed and nudged him for his cheekiness. They agreed on what notes they would take so they did not both cover the same aspect of the trial which had been a boon for readership.

'I think Mr Cowan is most pleased,' Lilly said of their editor as she sat back waiting for proceedings to start.

'It can be hard to tell most days, but I believe you are right,' Fergus said in jest. 'Have you invited your friend from the morgue along for tomorrow morning's session since I shall be out the front conducting interviews?'

'I have. She is from a funeral parlour, not the morgue. Her brother owns *The Economic Undertaker*. It was Phoebe who put me onto this case, so we owe her.'

'Ah, yes, of course, the friend with the handsome brother, I remember now. A very handy contact indeed,' Fergus agreed. They sat for a short while watching the court fill up. 'This is exciting, isn't it? So much better than doing shipping news.'

'I know. If I spent one more day on the births, marriages, and deaths column, I might have been on the latter list myself!' she proclaimed dramatically. Then her eyes lit up and she gave a small wave to a person at the back of the room. Fergus turned and did the same.

'Detective Payne is here but where is Detective Stone?' she asked looking around.

'Perhaps he will be called up today and is waiting elsewhere.'

'He will not want that; I believe he is still trying to prove neither man is the claimant and to get some inkling of what happened to the boy twenty years ago.'

'Good grief, that is a challenge,' Fergus whispered. 'The case was thoroughly investigated then. What can he expect to find now, twenty years later?'

'I don't envy him.' Lilly gave a small shake of her head and they both hushed as the court session began, and an air of excitement and expectation filled the air. They rose when Judge Miller – who would be presiding over the trial – entered, and they sat thereafter. Judge Miller did not waste any time getting right to the business at hand.

'The case against Mr Arthur Horton has been brought by the Tochborn family. The claimant must prove he is who he claims to be – the heir of the Tochborn estate – and the prosecution must prove his claim is fraudulent,' Judge Miller said.

There was no room left in the courtroom and people spilled out onto the streets, keen to be caught up in the drama. Some were fans of Mr Arthur Horton; others believed him to be a disgrace and imposter. Mr William Varsewell's trial was adjourned while waiting to hear from a relation based in England, and the judge had announced he was not sure that 'it would benefit the inmate, regardless of his real identity.' If Arthur Horton won, William Varsewell's family would have a fight on their hands to get a trial. Lilly secretly hoped that might happen – the thought of the stories that would require reporting excited her no end.

She returned her attention to the first witness – a man in his fourth decade – this was the man that the private investigator, Mr Bennet Martin, had secured. Lilly looked around finding Bennet sitting with two stern-looking men whom she deduced to be his client. He too was subtly looking around and their eyes locked; they exchanged subtle smiles, pleased to be front and centre for one of the most anticipated cases of the decade.

The man took the oath on the stand and proclaimed that he represented his uncle in Wapping, England, who personally and intimately knew the Horton family.

'I can say under oath that Arthur Horton was not a ship-boy nor was he orphaned,' the man declared in a loud voice. 'My uncle wrote to his father for years after they settled in Australia. This man is a fraud and perjurer!'

The gallery erupted and the judge slammed his gavel on the wood base on his desk. 'No need for theatrics, thank you,' he said to the witness before turning to address the prosecution.

'This is a matter of law and the facts alone are welcome. Brief your clients accordingly, I will have no grandstanding.' The judge turned his attention to the gallery. 'This court will not be delayed by the rowdy behaviour of those seated within it. I expect behaviour appropriate to a court of law.'

Everyone settled and quietened. Appropriately reprimanded, the English man gave a solemn bow to the judge and continued to make his case just as earnestly but without raising his voice to the gallery. 'I tell you unequivocally, your honour, that my uncle was a friend of the family for many years and Mr Horton senior came to Australia because his constitution demanded it. With his wife and son, who sits before you today, they arrived safely and he lived many more years in good health. This man here today,' pointing to the claimant, 'is the son of Mr Horton of Wapping and not Mr James Tochborn. He has no right to claim otherwise and should be sentenced for perjury!' He finished with a flourish despite his promise to the judge.

There were gasps, nods that the gallery was convinced – which would no doubt change several times during the trial – and two satisfied clients next to Bennet Martin from what Lilly could observe.

'Most convincing,' she whispered to Fergus who was hurriedly jotting down notes as he was assigned to take the first witness's account.

'He has me on side,' Fergus agreed. 'Who's up next?'

'I believe it to be a doctor who will speak of the deformity that Mr Horton has and that James Tochborn shared. A most delicate subject. Then, Arthur Horton will be challenged on his inability to speak French and a number of other characteristics that set him apart from young James Tochborn. I cannot wait until the man himself takes to the stand.'

'I suspect that will not be for a while,' Fergus said.

'I heard it was to be tomorrow.'

'No!' Fergus whipped to look at her. 'So soon?'

Lilly gave a nod as if she were the source of all knowledge. 'I heard from one of my legal friends that the prosecution did not want him speaking so early, but Mr Horton's legal team think he will win the jury over quite convincingly and they intend to play their trump card early.'

'He is by nature gregarious and I imagine they would benefit from his being on the stand,' Fergus agreed.

The pair smiled at each other, still celebrating their good fortune of landing the job everyone in the newsroom wanted, but neither believed for a moment that this trial would not drag on for weeks, if not more. And the longer, the better.

Detective Harland Stone was by nature polite, but on some occasions, it took great restraint to remain so. He did not care about the solicitor's solid reputation even though he was nodding with courtesy through Mr Kent's introduction to himself and his business, Kent & Jones. The only reason he was interested in the man was that Charles Kent, solicitor, had managed the estate of Mr and Mrs Tochborn for decades.

Harland was no stranger to pressure but he felt particularly under the pump with the trial starting and nothing of consequence to present. He still could not fathom why he was given the case; the brief was ambiguous at best and it took little effort to determine if Mrs Tochborn was poisoned, which mind you, was also indefinite. What was his superior expecting him to do with a case that had grown cold twenty years ago? And surely it was up to the court to determine the rights of the claimants, not the police. He refused to believe he was given the case to be derailed; his relationship with his superior was relatively new and his instincts claimed the man to be fair and reasonable.

He thought about Gilbert and knew his protégé would be taking copious notes at the trial despite his instruction to report only on anything that he believed might assist their case.

It was a relief that Gilbert was capable in that regard. Harland focussed on the man in front of him now that Mr Kent's speech was drawing to a close.

'Thank you, Mr Kent. I assure you my questions are very specific, and I am grateful for your history with the Tochborn family. No doubt you can assist me.' He was more than willing to provide the appropriate platitudes where necessary.

'Please go ahead, Detective,' Mr Kent said, leaning forward and giving Harland his full attention as Harland imagined the man had done across the desk for thousands of law cases and business transactions over the years.

'Could you furnish me with a list of all employees dismissed after the disappearance of young James Tochborn, please? I believe that to be 20 years ago in 1870.'

Mr Kent looked surprised and pushed his silver steel rim glasses further up his nose, putting a fingerprint smudge on one side of the glass.

'Well yes, I can,' he said rising and going to one of several large timber filing cabinets. Harland did his best not to tap his foot or drum his fingers as he waited patiently. Mr Kent returned with a file, sat down and licked his finger as he worked through the pages.

'I haven't opened this file for two decades. As you see, it is a wages file and includes termination and final payments. Would you like me to get my secretary to send you the names?'

'Could I take them down this very minute? It is a matter of some urgency,' Harland said and opened his pad, then fished a pencil from his jacket pocket and looked ready.

'There are only eight, so yes, I don't see why not. Mr Tochborn ran a tight ship and did not like excess.'

'Perhaps just the men,' Harland said working on a hunch.

'Only three then.'

'And if you have the information, I would welcome their age, occupation, and last known address?'

'I have that. Mind you, some of the jobs these men did twenty years ago do not exist anymore, we are becoming a progressive society. Everyone wants to work in manufacturing and be part of a union. It is very hard to get good domestic help,' Mr Kent said and sighed as if that was not a good thing. Harland did his best to feign interest. He wanted the names, nothing else, and quickly.

Jotting down the dictated names, ages, and addresses of the three dismissed staff, Harland looked up with gratitude. 'Mr Kent, your reputation is well deserved. I appreciate your thoroughness.' He circled one name, rose, and thanked the man again.

'Anytime, Detective, I am happy to be of service,' Mr Kent said with a satisfied look.

Harland headed to an address not too far from the solicitor's office, in pursuit of a Mr Isaac Elvin. Whether he or any family member remained there after twenty years was another matter.

Chapter 21

THE OLD FELLOW, MR Price, shook his head. 'Isaac Elvin! Well, there's a name I haven't heard for a very long time.' He dragged out the words as he looked skyward in thought, his clippers in one hand, his garden hat in the other, which he plopped back on his head before looking at the detective again.

Harland smiled not wishing to hurry the old man but pleased he recognised the Elvin name. 'The person whom I believe is living in Mr Elvin's former house said you had been here a while and might remember.'

Mr Price chuckled. 'That is an understatement, Detective... what was it, sorry?'

'Stone. Harland Stone.'

'Right, Detective Stone. Strong name. You look like you're a strong man, like a bit of boxing then?' Mr Price asked and moved his nose.

'I don't mind a dust-up in the ring,' Harland said with a grin. 'I've won as many as I've lost, so it's not all bad news, despite what my face says.'

Mr Price laughed as the two men spoke over the top of his white timber fence that came to waist height. 'Good for you, Detective Stone, keeps a man fit and lets some steam off.' He nodded as if he knew only too well how that could affect a man. 'So, yes, I've been here a while in answer to your question, in case you thought I was too old to remember it.' He tapped his temple. 'I was born in this very house and I'll die here too. I've seen them come and go, but it's always been a good neighbourhood.'

'Then you are just the man I need to help me, Mr Price. What you do recall of this man, Isaac Elvin?'

'He was a good, hardworking lad, and his mother a decent woman who kept a tidy home,' he said looking to the house on the corner. 'He lived in that house just there, as the folk inside told you.' Mr Price pointed to the one on the corner. 'But the Elvins are long gone.' He rubbed his fingers together in a pinching fashion. 'Their ship came in.'

'They came into some money then?' Harland clarified, most interested to hear this bit of news.

'A fortune! A relative with no immediate kin set them up for life.'

A very large ransom more like it! Harland though.

'What do you know of the family?' he pushed for more information. He'd never met an older person yet who wasn't happy to share their memories.

'They were battlers. Isaac's father worked hard but had bad lungs, and was dead in the ground before the boy passed childhood. There were four or five young ones from memory. His mother, let me think... May, that was her name, Mrs May Elvin, well she was a practical woman, and not afraid of labour. She took up housekeeping to make the rent, but her lad landed on his feet. Isaac was the eldest and he got himself a maintenance job with the Tochborn family. The rich lot whose son was stolen.'

'I know of them,' Harland told him, not wishing to interrupt, but giving some encouragement to continue.

'Well, the young man did a bit of everything for the Tochborns from what his mother would tell us, full of pride she was. He was there for years and lived on-site in quarters. He had a sweetheart who worked there too.'

Harland noted that and continued, 'But money was still stretched for his family back home?'

'That's right, Detective. There's always a need for money around here when you've got rent to pay, and mouths to feed. But Isaac came home on weekends to see his mum and brothers and sisters. She'd boast that he gave her a good chunk of his wages and mowed the lawn for her, did a bit of maintenance. She was mighty proud of him. He grew up to be a good man and I for one, couldn't think of a more deserving family to get a windfall,' Mr Price announced.

'So did Isaac leave the job when they got the windfall then?'

'No, there was a bad patch before that... they'd had their share of bad luck. It's like that in life, isn't it? That Tochborn boy was stolen and Isaac and several others were sacked.'

'Did you see much of him around that time?' Harland asked focusing on the time most relevant to his case.

'My word, we all did. He came back here to move in with his family, he had nowhere else to go until he got another job. He kept busy doing odd jobs in the neighbourhood including doing a bit of stuff for me. Then one day, they were packing. Mrs Elvin was as giddy as a schoolgirl with excitement. Mrs Elvin, or maybe it was Isaac, got a letter saying they'd inherited and they were off. And good on them, I say. I never begrudge anyone their good luck.'

'That's kind of you, Mr Price, very kind. Where did they go to claim this inheritance then?' Harland asked and held his breath, praying and hoping it wasn't overseas.

'Out in the country. A big farm they inherited where they would live off the land and be set for life, all of them. She told

245

me it came with everything they needed to make a good go of it. Oakey, if I remember right. Yes, it was in Oakey, about 100 miles from here.'

'Mr Price, you've been a great help, I thank you.'

He tipped his straw hat and smiled at Harland. 'Anytime. Nice to remember the old days.'

Harland bid him farewell and headed up the road on foot to hail a hansom. He didn't have time to trek to Oakey. If the trial had not started, he might have made a go of it, but 100 miles on horseback would take him four days, which he didn't have. He needed to telegraph the local police station in Oakey for information and to ask them to keep an eye on Mr Isaac Elvin if he was still alive and in the area.

Harland needed to know when the property was purchased – he didn't believe for a moment it was inherited – and how it was paid for... cash perhaps? He suspected Isaac Elvin had sent a ransom letter to the Tochborns and received the inheritance which led to the purchase of the farm, before telling his mother of the windfall. He must have convinced her they had inherited the farm; it wouldn't be hard to convince a desperate mother of good fortune. He shook his head in disgust. What became of the boy then? Young James would have known and trusted Isaac if they were all living on the Tochborn estate.

Harland stopped for a moment on the corner to study the house where the Elvins had lived. If Mrs Elvin was at work cleaning, and the youngsters were at school, could Isaac have had a chance to bury a young boy somewhere in the yard or under the house? The boy would have been the age of one of Isaac's siblings. How could he do that? The very idea was so abhorrent. A thought occurred to Harland and he raced back to Mr Price.

'Apologies for the interruption again, Mr Price,' he said as the man watered his rose bushes.

'Quite alright. I'm just encouraging my roses. This is the only season they do well, too hot here in summer for them.'

'They are doing very well.' Harland said, remembering to make the necessary small talk. 'It's a gardening and maintenance question. You mentioned Isaac helped around the house with duties. Before they moved, did he do any noticeable work around the house or garden?'

Mr Price rubbed a hand over his chin as he thought. 'Ooh, it's a long time ago, you are challenging me, Detective. Now let me think. It was a rental, so they didn't really do any more than was necessary, but now that you mention it, they did have a bit more bad luck.' He shook his head. 'Not sure that helps you or answers your question.'

'What was the bad luck then?' Harland asked hurriedly.

'Just before they moved, the tank out the back that they had for drinking water sprung a leak, or something like that, and flooded some of the garden and his mum's vegetables. I only remember because Issac made a joke about it saying they were going to give me some veggies before they left, but now there'd be lettuce floating down the street and we neighbours could help ourselves.'

'And he took it upon himself to fix it?' Harland asked.

'He did; the tank flooding had done some damage. He was digging and filthy but said he wanted to fix it himself so they were not delayed by waiting for the landlord to come and inspect it. I scored some of those veggies too, from memory. He was a good young man; said he could afford to do the repair now and it would be done right for the next tenant.' He nodded his head. 'Yes, a good lad.'

'So where was that exactly?' Harland pushed.

'Hmm, exactly, now I don't know that, Detective. I did offer to help when he brought the vegies out to the footpath and explained the flowing water to those of us around at the time. I'm a builder by trade and was working on that very house there,' he said pointing to a timber home two doors from Isaac Elvin's former family home. 'Isaac said he was almost done and had it under control.' Mr Price shrugged. 'I'm guessing the vegetable patch was out the back in front of the tank if it got flooded. She had a green thumb, his mum. I missed them when they moved.' His face reflected his melancholy at the memory.

Harland thanked him again. *Digging and filthy, making sure the neighbours knew why to not raise suspicion. Coming into some money*. It all began to fit very nicely. But surely the police looked at all employees at the time. As he walked, he recalled that Mr Price did say it was sometime after that their luck changed. Perhaps Isaac was smart enough to sit on the money for a while and to be seen looking for work and doing it tough. Inheriting property instead of cash was clever indeed to avoid assumptions being made.

He stopped at the house on the corner. It had been twenty years but was young James Tochborn, or rather James Hickling – twin brother of William, son of George and Frances – buried near the water tank in the former vegetable patch? It was an area where the dirt was regularly turned over so would not have looked suspicious. He pushed open the small gate and went to the front door again, knocking briskly. When the elderly tenant opened the door to him, she looked surprised.

'Could Mr Price not help you then?'

'He was a great help, Madam, I thank you for the recommendation. I wanted to have a look in your backyard, if I may?'

'Whatever for?' Her hand went to her heart and a look of alarm swept over her face.

'Just basic police work. Maybe some stolen goods were buried there a long time ago,' he said trying to be as honest as possible without alarming her or starting rumours.

She shook her head and exhaled with relief. 'Goodness, I thought you were accusing me of something criminal. By all means. Come through this way,' she said, and lead him from the front, straight down the hallways to the backdoor and backyard – a unique feature of the Queenslander style of houses for airflow. He thanked her and saw the yard was a reasonable size, and the water tank was still there and near the left of the house.

Feeling his eyes upon him, Harland walked around the area and then widened his area to study so she did not take it upon herself to start digging for treasure. Harland did not expect to find anything, it had been twenty years, but he needed to see the area for himself to determine if a body could be buried there, and ensure it wasn't now covered with a cement base or a house extension.

He re-joined her. 'Thank you, once again. I will do my best not to bother you again today,' he said with a dip of his hat and a small smile.

'Interruptions are always welcome, Detective, and I applaud you and the policemen of our city for the fine work you do.' She escorted him back the same way and out the front.

'Thank you, Madam,' he said again and departed. He had to inform his superior, but first, he had one more visit to make, and there was no time like the present.

Chapter 22

THE NEXT MORNING PHOEBE sat with Lilly in the press's allocated courtroom seats at the trial of Mr Arthur Horton. There was a buzz of excitement in the room, and while Phoebe felt like an imposter, she noticed there were a few other people scattered amongst the rows who were most likely not press representatives either. As the courtroom swelled with numbers, Phoebe realised nobody would notice anything untoward about her presence in the reporter seats – it was going to be packed.

'This is so exciting, thank you,' Phoebe said leaning into Lilly.

'No, thank you, Phoebe, we have this case because of you. Our second excellent story because of your tip-off,' Lilly reminded her. 'Fergus and I are quite the talk of the newsroom.

Now we just have to keep the stories coming.' She said the latter with a hint of anxiety.

'I am sure you will, Lilly, and you will be assigned stories too as your profile increases and your ability is applauded.'

Lilly squeezed her friend's arm in thanks.

'I do hope Mrs Tochborn gets her justice,' Phoebe said watching as the jury entered.

'You know what outcome she wants?' Lilly turned to study Phoebe who nodded.

'She wants her will to be honoured.' Phoebe lowered her voice. 'For the estate to go to her remaining family and the church. She is annoyed at Mr Horton's claim which she was just about to accept in good faith, only to find out now—'

'That he is a fake, as is Mr Varsewell,' Lilly finished Phoebe's sentence and then grimaced. 'But I understand the extenuating circumstances with Mr Varsewell. I am sure I would not mind if he benefited from it.'

'Nor I. Nevertheless, I feel the so-called brothers forcing Mr Varsewell to make this claim are as unscrupulous as Mr Horton.'

They studied the prosecution and the plaintiff's teams as they entered and the seats filled fast with legal experts and the public.

'Are you sure Fergus is not upset that I am in his seat?' Phoebe asked.

Lilly laughed. 'No, not at all. He will come in after lunch when you depart. As we did at the Beaming trial, our editor insists one of us reports from outside the courthouse and secures interviews with witnesses before or after they take the stand. We're also noting the public reaction.' She straightened, pad and pen at the ready. 'Now I will have to make copious notes during the testimonies, so forgive me for not being attentive to you.'

'Of course, disregard me completely,' Phoebe insisted. 'You have a very important job to do, and I am happy to observe.'

'I believe Mr Arthur Horton is to take the stand first today,' Lilly said, 'and then Detective Stone will be called.'

Phoebe's expression radiated her delight. 'What an excellent time for me to be in attendance.'

Lilly agreed and then bit her lip with hesitation. 'I hope the detective has found something substantial. I can only imagine how frustrating it is for him to be given such a difficult case with a boy stolen and never found, and the two claimants relying on the real James Tochborn remaining that way.'

'Not to mention someone has got away with murder,' Phoebe said in a low voice. 'There is Detective Payne but no sign of Detective Stone.' She looked to the far left and gave him a small wave as the young detective sat and looked around the gallery. Seeing the two ladies he broke into a smile and acknowledged them with a wave and a tip of his hat.

'He is so lovely,' Phoebe said and smiled.

'He is. They are odd colleagues, but also, somehow well-paired,' Lilly observed.

'I completely agree. Ooh, we are starting.'

They rose as Judge Miller entered, and sat again, ready to be transfixed by the morning's proceedings. As Lilly anticipated, Mr Arthur Horton was called to the stand and he took the position in all his sartorial splendour. It was quite a performance as Phoebe observed. He was dressed in a manner befitting an heir, in clothes that a butcher would not have been able to afford. Mrs Tochborn's allowance served him well. Arthur Horton took the oath and then the questions began.

'Will you tell us why you believe yourself to be Mr James Tochborn?' the prosecutor enquired and stood back as if to give Arthur Horton the stage.

Sitting forward in the witness box, Arthur Horton looked at every jury member making a personal connection. He is very, very good, Phoebe mused.

He spoke loudly as if projecting his voice from the stage to the back seats of a theatre. 'I had a displaced childhood, my memories of anything before the age of ten are at best sketchy. But I always told everybody I met, in the town I came to know as home – Wagga Wagga – and, indeed, anywhere I travelled, that I was connected with a good family and that I was superior to the position I was then holding.'

There were some laughs, snickers and applause from the gallery as the judge called for order.

Lilly whispered to Phoebe, 'I've been saying that for years, but no one takes any notice of me.'

She suppressed a laugh as the judge warned the gallery that interruptions would not be welcomed.

Mr Arthur Horton continued, 'I believed I was of a good family,' he said again for emphasis, 'and that ultimately, I should come into great riches. There was not, however, a word of truth in the statement, because I was nothing but a poor man at the time. Up to this time, I had never heard the name of Tochborn in my life. I didn't know who he was, what he was, or where he came from.'

The prosecutor asked, 'But you must have thought you could be James Tochborn, as you answered to the description of this advertisement,' holding up Mrs Tochborn's public notice, 'and you contacted the lady herself, Mrs Tochborn.'

'I did. After seeing the notice, my heart went out to the poor lady, and I could not forget it. It was as if my pain was the same, a pain born from the separation of a mother and child,' he said in a shaky voice, appearing to be close to tears.

'Goodness,' Lilly muttered, 'what theatrics.'

Phoebe giggled behind her hand but was not willing to speak lest she was evicted from the courtroom.

The prosecution continued his attack, 'The reason you wrote to Mrs Tochborn was because you were hard up and saw an opportunity!'

'I did nothing of the sort,' Mr Arthur Horton thundered. 'Why even my own mother – forgive me – Mrs Tochborn – said on her deathbed that she would own to me.'

His purposeful slip of calling Mrs Tochborn his mother enraged some and made others more sympathetic. Phoebe studied the jury and found that the expression on the lady jurors' faces was more sympathetic to his cause.

Arthur Horton reached into his pocket and waved a piece of paper. 'The lady I call mother was about to sign this note before she passed away, and in her own words she dictated the following: "I am certain as I am of my own existence, that the plaintiff is my first-born son." There, I swear to you all here today of this truth.'

'But she did not sign it, nor did Mrs Tochborn present such a declaration to her solicitor, so we will never know if it is the truth,' the prosecutor said drily. 'But she did receive this correspondence from you when you initially made contact and the first thing you did was to ask her for money. Ladies and gentlemen of the jury the first letter of contact reads: "My dear mother, I have no doubt after so many years have passed you will have some difficulty in knowing whether it is me that is writing to you. But believe me to be your son. I would value the chance to be reunited, but as I lost £1500 at cards just recently, I will require your generosity for the fare. I assure you of two signs that you may know I am your son – I have a brown mark on the left side of my face, which you will remember, and a delicate condition in the lower regions. I look forward to the day of our reunion. My fondest regards, your son, James Tochborn".'

Conversations, exclamations, and cries broke out in the court and Judge Miller silenced the gallery in his usual style.

'The mark and the condition you write of were no secret between mother and son. You could have obtained that information by sourcing the news stories from twenty years ago.'

'But I did not, Sir,' Arthur Horton angrily addressed the slight against his character even though he was not asked a question.

The prosecutor continued, 'Could you tell the jury please, Mr Horton, how your first meeting went with Mrs Tochborn? Perhaps tell us of it in French.'

Again, the courtroom erupted but the prosecutor continued regardless, raising his voice above the noise. 'We understood that the real James Tochborn spoke fluent French.'

Everyone hushed to hear what Arthur Horton would say.

'If I did speak French to the age of ten, I cannot recall it now, any more than I can recall my childhood. There are some things my memory simply will not bring top of mind,' Arthur Horton said holding his head high and proud. 'I am sure there are medical men who can attest to how trauma might result in a forgetful condition.'

'How convenient,' the prosecutor said. 'And can the same be said of your ability to play the piano?'

'If you bring one in, Sir, I am sure I could entertain you,' Arthur Horton said to the amusement of the gallery, but not the prosecutor.

Behind them, the court doors opened and everyone turned to look towards the doors, a hush descending over the room. Detective Harland Stone appeared looking every bit the figure of authority. He motioned for Detective Payne to join him. The young man jumped from his seat to stand beside his superior.

'What is going on?' Phoebe asked, watching the drama unfold.

'I believe Detective Stone has something! Imagine if he has found evidence to close this trial down. Goodness,' Lilly exclaimed excited for a news headline.

'Your honour, forgive the interruption. Detective Harland Stone and Detective Gilbert Payne from the Roma Street branch requesting an audience. We believe we have evidence that will put an end to this trial immediately,' Harland said.

'That I would welcome,' Judge Miller said drily. 'Please approach. Alone,' he added with a look to the legal teams.

Both ladies leaned forward eagerly as the two detectives approached Judge Miller at his bench. The men spoke briefly and then stepped back.

'Ladies and gentlemen of the jury and press, we will take a short recess and return, calling Detective Harland Stone to the stand. You may stand down, Mr Horton.'

Phoebe noticed Arthur Horton looked most disappointed like an actor pulled from the stage. The judge rose and hurried to his rooms, the two detectives exited the way Detective Stone had entered and just as quickly for fear of being mobbed by the press before they presented. The noise in the courtroom was deafening.

'I best go tell Fergus to prepare, and to send a note to our editor to tell him to hold the front page – a story is about to break,' Lilly said, jumping to her feet.

'I will leave and let Fergus resume his seat,' Phoebe stood beside her.

'No, he needs to be on hand outside to cover the reactions of the claimant and Mrs Tochborn's family. Please stay, Phoebe, and mind our seats. I will be back promptly,' Lilly promised and hurried off, leaving her notepad on her seat and Phoebe next to it.

How exciting, Phoebe thought caught up in the moment and the thought of the very handsome figure of Detective Harland Stone as he strode in so confidently. The sight of him so in control made Phoebe feel quite heady. Imagine if he were to favour her with his affection.

Phoebe was most excited for him, but just what had the detective found and would it be enough to give Mrs Tochborn her last wish?

Chapter 23

M ARY SIGHED AS SHE finished pinning the hem on a
mourning dress that was draped around a dressmaker
mannequin. 'I am sure the men will look so handsome at the
ball in their formal attire. I would be swooning so much as to
find myself incapable of dancing.'

'Well, you are welcome to come, Mary,' Violet said, 'I could
try and secure a ticket for you and Mrs Shaw.

'Oh no, I couldn't, Miss, but thank you. My father says I am
not to attend balls until next year. My mother is keen to marry
me off and my father wishes me to remain at home for a while
yet.'

'He must love you very much to not want to hurry you out
into the world,' Mrs Shaw said and gave the young girl a warm
smile.

'Perhaps,' Mary said, 'but I think he doesn't want to be home alone with Mum. I am the youngest and last to leave home.'

Both Violet and Nellie Shaw hid a smile knowing Mary's father would not be the first man to find himself in that situation; the pubs at night were full of such men.

'Would you like to come to the Hospital Ball, Mrs Shaw?' Violet asked, looking across at her assistant manager as she finished some hand stitching on a bodice.

'You are too kind, Miss Forrester, dear. But I am content in quiet solitude these days and my husband is not well enough for company. My days of balls and dancing are behind me. Unless it is a wedding of course. I am sure I can muster for that.'

'Of course,' Violet agreed smiling at Nellie's teasing.

Mary stood and moved away from the mannequin, circling it slowly to check the hemline. 'That is ready for sewing, I believe, Miss,' she said and moved to the cutting board to begin her next chore. She sighed again as her imagination took over. 'I am sure I would die if Mr Julius Astin or Mr Ambrose Astin looked at me, let alone asked me to dance.'

'We have quite enough of dying around here, young Mary, so please refrain from doing so,' Nellie scolded her and Mary giggled.

'Alright then, I shan't succumb to death, but I don't know how you bear it, Miss.' She looked at Violet. 'They are so very handsome and you have had to meet with Mr Julius Astin on several occasions. I could not form a sentence in his company.'

'I have a strong fortitude,' Violet said and the ladies laughed.

They heard a sharp rap at the back door and it opened before one of them could rise to answer.

'May I come in?' a male voice called.

'Most certainly, come through,' Mrs Shaw called out and the ladies straightened themselves to look even more industrious, as they waited to put a face to the voice. Mary's eyes widened in disbelief as Mr Ambrose Astin – one of the men whom she had just been swooning over – entered.

'Miss Forrester, Mrs Shaw, Miss Pollard, forgive the intrusion if you will?' he said with a friendly smile and a small bow.

'A most welcome intrusion, Mr Astin,' Mrs Shaw said. 'How may we be of assistance?'

'I have just been to collect a supply of coffins from cousin Lucian and Tom asked me to pass a message to his sister,' Ambrose said turning to Violet who coloured slightly.

'How impudent of him,' she tutted. 'I apologise Mr Astin and will remind him this very evening that you are not his messenger.'

Ambrose laughed. 'That is not necessary, I was happy to do so, and the fault is partly mine. Lucian was speaking of seeing a boxing match tonight and Tom expressed the wish to see it. I invited him along. I will ensure he does not drink if you have no objections to his attending?'

'Thank you, Mr Astin. I suspect he attends many things without my knowledge on the ruse of seeing his friends,' she said narrowing her eyes. 'But if he is in the company of his employers, I will not worry.'

'Excellent. He said you would say that, and to tell you he will be home at ten.'

The ladies laughed.

'How presumptuous.' Mrs Shaw smiled with a shake of her head. 'He knows how to play you, my dear,' she said to Violet.

'Don't all men know how to play we ladies, Mrs Shaw?' Violet said and all three ladies turned their faces to Ambrose with a look that required a response.

'I know no men in my acquaintance that answer to such a charge,' he teased and they all laughed, easily charmed by Ambrose.

'Sir,' Mary spoke up, causing Violet and Nellie to turn suddenly toward her, knowing she was most shy and tongue-tied around the men.

'Yes, Miss Pollard?' Ambrose turned his attention to Mary which made the poor girl forget her question for a moment.

She coughed lightly and spoke up, 'If time permits now, Sir, will you tell me please what you will wear to the Hospital Ball, if I may ask? From a seamstress's point of view, I am most interested.'

'Oh, I am sure Mr Astin is too busy—' Mrs Shaw began.

'No, that is quite alright, and curiosity in one's profession is always welcome, is it not?' he asked Violet.

'Absolutely. Just don't tell Mr Astin – Mr Julius Astin that is – or he might start Mary making menswear,' Violet said with a teasing smile which Ambrose returned.

He looked to Mary. 'Well, let's see, Miss Pollard. Being the sharp dresser that I am known to be,' he said with a smile and wink in her direction which brought on a giggle from her and the utmost look of being charmed while Violet made a face.

'I saw that look, Miss Forrester,' Ambrose said making Violet laugh. 'While I don't profess to be a fashion doyenne like yourself or Mrs Shaw...'

Both ladies laughed at his antics.

'I believe I can hold my own. So, Miss Pollard, and I thank you for your question, I shall be wearing a dark tail coat and trousers with a white bow tie and a white shirt with a winged collar. My waistcoat will be lighter in colour and feature hand-stitched flowers in gold and blue stitching.'

'Oh my,' she said, 'that sounds so handsome.'

'Yes,' he sighed, 'I feel sorry for Julius and the other men in my company who have to compete, but so be it.'

The ladies laughed and teased him, and with a grin in Violet's direction, who in turn blushed that he should look at her whenever he spoke of Julius, he bade the ladies good day and exited the way he came. Mary picked up her scissors and began cutting with gusto and a smile on her face, and Violet and Nellie exchanged smiles.

'I am sure as handsome as Mr Ambrose Astin will be on the evening, his brother will give him a run for his money,' Nellie said and laughed as Violet shook her head at the teasing she endured.

Chapter 24

Detective Harland Stone took the oath and felt the heady mixture of excitement, nerves, and justice about to be delivered. He was not a man who sought the limelight and would ensure his partner, Gilbert, received due recognition. Equally, he would take responsibility if an error was found, as a good supervisor should if he was worth his salt. As everyone settled, he looked up only to lock eyes with Miss Phoebe Astin, whom he did not expect to see in court. For a moment he was displaced but regained himself. She was sitting beside Miss Lilly Lewis and he gave them both a subtle nod of acknowledgement.

Seeing Miss Astin had the effect of making him a little more on edge, and also strangely assured as if she anchored him. It was, after all, the result of her client's testimony from beyond the grave that had brought them to where they were today and he was grateful for it, and not just because it would once again assist his career. This was a case where much heartache had been endured and it was time to put it to rest.

The prosecutor welcomed the detective most heartily as expected, and asked him to share his information with the jury.

Harland addressed the judge and jury as he began. 'Your honour, ladies and gentlemen of the jury, I believe my partner, Detective Gilbert Payne, and I, have found substantial evidence that proves neither the claim of Mr Arthur Horton nor Mr William Varsewell is legitimate.'

The judge banged his gavel and called for order as the gallery erupted in noise. Mr Arthur Horton jumped to his feet and waved his fist in the direction of the detective and supplied a few colourful words.

'I will have no further interruptions in my courtroom or to the detective's testimony,' Judge Miller exclaimed. 'Mr Horton, I suggest you sit down or you will be evicted post-haste.'

The large man dropped back into his chair and his legal representative offered a hasty apology to the judge and whispered what appeared to be a warning to Mr Horton.

'Please continue, Detective,' Judge Miller said, 'from the beginning with your proof front and foremost.'

Harland nodded. He was not an actor like Mr Arthur Horton and silently resented the judge's implication that he would be making theatre of his appearance. However, he knew this would take some time, as what he was about to say would fire up the gallery and press present, not to mention the families, supporters, and the claimant himself, and interruption was inevitable.

He continued, 'We discovered that the son of Mr Leo Tochborn and Mrs Henriette Tochborn was a fake child.' Instead of an outcry, there were gasps and hushes as everyone waited to hear what came next.

'So, you are saying there never was a child or a kidnap victim?' the prosecutor asked but the judge intervened.

'Please allow the detective to deliver his testimony and hold the questions until the end. He does not need prompting.'

The prosecutor nodded and made a show of waving his hand to give Detective Stone the floor as he dropped back into his seat. Harland's eyes briefly went to Phoebe who gave him a supportive look and a small nod of her head, no doubt understanding his frustration.

Harland resumed his testimony. 'There was a child that was kidnapped and never returned but the child was not the son of the Tochborns.' He hurried on now, not stopping which forced the court attendees to be quiet and listen without interruption. He kept his focus on the judge and the jury.

'The Tochborns desperately wanted an heir and they were unable to have a child. Mr Tochborn believed it was only a matter of time, but he wasn't a well man and he wanted to ward off family members securing his fortune, or his wife remarrying and another man coming into his money. Consequently, he created a fake heir and honestly believed he would soon have a son of his own and the other child could meet a fake tragedy, his real son then stepping into his shoes.' He stopped to draw a breath and let the jury catch up as several were taking notes.

Harland continued, 'Mr Tochborn was not a man who sought company, and he did not want any more staff than absolutely necessary on his estate. His staff was paid handsomely to stay in his employ and all resided on the estate in separate quarters. Mr Tochborn's stable manager, George Hickling married the cook, Frances, and they remained working and living on-site. They had twin boys, William and James.'

As the gallery realised the connection, audible gasps and discussions broke out. Arthur Horton looked outraged at the very idea of it, and his supporters began to look at him with similar expressions of outrage for being deceived.

When the judge had finished calling for quiet again, Harland moved to the next part of his story. 'Mr Tochborn entered an agreement with George and Frances Hickling, that he would educate their two boys and provide for them if one of them would pose for a family photo and the occasional appearance as needed. The offer was too good for the Hicklings to ignore, as they were parents who wanted the best start in life for their sons.'

He looked away for a moment and up to Phoebe and the press gallery. Everyone was riveted by his tale and Lilly was smiling, already knowing most of this story and having it ready to hit the press.

'James Hickling appeared in two studio portraits with Mr and Mrs Tochborn, at the age of three and again at the age of ten, not long before he disappeared. In a shocking crime, a kidnapper removed the young boy from his family and demanded a ransom, which was hastily paid by Mr Tochborn hoping to shut down the attention the family was receiving. The Hickling family was distraught but were part of the deception and feared they could not tell the truth. Mr Tochborn also threatened to turn them out with no assistance to find the boy, if they revealed all.'

There were gasps of shock and hissing from the audience towards the Tochborn family in attendance. Arthur Horton was also getting his share of attention with curious eyes determining if he could still be James Tochborn, or rather James Hickling. There was much head shaking amongst the attendees and then Arthur Horton jumped to his feet.

'I am that boy, James Hickling, and deserve to be recognised as the heir, James Tochborn, for suffering separation from my family and the despair it caused my parents.'

The judge glared at Arthur Horton and bellowed, 'Sit down Mr Horton or I will have you arrested immediately for perjury. Enjoy your last moments of freedom. Go on, Detective.'

Arthur Horton glanced around nervously, his tongue darting over his lower lip but then as if someone flicked on the stage lamps, he sat down stretching taller, chin up, prepared to play the role of the much-maligned, James Hickling to his best advantage.

'Your honour,' Harland began, 'We have on good authority that Mr Tochborn wanted to substitute the identical second son, William, for the first and to say the boy, James, had been returned.' He raised his voice to speak over the gasps and cries of outrage. 'His parents refused as one might imagine and the remaining Hickling family – George, Frances and their son, William – were turned out.'

Harland swallowed and continued, 'As we know now, twenty years later, the ransom was paid, but the boy was never returned and the kidnapper was never caught. Thus, there is no James Tochborn, nor has there ever been, and the staff was prepared to keep this secret, especially for the sake of George and Frances Hickling. The despair of losing their son and no progress from the investigation saw the decline of Mr George

Hickling who died shortly after and Mrs Frances Hickling was institutionalised after a breakdown and died several years later. Their remaining son, William, was sent to an orphanage where eventually, Hickling family members retrieved him out of duty.'

Harland took a sip of water. 'William eventually went the way of his mother and was not able to cope with all he lost – his twin brother and his parents. We believe him to be the second claimant, Mr William Varsewell of the Woogaroo Lunatic Asylum.'

The courtroom erupted and while the judge tried to establish order, Harland was able to take a few moments to rest and study his surroundings. Several of the pressmen ran out to report what had come to light, but there was more to come. Harland saw the look of sadness on Phoebe Astin's face and her hand moving to sit over her heart, even though she knew of the outcome of William and James. When the noise had lessened and invited by the judge, he cleared his throat in preparation.

'However,' Harland spoke in a louder voice until he could speak normally again, 'Mr Tochborn was unable to do further harm as before their departure from the Tochborn estate and their decline, Mr and Mrs George Hickling had the foresight to write down all they knew about what happened, incriminating Mr Tochborn who was bedridden by this stage. They put this letter in safekeeping with someone they trusted and advised Mr Tochborn that the letter existed and that if anything should happen to any of them – Mr Hickling, his wife, or young William, the letter would be given to the law and a copy to the press.'

Harland turned to Gilbert and nodded. Gilbert rose and came forth with a letter in his hand.

'Your honour, my partner, Detective Payne has that very letter and we have the recipient of the letter here and present should you wish to hear her account in person.'

Gilbert handed the letter to Judge Miller who opened it and read the document while the court was hushed. Gilbert resumed his seat and eventually, Judge Miller looked up at the two detectives. 'Excellent work, Detectives, excellent. Yes, I want on the record the name and account of the letter holder. Who is the person present who has safeguarded this letter for all these years?'

'It is an innocent lady, your honour, who was a close friend to Mrs Frances Hickling and loved the twin boys. She also held in high regard her employer, Mrs Tochborn, whom she served from the first day of Mrs Tochborn's marriage. It is Miss Rachel Temple, your honour.' Harland looked at the lady sitting next to Gilbert and indicated her to the judge. 'Miss Temple has been Mrs Tochborn's maid and companion these past thirty years.'

There were sharp intakes of breath, stretching of necks, and much jostling to see the diminutive lady with her tight bun of grey and brown hair, seated next to the young detective. She wore a black mourning dress, in respect for Mrs Tochborn.

'Miss Temple, thank you for attending,' his honour said mindful of the lady's state of mourning and her look of frailty. 'I would like to hear your testimony shortly.'

She gave a nod and looked as if she might expire from the attention but Gilbert patted her hand and she gave him a nervous smile. By now, Mr Arthur Horton was somewhat forgotten as the drama played out in court.

Judge Miller spoke to Harland. 'There is more, is there not, Detective Stone?'

'Yes,' Harland answered. 'I believe we may have identified the boy's kidnapper and murderer, who was once acquainted with Miss Rachel Temple and in the employ of Mr Tochborn, and we have a lead on where young James Hickling might be buried.'

There was no getting order back in court after that announcement as Arthur Horton tried to run out of the courtroom, members of the press did race out except for those that tried to speak with Detective Stone directly, the jury stood bewildered as to their role now, and Judge Miller threw his gavel down in annoyance.

'Detectives,' he called them both to his bench and Gilbert called on a Tochborn family member to sit with Miss Temple. The men approached with as much haste as possible via the now crowded aisle, and the judge leaned close to speak with them holding up a hand to ward the legal teams back. 'The matter of finding the murderer and the boy is not for this court as we have established Mr Arthur Horton is not James Tochborn and that was our purpose. If you do not find the boy, and there is a chance Arthur Horton is James Hickling, he is still not the Tochborn heir. I thank you for your impressive detective work and relieve you from court to continue your investigation.'

Harland thanked the judge and looked to the swarm of people waiting for him and Detective Gilbert Payne.

'Perhaps you would like to depart through my office and out the side of the building?' the judge asked and the men hastily accepted his offer.

Now, it was time to bring the murderer to justice and close the case for good. Before departing, Harland glanced at Phoebe and returned her smile of relief. He turned his attention to Lilly and with a subtle inclination of his head saw her nod her understanding; he had a scoop for her. With a smile to his partner, Gilbert, they made their exit.

Chapter 25

THE *VEXED VIXENS* WELCOMED a new member to their party in the form of Miss Violet Forrester, who arrived with Phoebe to meet the ladies. They agreed to keep their group small for intimacy's sake and invite those ladies most open to views more liberal, or occupations more diverse. Tonight's meeting was being hosted by Emily at her small and very tasteful townhouse in Bowen Hills on Montpelier Hill. Emily hosted more so than the other ladies as she was the only lady with her own abode, thanks to a generous aunt who had few other relations to bequeath it to, and she was quite fond of Emily.

As the five ladies – Phoebe, Lilly, Kate, Emily and Violet – sat around the dining table relaxing in each other's company and filling their dinner plates from the spread in front of them, Emily welcomed Violet.

'The pleasure is mine,' Violet said. 'My brother is out at a boxing match this evening and I am grateful for the company. However, I fear I am vexed by very little at present, so perhaps you will dismiss me from the group before I truly settle in.'

Kate, the photographer, laughed. 'Fear not, Violet. It is not a requirement that you must discuss vexing matters at every meeting, but rather an opportunity to share if you so choose and get it off your chest, so to speak. I am sorry to hear of your recent loss, but very much admire you for not wearing black.'

'Thank you. I confess I feel very torn about disrespecting my grandmother,' Violet said and thanked Phoebe as she passed a platter of vegetables. 'But I made a promise to her that I would not wear black as we were just out of mourning for my parents. It does not sit right with me so I find myself wearing the half-mourning colours.'

'An excellent compromise,' Phoebe agreed. 'I am not fond of young people wearing black. Goodness, I sound like I am ancient, but you know what I mean, I am sure.'

'I agree completely and if I did not look so good in black, I'd happily make that promise too, if the situation presented itself,' Emily said and made them laugh. 'Well, after your day in court and that startling outcome, I did not expect to see you here on time, Lilly.'

'We made the early edition of the paper and my work was done. Until tomorrow of course. Detective Stone is letting me attend the site where they believe the young boy might lie. The detective has been true to his word and most supportive of Fergus and me,' Lilly said.

'Of you, most likely.' Kate snorted.

'No.' Lilly shook her head. 'I don't believe there is a spark of interest between us, it is purely a professional relationship and most satisfactory.'

Phoebe silently breathed a sigh of relief. Of course, she would claim no interest in Detective Harland Stone if Lilly did, but she rather hoped to attract the detective's eye, as she imagined most of the ladies of the town her age did. Her eagerness to attend the ball was due to the promise of his attendance and she imagined he had no idea of the fluttering he created within her with his presence.

Emily said as if she read Phoebe's mind, 'Before we talk of the ball and other matters, is anyone vexed?'

'I think you should go first as you are the hostess,' Phoebe encouraged her, 'it is only fair.'

Emily smiled and needed no further endorsement. 'Thank you, I shall then. These past few weeks I am finding it very vexing having carpenters in my townhouse. They are combining two of my smaller rooms into one large room so my students can practice dancing,' she added for Violet's benefit.

'Ooh, at the *Miss Emily Yalden School of Deportment*?' Violet asked recalling the information Phoebe gave her on each of the ladies.

'The very place indeed. One of the young men has taken it upon himself to flatter me every day with a smile, a wink, and a kind remark, and the two other young men appear most uncomfortable in their surroundings. As to my students, you would think they had never seen a person of the male species before. They are ridiculously silly about it. The simpering and smiling, flirting, tugging at their hair and so forth. I am sure the poor fellows can not get out of my residence quick enough at the end of the day, except for Mr Flirt. We are a society hell-bent on partnering.'

'Mr Flirt?' Lilly laughed. 'Do tell then, are you likely to succumb to his charms?'

'Goodness no, and mark my words, he will be doing this to some poor unsuspecting woman at his next job location, no doubt.'

'Do you wish to marry, Violet?' Lilly asked abruptly.

'Me?' Violet started with surprise. 'I do, very much, but for love. I believe I can provide for myself, especially at the moment in my current employ, and like you ladies, that means I can make a love match and not a match for company or comfort.'

'We are lucky,' Phoebe agreed. 'Although I worry what will happen to our male friendships when love is denied.'

'You are thinking of Mr Bennet Martin?' Emily asked. 'I look forward to setting eyes on him at the Hospital Ball.'

'The private detective who visits so often? He is very handsome. Is he not a close friend of your brother?' Violet asked.

'Yes, and Julius tells me he believes Mr Martin will ask to court me.' Phoebe sighed. 'It is such a shame because I enjoy his friendship and I wonder if he will withdraw it should I decline him. And I intend to decline his interest.'

'Very problematic,' Violet agreed sympathetically and the ladies exchanged a small smile as confidants.

'My turn, if I may,' Kate said not waiting for agreeance, 'and it too is related to matters of the heart.'

Emily sighed. 'And we said when we started this group, we would not spend our time talking of men and romance.'

'Well not exclusively, anyway,' Lilly reminded her. 'I think we can enjoy a little happiness of heart, especially if you get hitched to a carpenter, Emily,' she teased and Emily made a scoffing sound.

'Miss Emily Yalden! Young ladies do not scoff or snort. You of all people should know better,' Phoebe reprimanded her with a rule from the *Miss Emily Yalden School of Deportment* and the ladies giggled.

'A fall from grace,' Emily said in good humour. 'Kate, please tell us what has you vexed.'

'Yes, thank you, Emily. I find it vexing and very awkward when everyone is constantly watching and pairing you with people in your circle. Is that not most uncomfortable? I am sure I don't know where to look and I am more tongue-tied for it than I would be if everyone relaxed and minded their own business.'

Phoebe glanced at Violet and wondered if she felt that way about working so near Julius and the constant interest the pair were creating. She would hear what Kate had to say and if needed, vowed to watch herself and warn Ambrose to not tease the pair lest it should separate them.

'Provide us with an example of what you mean,' Lilly requested taking up the conversation thread.

Kate sipped her punch and said, 'Dr McGregor, the coroner, is a pleasant and outgoing man, but any time I am called on to photograph a death scene in the absence of the police photographer, he only has to show me a little interest and everyone is smiling and nudging both Dr McGregor and myself. It has put me off attending, even though I want the work. I cannot put the camera close to my face quickly enough to hide my blush. But he does not seem to mind the attention and makes a sport of it.'

'But I thought he liked you, Lilly?' Phoebe asked, looking from Lilly to Kate in confusion. 'Ambrose said he has made no secret of his admiration for you, Lilly.'

'Perhaps he just enjoys the attention of lovely ladies,' Emily said. The ladies gave up in exasperation and continued around the circle now turning their attention to Violet, who brightened.

'I have come up with one – a vexation! It is perhaps a little selfish and may offend, but it is in keeping with what Kate was saying previously about my choice of dress colour in mourning.'

Phoebe noticed Violet said everyone's names with hesitation, having been invited to address everyone intimately but being an acquaintance at best.

'Please do go ahead, your first vexed moment in the *Vexed Vixens*!' Emily announced ceremoniously, holding up a glass and the ladies raised their own to clink together. Violet laughed and thanked her.

'Now that you say that, I should wait for something better,' Violet frowned and then smiled as they all encouraged her. 'Well, as mentioned it is about mourning. Of course, I do not want to look a gift horse in the mouth when my income now comes from making mourning clothing, but why do we insist on such shows of grief? One year of wearing heavy black clothing, another six months of wearing the dullest of colours and for what? To show respect and to show we are missing someone? I shall miss my family for years and years to come and no colour will make any difference to that.'

'That is so very true, Violet,' Phoebe agreed. 'I think of my parents often, and what life we might have had as a family, and I know Julius, who was the eldest and best remembers his relationship with our mother and father, still carries the pain of their death in his heart.'

Emma agreed. 'It is all for show and tell. I know wives and husbands who led very separate lives and, in some cases did not even like each other but succumbed to putting on this charade of grief at the time of death.'

'I for one would like to wear what I feel,' Violet said. 'Some days I might wear black, or perhaps red because it was my mother's favourite colour, or blue if I feel that way.'

'That is a lovely thought,' Phoebe agreed. 'I wonder if it will ever change. If so, you will have to change to a ladies' fashion store instead of mourning wear.'

'Your brother thought we might have the opportunity to do just that in due course,' Violet said. 'Oh, I hope that was not said in confidence.' She gave a small shrug, 'Well that will teach Mr Astin to share his confidences with me. Regardless, it would not be withheld from you, Phoebe, so Lilly, Kate, Emily, please forget I said that.' The ladies happily agreed.

'Well done and welcome, Violet, a fine contribution. Your turn, Lilly,' Emily said.

'I have been too busy to be vexed or rather too focussed on all that was happening with the case and the pressure of writing daily stories with new angles. So, it has just been the usual round of vexations – the office bachelor, Mr Lawrence Hulmes, asking me to dinner every day I am in the office; the men thinking him so very amusing, and my father is now more concerned than ever that no man will marry me given my profile and outspokenness. It would be nice if instead, he recognised my work and ability.' Lilly sighed dramatically.

'I am sure my grandfather is concerned for me too,' Phoebe said. 'He is always so supportive but I have heard him ask Julius if my style of dress or wearing my hair down might prevent a good match.' She smiled. 'It is meant in kindness and with care; he is a different generation.'

'He is a kind soul,' Violet agreed.

'You will meet my grandmother at the Hospital Ball,' Phoebe said. 'I am very much looking forward to the evening.'

'I have room in my ride if any of you ladies need a lift. It is just my cousin – a solicitor,' Emily added for the benefit of Violet who missed the original discussion on suggested attendees, 'and myself. We could fit one more lady.'

'I am going with my brothers, but thank you, Emily,' Lilly said.

'My father will drop off my two sisters and me, and pick us up strictly on time later,' Kate said with a roll of her eyes.

'I will go with my grandparents or Ambrose,' Phoebe said, and all eyes turned to Violet.

'I believe Mr Astin is collecting me,' she said and all eyes widened at the news.

'Julius,' Phoebe confirmed.

'Lucky you,' Lilly said and almost pouted but checked her expression. Violet glanced at her, concerned for Lilly's feelings.

'I am sure it is just a courtesy as he knows I am attending alone.'

'But as part of our party,' Phoebe said reaching for Violet's hand.

Lilly shook her head. 'I am convinced Phoebe's handsome brother has no fascination with me, sadly.' She huffed dramatically, not noticing Phoebe's surprise at her bold and honest declaration.

'You will win many hearts,' Kate declared. 'And Violet, prepare yourself because your entry with Mr Astin will set tongues wagging, I am sure.'

Violet gave a small smile that Phoebe could not read as one of pleasure or dismay. Emily interrupted her thoughts.

'And aside from the ball, do you have a vexation to share, Phoebe?'

'Oh yes, my vexation. Well, I am vexed by my Uncle Reggie.'
She explained, 'He is my grandfather's brother and don't get
me wrong, I love him dearly and I like him a great deal too. He
is a light-hearted and fun soul, like Ambrose. But he is taunting
Julius more and more, and he is around at work more so than
usual. I don't know what to do for him, nor will he say. It is
most exasperating.'

'There must be a reason, everyone moves on in good time,
or they have up until now, have they not?' Lilly asked studying
her friend. 'And he will not reveal why he is in attendance?'

'No, and it is futile for me to ask him, although I have subtly
tried without inferring that I want him to move on, of course.
He has to tell me in his own good time, that is how it works,'
Phoebe said. 'Oh well, it will sort itself, it is nothing new, just
frustrating and I fear it distresses Grandpa. He loves him so.'

Violet looked confused. 'But if he is family, is he not staying
with you? I have not seen him around the business.'

'Oh!' Phoebe glanced at her girlfriends, her hand going to
her mouth, and lowering it, she turned back to Violet. 'Of
course, you would not have seen him around.'

Violet regarded her with a miffed expression.

'I do forget sometimes that it is a small and trusted group
that knows of my spiritual proclivities. Dear Violet, if you
promise to keep my secret close to your heart and only
speak with those who know about it, namely my immediate

family and the *Vexed Vixens*, I shall tell you about my visitors including Uncle Reggie. But if you prefer not to know, we will say no more and I will deny everything,' she added with a grin.

'Goodness,' Violet said and with a small laugh at the amused looks of the ladies around the table, returned her attention to Phoebe. 'Your secret is safe with me; I assure you of my discretion. I cannot wait to hear this. Please, Phoebe, proceed.'

'Well, to begin with, Uncle Reggie is quite dead... it is just his spirit that insists on staying.'

Chapter 26

I T WAS BEFITTING THAT it was a grey day threatening
rain – befitting the solemnity of the occasion. Detective
Harland Stone had received word that morning that Mr
Isaac Elvin had been detained on his property by the Oakey
police and unable to provide the legitimate information
for the source of his inheritance, Mr Elvin was being
transported to the Brisbane watchhouse for the detective's
further questioning.

Now, back in the street where Isaac Elvin's family lived – the
small timber house with the water tank at the back – Harland
hoped his hunch was right and he had not called for a team
to dig up remains that were not there. Harland felt there were
detectives at the station only too keen to see his downfall after
his last success. Not all, of course, some mature detectives

encouraged the new young team and remarked how much they reminded them of themselves when they first began. That was appreciated.

He saw the elderly neighbour who assisted him, leaning over his fence and looking to see what all the excitement was about. Harland acknowledged his presence with a wave. The current residence had agreed it best she visits her sister for the day and with the assurance that a policeman would be on duty and her personal property safe, she reluctantly left the small team in her backyard.

Harland moved down the side of the house and stood where he could see what was going on in the front and backyard. A constable was posted on the gate, and a team of three men had arrived with shovels to begin work. His partner, Gilbert, showed them through to the backyard and the men looked around the tank area. There was nothing to indicate where the body might be or where to start digging – it had been twenty years after all. Harland had guessed where the vegetable patch might have been – against the fence and near the tank was all he had to go on from what the neighbour had said.

Harland recognised the gruff man who leapt down from a hansom cab and told the driver to wait. It was a senior detective – Detective Bell – one of the men who worked on the original case twenty years ago when he was a younger man. He had not been forthcoming with assistance and bullied his way past the constable. Harland waved him in.

'Just on my way to a case and curiosity got the better of me,' Detective Bell said. 'Found a body yet?' He said the words in jest as if he did not expect a result and looked forward to the young gun detective falling flat on his face.

'We haven't started the dig yet.' Harland lowered his voice. 'You know this is not about showing anyone up, Detective.'

The older detective gave a short, sharp and dismissive nod, and looked over Harland's shoulder.

Harland continued, 'Mrs Tochborn's death and the claimants coming forward unearthed some old secrets and new information.' He shrugged. 'Fortunate for us.'

Detective Bell grunted in reply. 'I guess you need a break given the partner you were saddled with, better you than me.' He laughed and said the words loud enough that Harland believed Gilbert and the men on-site might have overhead him, which angered Harland no end.

'Detective Payne's eye for detail and factual knowledge unearthed several valuable clues; I would not give him up for the world and would fight against his transfer unless it was a promotion.'

He felt Detective Bell's scrutiny and then the man shrugged. 'Well, good luck then.' He looked toward the men with shovels one more time and with a tip of his hat to Harland, departed as quickly as he came. Harland exhaled and tried to put himself in Detective Bell's position. Would he be defensive? Probably, he conceded.

Harland saw Miss Lilly Lewis arrive and gave the constable on the gate a nod to let her in. She walked down the side of the house to join him.

'You must be most anxious, Detective,' she said by way of greeting.

'That is exactly how I feel, Miss Lewis.' He explained what he was looking for and the very real possibility that nothing might be found. Gilbert approached.

'Good morning, Miss Lewis.' He acknowledged Lilly, who looked suitably demure in a dark skirt and grey and white pin-striped blouse, with a straw hat perched on her head. 'You look dressed for a dig,' he joked and she laughed.

'Good morning, Detective Payne, very true. I've come prepared should there be mud flying.'

Gilbert turned to his superior. 'Sir, I heard what you said. Thank you.' He moved on quickly. 'May I make a suggestion?'

'Please do,' Harland invited the young man's observations.

'If the neighbour's memory is correct and we are looking for an old vegetable patch, I believe the strip closest to the tank stumps is our best bet.' He indicated with his hand. 'You see, if you observe the yard, a vegetable patch needs sunshine for a full day ideally, and that area is out of the shadow of the house and tank. It is also higher so water drains away down the yard to the front, which is ideal.'

'And if there was a leak in the tank, or one was created for a ruse, the water would also run to the street,' Harland said thinking on the neighbour's recollections of the damaged tank being repaired.

Gilbert looked at the area. 'Yes, if the water was excessive it would rush to the street. But that is where I would put a vegetable patch as it is more likely to sustain vegetables and a good gardener would know that.'

Harland grabbed Gilbert's shoulder. 'Your fact-gathering has proven to be very useful yet again, Gilbert. I thank you.' He strode over to the men with shovels and suggested they begin digging in the area that Gilbert had outlined.

Now, they waited.

Late afternoon edition
BODY FOUND
TWENTY-YEAR-OLD MURDER SOLVED BY
DETECTIVES
CLAIMANTS BOTH FAKES!
The Courier presents an exclusive report
by Lilly Lewis and Fergus Griffiths.

The mystery of the tragic disappearance of a young boy held for ransom twenty years past has been solved thanks to the fine work of the Roma Street detective team, Harland Stone and Gilbert Payne. *The Courier* has been updating you daily on the historic murder and the claimants who raised their hands to be recognised as the heir to the Tochborn estate. The process stalled for a brief time with the recent death of Mrs Henriette Tochborn who we understand was intending to support the claimant, Mr Arthur Horton.

But early this morning, the corpse of the ten-year-old boy, James Hickling, who played the role of James Tochborn for family portraits, and was kidnapped as a result of his family's deception, has been found, buried in the garden of a Brisbane backyard. His kidnapper and murderer is believed to be Mr Isaac Elvin, a former employee at the Tochborn estate, a man admired by friends and neighbours, but who hid a dark secret. The ransom received for his dastardly deed, he claimed to be an inheritance and duping all who knew him, Mr Elvin relocated his widowed mother (deceased) and siblings to a large farming estate in Oakey, where they would want for nothing ever again.

Mr Elvin was initially hired as a labourer and handyman to the Tochborn family, the job was a great boon for his family and his mother was immensely proud of his employment. But the temptation and the secret of the fake child – which this newspaper covered in detail yesterday – proved too much. One can only assume as Mr Elvin knew young James through his friendship with fellow employees, the cook and the stable manager, that he coaxed the young boy away with some false incentive. James, innocent and trusting, may have readily gone with Mr Elvin, unaware of his destiny or the ruse at hand.

Mr Elvin was courting Mrs Tochborn's maid and companion, Miss Rachel Temple, at the time of the boy's disappearance, and along with a handful of staff was dismissed from his employ when the boy was not found. According to a neighbour, Mr Elvin played the role of a down-and-out man looking for work and willing to do odd jobs, while he must have been stashing the huge inheritance and secretly buying the farm. Then, when the investigation cooled, he proclaimed an inheritance, deserted Miss Temple citing the family commitment must take precedence, and departed for his new life. Miss Temple remained in Mrs Tochborn's service until the death of the senior lady recently.

As for Mr Arthur Horton, the claimant, he will face court on charges of perjury. The judge has advised that he is unlikely to pursue the same charge against asylum resident, Mr William Varsewell, as he is believed to be the twin brother of the murdered boy, and is safe in his current surrounds with no desire to seek release. His extended family may seek monetary compensation on his behalf from the Tochborn estate.

It was a most tragic moment to hear the cry of the men digging and the call to halt work as the bones revealed themselves, and neither of the detectives was of a mind to celebrate their find and solving another case. Mr Elvin is currently in a Brisbane holding cell and the mystery of what became of James Tochborn, a fake child, has been put to rest.

Ambrose stopped reading and put the paper down, returning his focus to Mrs Dobbs' egg and bacon pie and the generous portion she had placed before him.

'It would break your heart, would it not?' she said with a sigh, pushing another piece of pie towards Julius as he rifled through paperwork. Both men had come in early for work – Julius to meet with his bookkeeper and Ambrose to begin collections – and Mrs Dobbs had insisted on feeding them; neither was complaining.

'I don't seem to have Lucian's accounts for the month,' Julius said, his brow furrowing with impatience as he looked around his piles of paperwork. Behind him, his grandfather entered the room.

'Good morning, all. Lucian's accounts,' he said placing them in front of Julius. 'Just dropped in.'

'Ah, good.' Julius relaxed again. 'This is excellent pie, thank you, Mrs Dobbs.'

She flushed with pleasure. 'My mother's recipe. A slice, Mr Astin?' She looked to the senior Astin.

'I've breakfasted but thank you, Mrs Dobbs. And thank you for feeding this brood. Did you not eat before you left this morning, Ambrose?' Randolph asked.

'Yes, but fortunately I managed to fit in a slice, or two,' he said earning a delighted look from Mrs Dobbs.

Randolph chuckled and addressed both of his grandsons. 'Now lads, I need to warn you that your grandmother intends to introduce you to everyone in her acquaintance at the ball tomorrow evening.'

Neither dared groan, but it took some restraint.

'I believe she has already introduced me to all and sundry at her last charity ball six months passed. Thus, the focus will be on you, brother,' Ambrose said with a smile patting Julius on the shoulder.

'It is the first ball you have deigned to attend, Julius, so bring your most charming self,' his grandfather requested.

Now he did groan. 'I feel exhausted at the thought.'

'Yes, not everyone is naturally charming like me,' Ambrose conceded, 'and I can't be there to cover for you all night, Julius. Just do your best.'

Julius gave him a grimace which had Randolph and Mrs Dobbs chuckling.

'Do you want the stable lads to prepare the trap for you and Miss Astin?' Randolph asked.

'No, but thank you. I will take a hansom to collect Miss Astin and drop her home afterwards.'

'A much better idea, but it might be worth tipping the driver handsomely to collect you after or you may be waiting in quite a line-up. I shall organise it for you while you are in your meeting.'

Julius looked up from his paperwork, surprised. 'That would be great, thank you, Grandpa.'

There was a knock at the front door.

'Ah, the dead are keen this morning,' Randolph joked.

'If it is anyone for me other than the bookkeeper, I am unavailable,' Julius called behind his departing grandfather.

Moments later, he heard the voice of Miss Violet Forrester and both men rose to their feet as she entered the kitchen behind Randolph.

'Miss Forrester, is everything alright?' Julius asked, concerned to see her so early.

'All is well, I assure you, Mr Astin. I just hoped for a private word if you have time, but I understand you have a meeting shortly?'

'The bookkeeper can wait,' Julius said ignoring the surprised and amused looks of his family. 'Shall we—' He looked around for a private meeting area.

'I need to get the day's roster, Grandpa,' Ambrose said, rising.

'Right this way,' Randolph agreed, and the two exited the room hurriedly.

'I am just dropping some biscuits to the lads in the stables,' Mrs Dobbs declared, grabbing a small tin and departing just as quickly.

Julius gave Violet a smile that bordered on a wince and she laughed.

'Something we said?' she asked.

'I suspect so,' he agreed and offered her a seat.

'I shall stand and only take a minute of your time, thank you, Mr Astin.'

He nodded for her to proceed, not taking his eyes from her face, and attracted beyond all measure by her large blue eyes that seemed lighter with the pale grey dress she wore.

'Last night I had the pleasure of Phoebe's company and that of her friends.'

'Ah, you were exposed to the *Vexed Vixens*,' he said and smiled. 'I hope you were able to contribute?' he teased.

'I did my best,' Violet said with a small laugh. 'Emily, that is, Miss Yalden, offered to share her ride and that of her cousin's with me to the ball. When I mentioned you were collecting me, it was suggested kindly, that it could set tongues wagging.'

'Ah, I see,' he said, disappointed and very much looking forward to having the journey before and after, and the three waltzes, with Miss Forrester. He tried to hide his regret and straightened. 'Of course, I understand you wish to avoid that.'

'Oh no,' she said, 'I just thought you might wish to do so, and your offer to transport me was based on kindness for my situation without thinking of the consequences.'

'I did not think of the consequences,' he answered honestly, 'nor do I care for my own sake. But of course, I see it from your perspective.'

If she wished to extend her social circle and enjoy the company of other gentlemen, they may assume she was spoken for should they arrive together.

'Whatever you think is best, Miss Forrester, I will respect your decision.'

He saw the look of frustration cross her face and then she said, 'Mr Astin, may I speak frankly.'

'I would welcome that,' Julius told her and gripped the top of the chair in front of him, wondering what might come next. A rebuff? A reminder of her state of employment at his mercy and the wish to remain purely professional?

'I very much look forward to you collecting me and delivering me safely home thereafter, and our shared dances. It is of no concern to me what anyone thinks, as I shall be happy. But now that you see the bigger picture, if you wish to make other plans, please inform me and I shall accept Emily's offer.'

Julius was surprised by her frankness and pleased for it. He smiled at her.

'Miss Forrester, if I may be so bold, the only part of the ball that I am looking forward to, is the time in your company.'

He saw her smile, then attempt to hide it, while colouring very prettily. She gave a quick bow and said, 'Tomorrow evening then. Thank you, Mr Astin.'

'Thank you, Miss Forrester,' he said, with a small bow and hurriedly followed her out of the kitchen to the front office door where he held the door open for her, knowing his grandfather and brother were watching the scene with great interest. His bookkeeper arrived at the same time, and Julius left the man waiting a few moments while he watched Miss Forrester make her way to the business next door, and then with a light heart, returned to his duties.

Chapter 27

C ENTENNIAL HALL HAD BEEN turned into a glamorous ballroom for the annual Hospital Ball – one large area was designated for ballroom dancing and an equally large section was set aside for supper with long tables filling every inch of the room. By the time Ambrose entered the ballroom with his sister, Phoebe, the crowd numbers had swelled to almost capacity. He nudged her to indicate members of their party and they made their way to the group, undertaking introductions to brothers, sisters, and cousins of the *Vexed Vixens* who had coordinated the large gathering.

Before he could put his plan in place – to secure a dance with Miss Lilly Lewis – the national anthem struck up and everyone stood respectfully to participate. The band that played the anthem would play the dance music for the evening, and looked keen for the fun to start. Once the anthem was completed, Ambrose left Phoebe in the company of Bennet Martin and her friend Emily, and sidled up to the enchanting Miss Lilly Lewis who smiled and studied his attire.

He was captivated, as he always was by the sparkle in her blue eyes, the silkiness of her brunette hair, her creamy skin and her endearing smile. Tonight, she wore a pale blue, off-the-shoulder ball gown with cream pearls and matching earrings. She was more beautiful than ever, although Ambrose would not have thought that possible. Before he could compliment her, Miss Lewis admired his attire.

'My, you look most handsome, Mr Astin,' she teased.

'It's my natural state,' he said and made her laugh. 'And you, Miss Lewis... look beautiful.' He said no more. No teasing, no winking, nothing but sincerity and her expression reflected her surprise.

'Thank you,' she said a little belatedly.

'May I have the honour of your first dance?' he asked.

'That would be my pleasure,' she agreed and Ambrose felt her studying him as she offered her pencil and he filled in her card.

'Aye, I was just going to claim that dance,' Dr Tavish McGregor appeared resplendent before them in his formal wear, with a tartan sash.

'Beaten by a better man,' Ambrose joked and handed him the pencil to claim another, Miss Lewis permitting.

'You are the belle of the ball without rival, Miss Lewis,' Tavish said to Ambrose's frustration as he was just about to embark on a similar flattering remark.

She laughed and appeared to dismiss them both as if their comments were nonsensical, destroying the brief moment of intimacy Ambrose had shared with her. Before he could broach a subject, a man's voice called for attention and the Governor and his wife were welcomed. Ambrose shifted from foot to foot, then remembered to stand still, and glanced around to see if his grandfather had sent that message to him, hearing his voice say it over the years. He found his grandparents in the crowd; his grandmother was called forth with other lady board members to be presented with a bouquet for their efforts.

Ambrose was envying Julius for missing this boring part of the evening. With formalities over, the Governor and his wife launched the ball with the first dance – a quadrille, and Ambrose offered his hand to Miss Lewis.

'Shall we, Miss Lewis?'

'Let's show them up, Mr Astin,' she said and laughed as they moved to the dance floor to take their position with the other couples. As Ambrose stood opposite the woman of his desires, he was mesmerised. Imagine if she was his, he thought.

Imagine if every day he had the honour of seeing her, walking beside her, providing for her, and helping her choose her hats and fashion on the pretence of being near her. Imagine loving her physically, and the thought made him swallow and look away for a moment while he regained himself and they waited for the music to start.

She leaned towards him and he returned his attention to her.

'Is your brother coming later? I heard he was collecting Miss Forrester?' she asked, with a glance around the room.

And with those words, he returned to being her friend with no prospects and the music started.

'Did you wish to give me any warnings or ask me to have your sister home at a respectable hour?' Julius teased Tom as they stood on the verandah of the Forresters' small, rented home, waiting for Violet to finish her dressing. She was a punctual young lady, Julius knew that of her, but he had arrived fifteen minutes early, undeterred by other carriages on the journey. Julius was happy to have the time to talk with her brother, and the driver was equally pleased to wait since he was being paid handsomely for it.

Tom laughed. 'I won't lay down any rules for you if you do the same for me,' he said with a glance inside.

'Oh, and what does your sister think you are up to tonight?' Julius asked eyeing the young man suspiciously who grinned at him. Tom was a working man now with his own income, and in effect the man of the house, but he was a lad of fifteen with no male influence.

He looked down the street and nodded towards a house. 'Just spending the night with some of the boys. Don't worry, I'll be home before you two are tonight. He looked Julius over. 'You look sharp. Violet likes you.'

'I hope so.'

'I mean, she likes you a lot.'

Julius nodded his understanding and keep his emotions steadfast. He was not one for displaying his feelings, not like he did when his parents first passed. He would never be that emotional again, especially in public.

'I will protect her, fear not.' He realised Tom wanted more than that and added, 'I feel the same for her. Is that permitted?' Julius smiled.

'Sure. Rather you than some idiot.' Tom grinned like he had a great secret to tell her later, and Julius laughed at the odd compliment.

They turned on hearing Violet, and Tom gave a low whistle as she appeared in the doorway wearing a striking ballgown of pale grey. It was a gown chosen with a colour befitting light mourning, but it shimmered like fluid satin, making her skin glow, making her appear feminine and ethereal. Julius knew she was all that, but strong and determined too.

'Miss Forester,' he said and cleared his throat lightly. 'You are breathtaking.'

She gave a wide grin and thanked him, before turning to her brother. 'And what say you, Tom?'

'You look great. No one would ever know we are not top shelf.'

She flushed a little with embarrassment at his words, reminding her of the area they lived in, the house they survived in week to week. Violet was about to respond when Julius said to her, 'You are out of my reach, but I will aim for the stars, regardless.'

Violet's eyes widened with surprise at his compliment, and she appeared momentarily flustered; Tom gave a sharp laugh.

'He's right, Sis, you are a good catch. I just wish Grandma could see you in that dress. She'd love it.'

Violet gave him a warm smile and thanked him. 'I hope so. That is why I am not wearing black, to please her.' She turned the attention from herself. 'Are you sure you will be alright, this evening?' she asked her brother.

'I'll be fine, don't worry. I'm just going to be down the road with the boys.'

'Do not stay out late.'

'I won't.'

'Be home when I get home.'

'I will be.'

'And I don't mean running in the backdoor as I am coming in the front,' she said narrowing her eyes at him, knowing him only too well.

'When did I ever?' he asked and then laughed when he saw her expression.

'Be careful, we only have each other,' she said in a lower voice and Tom nodded then turned to Julius with an imploring look which he understood and stepped forward.

'Shall we?' Julius asked and offered his arm, as Violet had not made eye contact with him since his compliment. *This will be interesting*, he mused. *Have I rendered her speechless?*

Julian looked back to Tom. 'Have a good night and stay out of trouble for your sister's sake,' he teased and Tom laughed again.

'Yes, Dad.'

Julius chuckled, shook his head and said, 'Young ones,' making Violet laugh. He led her down the steps and she waved to a few neighbours who had come out to admire her dress and the handsome man who had come to collect her.

Julius handed her into the seat of the hansom cab and waited while she arranged her dress before joining her. Violet gave Tom a wave, and then they were alone.

Harland Stone arrived at the ball with his ticket and invitation as part of the Astin party. It had been several years since he had attended a ball, but his formal attire returned from cleaning and pressing looked fresh. He was a man comfortable in all manner of clothing. Years of private schooling and wearing a police uniform thereafter had given him a discipline for dress.

He arrived just as the final bouquet was being presented to the ladies of the board and scanned the crowd. He drew attention; not only because of his recent success on two high-profile cases, but he was a single young man of stature. Handsome, well-presented, and well-employed. His eyes immediately sought Miss Phoebe Astin, finding her. She returned his gaze as if she too were looking and waiting for him, but that was just wishful thinking, he mused. He gave Phoebe a fleeting smile; Bennet Martin was speaking with her and looked in his direction, waving him over. Would Bennet be so keen to see him if he knew how off his balance he was around Miss Astin?

Harland began to wade through the guests toward where his party gathered only to be stopped numerous times by people who wanted to pat him on the back, shake his hand and congratulate him. He came within a few feet of a senior man he recognised – Randolph Astin – and was grateful for the rescue.

'You are famous, Detective, but I'm gathering you want to get to your party,' Randolph said, shaking his hand.

'Mr Astin, good evening. I'm determined to get there,' Harland said in jest.

'Then pretend you are engrossed in a conversation with me as we walk that way.' They did so, with Harland nodding his thanks to those who did not interrupt but slapped his back or applauded as he passed. He felt embarrassed and uncomfortable but knew it would soon pass once he had been there some time.

'Ah, here's Miss Kirby,' Randolph said greeting Kate as she passed with a glass of punch. 'You two are acquainted are you not?'

'We are. Hello detective. We met on your earlier case at a crime scene when I was called in to photograph it in the absence of the coroner's man.'

'Indeed. Hello Miss Kirby, you look lovely this evening,' Harland said giving the expected compliment.

'I shall leave you young people to it,' Randolph said accepting Harland's thanks and moving away, and Harland found himself escorting Kate over to the group The dancing had begun and he saw Ambrose and Miss Lewis dancing. He wondered if he could ask Miss Astin for a dance or if Bennet would dominate her attention this evening. The thought made him wish he had not agreed to attend.

Chapter 28

VIOLET WANTED TO BE present in the moment but Julius's beautiful words about her being above him left her stunned and grateful. She wanted to remember the sentiment and think back on it later. Perhaps the gulf between them wasn't as vast as she thought. Tom had told her the story Julius shared about his modest beginnings – how his grandfather and grandmother struggled to bury his parents and keep the three of them. Maybe their lives had run parallel at one stage, even if he was hugely successful and wealthy now. Not that Julius acted that way, he had worked for everything he had. As Julius was not driving, they had less distraction and Violet felt keenly aware of his proximity.

'Thank you for collecting me, Mr Astin,' she said. 'I hope Tom did not grill you on your intentions this evening.'

Julius smiled, which she studied with great interest. He seemed to do that more of late, not that she knew him very well, but he was more disposed to sternness unlike his brother, Ambrose, who smiled and joked readily. She felt it was a personal victory to make Julius smile and if he laughed, it was even more delightful.

'I gave him the chance to read me the Riot Act,' Julius informed her, 'but he undertook negotiation instead. He is a bright young man.'

Violet huffed with amusement. 'I can just imagine the negotiation too. A bid for freedom and you may do as you wish?'

'I cannot reveal the outcome of our confidential agreement.'

Violet laughed and shook her head at him.

'Miss Forrester, I hope you will permit me to give you a small gift this evening before we arrive at the ball.'

'But why?' As soon as the words escaped her, Violet realised that was less than gracious but curiosity overtook her. She thought a bouquet or a corsage might have been appropriate if he had wanted to arrive with a gift but neither was in sight.

'Because you look beautiful and it would give me pleasure.'

'Oh. Well thank you but is not necessary. You, that is, your company, has already provided me with a complimentary ticket for the evening and my safe delivery. That is gift enough.'

'Nevertheless, I hope you will accept this and wear it,' Julius said and reached into his pocket withdrawing a black velvet pouch and offering it to Violet, placing it in her hand.

She looked at him and then to the pouch and opened it with curiosity, pulling out her grandmother's black pearls which she recognised immediately from the engraved clasp. Violet gasped.

'Mr Astin, how did you know? Where did you find them?'

'Will you accept them and wear them tonight? They will go perfectly with your dress.'

'They will.' She said in awe touching them lovingly. 'They mean a great deal to me. Thank you, this is the kindest gift I could ever hope for, thank you.' She blinked away tears and kissed the necklace before realising how silly that must look. But Violet could tell Julius felt genuine pleasure in giving them to her and her reaction would not have disappointed him. She turned as she placed them around her neck for Julius to affix the clasp. 'Will you please?'

'Of course.'

It was unavoidable that his fingers would brush the bare skin of her neck as he fastened the clasp, and she felt her skin tingling once his hands were removed. Violet turned back, touching the pearls around her neck and sighed with relief. 'I felt so terrible parting with them. How did you know?'

'I saw you... it was the morning you were coming to meet with me and I had to delay our meeting but we passed you. I made Ambrose wait while I raced in to retrieve them for you – Tom mentioned you were going to sell them and I recognised the store you entered. They belong with your family. I would have advanced you your wages so you did not have to sell them.'

She blushed. 'I did not know you paid weekly or I would not have sold them. I thought I might have to wait some weeks or a month and with the funeral cost...'

'I understand, but we have payment packages for those who can ill afford a funeral, and I am sorry for not informing you of our wage arrangements.'

She laughed. 'Mr Astin, you are a most generous employer, and no apology is necessary. It is an extravagant gift; I am very grateful.'

'The pleasure is all mine.' And then Julius blurted out, 'I too have sold things when I needed to supplement my lack of income. I once sold my bicycle... and a few things that didn't belong to me.' He looked sheepish.

Violet laughed. 'No?'

He shrugged. 'Boys will be boys, besides if I needed anything, I didn't like to ask my grandparents for it when times were tight, so I found ways and means.'

'Goodness,' she said. 'I may have to turn you into Detective Stone.'

Julius grinned. 'Now you have something on me.'

'Now I worry what Tom is up to!' She bit her lip. 'I did go back to get the pearls that very evening I was paid, but they were gone. I was quite devastated.'

'They were in safe keeping,' he said with a smile.

'Thank you, Mr Astin.' Violet could not help but touch the pearls, the delight of having them back was so great, but her mind went to Julius.

He likes me with more than a casual interest. There was no denying it now or thinking he was just being kind or feeling sorry for her, and thus she had a decision to make. Accept his attention at the risk of her job, or choose her employment first and foremost. In Violet's head, the decision was easy – protect her employment, but her heart would have none of that. There were other jobs she could get, and Tom no longer needed her complete financial support, he had his own apprenticeship.

Violet had to admit that she could not imagine what it would be like to see Julius courting a lady, someone other than herself.

I suppose I will see that tonight when he dances with others and it will be telling on my heart, she thought.

She was not so vain or presumptuous to believe Julius's name would not be on several dance cards with women better connected and with more to offer.

The hansom cab stopped; they had arrived.

'You will not forget I have taken your three waltzes and I won't negotiate with anyone trying to take them from me,' he teased as he stepped down to assist her from the hansom.

'I will not forget nor forfeit them to the highest bidder, I assure you.' She leaned on Julius needing more help than one would when wearing conventional clothing, the layers of delicate fabric made descent that much more perilous.

Once righted, she accepted his offered arm and they entered the hall, their expressions revealing their surprise at the numbers in attendance and the glamourous decorations. The first dance had begun, the music swelled and the noise of the ballroom was engaging and exciting.

'Oh, how lovely,' Violet exclaimed. 'There is your brother dancing with Lilly, and Emma is dancing also.'

'That is Tavish, Dr McGregor – the coroner – who is partnering her,' Julius said leaning lower to talk near her ear to be heard above the noise.

Violet saw Julius acknowledge Bennet's wave but before he could lead her to their friends, they heard a voice behind them.

'Ah, here's Julius and Miss Forrester now.' They both turned to see the senior Astins and Violet was introduced to Julius's grandmother who looked more like Phoebe than Julius. The first dance finished and Violet saw Dr McGregor bow to Emily and take Lilly from Ambrose's clutches, thus releasing the younger Astin brother who made his way to Julius.

On Ambrose's arrival, Mrs Maria Astin stepped in and organised the young people. 'Ambrose, will you escort Miss Forrester to your friends? Forgive me, Miss Forrester, but I need to introduce Julius to a selection of business people before he disappears on me for the night,' Mrs Astin said.

'Of course, Mrs Astin, a perfect opportunity,' Violet said and offered his grandmother a conspiratorial smile.

'The ladies are conspiring against you, dear brother,' Ambrose said to Julius and obliged his grandmother. 'Come, Miss Forrester, let us greet the others. That is a beautiful necklace,' he added and Violet saw the look he gave his brother. She touched it and smiled at Julius.

Julius gave Violet a small bow and they were separated by the crowds. For the next twenty minutes which felt like two hours to Julius, he was introduced to the hospital board, reacquainted with business leaders he had not seen for some time and endured with good grace the endless round of comments such as 'good to see you above ground', 'See you again, hopefully not when I am a client' and 'I hope you are making a good living' often delivered with a nudge or wink.

Seeing the cracks in his patience, his grandmother thanked him with a kiss on the cheek and dismissed him. He may be a grown man, but he knew it was important to her and he owed his grandmother that and much more. When he joined the group, his eyes searched for Violet – not that she had been long out of his sight – and he found her dancing the quadrille and partnered with Ambrose; his sister Phoebe danced with Bennet.

'I believe congratulations are in order,' he said to Harland after meeting and greeting the group appropriately.

'It was a good outcome,' Harland acknowledged. 'Hopefully, we will both have the rest of the night off now.'

Julius gave a small sigh of relief. 'My duty is done but I suspect you will be the novelty of the evening. Do you intend to dance?'

Harland looked to Julius. 'Are you asking me?'

Julus chuckled. 'While you look presentable, there is no attraction,' he said in jest making Harland laugh. 'I have committed to three dances which I am very much looking forward to, but aside from that, I like to see everyone suffer accordingly.' He gave his friend a wry look. His intentions were more honourable, he hoped to see his sister happy and he knew she would like the detective to ask her.

'Unlike Mr Martin and your brother, I am not a natural, believe it or not?' Harland joked. 'But years at boarding school with strict practice in the social arts means I am at least capable. I suppose I could inflict myself on some poor unsuspecting lady.'

Julius saw the detective watching his sister but he had promised Phoebe not to interfere, especially if the interest was not mutual and she might read more into the dance than intended. How to introduce the subject? He tried again.

'The brothers have stepped up. Ambrose with Miss Forrester and Bennet with Phoebe.'

Harland looked at him, then back to the handsome pair similar in colouring – Bennet and Phoebe. They looked to be enjoying themselves and made an attractive couple.

Julius continued, 'That is, my sister regards Bennet as akin to a brother, even though they have only known each other for a brief time. They have a comfortable friendship.'

'I see,' Harland said.

Duty done, Julius thought. There is nothing he would not do for his brother and sister, and soon it was time to claim his waltz.

Chapter 29

P HOEBE THANKED MR BENNET Martin and allowed him to escort her back to her friends. She felt she looked the best she could in her dusty pink ballgown accessorised with cream pearl earrings and necklace. The dress was a gift from her grandparents, the jewellery once belonged to her mother, and she was delighted at last to have the chance to show them off. Phoebe was not oblivious to the heads she turned, but her profession often startled some. Tonight, she only wanted to turn one head.

On Bennet Martin's arm, she arrived back to where their friends were gathered. Detective Stone was a short distance away talking with a group of men she did not know. Phoebe had seen Julius talking with the detective earlier – she was torn between wanting Julius to say something to encourage the detective's suit, and being mortified should he not be interested. It was best left to the detective; he was a man of strength and character as she had seen in the courtroom, and she imagined he would not shy from making advances to a woman he desired. The thought made her colour slightly and she returned her attention to the ball and her group of lady friends as Bennet departed to fetch refreshments.

'Violet is dancing with my solicitor cousin, Lilly is dancing with Kate's brother, and Kate is taking a turn around the floor with Dr Tavish McGregor,' Emily said filling Phoebe in on what she was missing and how the *Vexed Vixens* were currently occupied.

'Ah, the coroner has arrived then,' Phoebe observed the dancing couples.

'Yes, so has Detective Stone.'

'I noticed,' Phoebe said and gave Emily a small smile.

'Your dress is lovely, Phoebe, you look very becoming.' Emily was not one for overt flattery.

'Thank you, Emily, it is a sentimental dress, as is my jewellery. I feel rather empowered wearing them,' Phoebe remarked. 'Your gown of green is also most becoming on you; it is your colour.' She leaned in and whispered, 'I can't recall, but did Kate like Dr McGregor or not?'

'She did not say, but Lilly was not interested in pursuing his interest.'

'Ah that is right,' Phoebe said and hurriedly changed the subject seeing Detective Stone approaching them. She asked Emily, 'Did your week conclude on a high note?'

'Well, two young ladies graduated and I am tempted to give one her money back, but I am nothing if not persistent.'

Detective Stone grinned on hearing her last words. 'It seems to be an admirable trait with Miss Astin and her friends.'

'Well thank you, Detective Stone,' Phoebe said smiling up at him. 'May I present Miss Emily Yalden?'

'Miss Yalden, a pleasure,' the detective said. 'And may I ask who you are tempted to refund?'

'A baby hippopotamus attending my deportment school, detective.'

Harland laughed and Phoebe smiled enjoying his unguarded reaction. She imagined he needed a night amongst friends and some humour after such a dark trial.

Bennet joined them returning with a drink for Phoebe, and Harland offered to fetch one for Emily who declined with thanks; the four friends spoke over the sound of the orchestra and din of the guests.

Phoebe glanced at the detective several times only to find him watching her and looking away just as quickly. She was sure that there was something between them, a tension or energy she had not experienced with anyone else before, but could anyone else see it? Bennet clearly did not as he continued to engage her in conversation. The constant banter and energy to respond was rather exhausting given she could spend many a day saying very little. She would have preferred to observe the dancers, enjoy the music, or take to the dance floor with the detective who did not ask anyone to dance but rather stood in a dignified, disciplined manner watching all around him – an occupational trait she imagined.

Goodness, get a hold of yourself, she scolded herself and did her best not to look at the detective again unless he was speaking.

'Do you not dance, Detective?' Kate asked arriving slightly breathless after her dance set with Dr Tavish McGregor.

'Of course he dances, like he owns the dancefloor,' Tavish answered for him and laughed at Harland's expression.

Phoebe couldn't help but grin as the detective grimaced at the coroner before responding to Kate.

'Not if I can help it, Miss Kirby, and trust me, the ladies are grateful for that.'

'Oh phooey,' Kate said. 'I do not believe that. You cannot come to a dance without dancing.'

Emily shook her head slightly. 'At this point, Detective, I would be telling my students that young ladies of good breeding do not say "phooey" nor do they force a gentleman to dance.'

Kate laughed. 'Oh dear, I would fail terribly at your academy, Emily. What say you, Detective, will you dance? I promise to forgive you should you stand on my toes.'

Phoebe turned to see what he would do. It would be churlish to turn down her friend, Kate, who had been brave enough to ask, but Phoebe would be disappointed if Detective Stone took to the dance floor and not with her. Well, a little more than disappointed.

'Let's make a group of it,' Tavish announced.

'Yes, good idea,' Detective Stone said and with a glance at Phoebe, he inclined his head politely to Kate. 'It would be a pleasure, Miss Kirby,' he said and offered his arm.

'Come then, Miss Astin, are you up for a turn about the dance floor?' Tavish asked.

Phoebe hid her disappointment and accepted Dr McGregor's invitation with enthusiasm and grace. She could see Ambrose and cousin Lucian heading to the dancefloor with sisters who appeared to be twins and very pretty. On Dr McGregor's arm, she followed Detective Stone as he escorted Kate to the dance floor. Phoebe found herself feeling a little jealous and irrationally saddened, and she did not look at him once lest the detective should be enjoying himself far too much.

As much as she enjoyed a second dance with the handsome and charming, Ambrose Astin, it was the dance with his brother that played most on Violet Forrester's mind, and then, at last, the waltz was next on her dance card. Ambrose departed to claim the dance Miss Hannah Reed had pencilled in for him when he invited her to select a dance of her choosing. A clever move on her behalf but not surprising. He told Violet he could not complain, given he had thrown himself on his sword in the office for his brother, so he would see the sacrifice out. Violet laughed at his fake heroism and coerced an admission from him that Miss Reed did look rather lovely so it would not be too awful.

Violet watched as Julius came across to claim her. Those who knew of the eldest Astin also watched with interest. He was not known for dancing despite the enthusiastic attempts by the ladies for his attention at the occasional ball he deigned to attend.

'Miss Forrester, do you still have the stamina for our dance?' he teased, offering his hand and she placed her small hand within his.

'Oh, I assure you, Mr Astin, my stamina on the dance floor will likely outlast yours,' she teased in return.

'On that, we agree.'

As the dance began Julius moved to hold Violet in the accepted position for the waltz and she leaned into him, placing her hand on his shoulder. She looked up at him, forgetting about the other dancers but conscious his family appeared to be watching with undisguised interest.

'The floor is rather slippery, I have discovered,' Violet said. 'Do not let me slide off if you would be so kind.'

Julius shot her a small smile and secured his hand around her a little tighter. 'I have you, Miss Forrester, of that you can be sure.'

I hope so, she thought feeling a little frightened and undone with wanting him. *I truly hope you do, as no one will be comparable after you, Mr Astin. No one.*

Chapter 30

ON MONDAY MORNING, AMBROSE paced around Phoebe's workroom, touching things to her annoyance, as she was quite methodical with her tools and preparation.

'So, he said nothing to you of the evening?' he asked again.

Phoebe sighed. 'No. I saw him for the same amount of time that you did when he came by for lunch yesterday. He did not engage in any private discussions with me. But he seemed happy, did you not think so?'

'For Julius, definitely.'

Uncle Reggie appeared in his usual seat by the window and asked, 'Is my eldest nephew in love then?'

Phoebe turned to Ambrose. 'Uncle Reggie is here and asks the same question as you. Good morning, Uncle. We are none the wiser.'

'Perhaps I should go next door on some false errand and see how Miss Forrester fares this morning,' Ambrose mused.

'I believe that would be most obvious.'

'How was your evening, Phoebe, and your brother's?' Reggie asked. 'I am sure you were the belle of the ball, young lady.'

'Thank you, Uncle Reggie, but there were many belles there, especially Violet – Miss Forrester – she was strikingly beautiful. But it was a pleasant evening and we both enjoyed it, did we not, Ambrose?'

'It started well but...' He waved his hand.

Phoebe nodded. 'I am sorry Lilly does not return your affection but perhaps she is unaware of it.'

He made a sound that spoke of disbelief. 'Probably because she cannot see past Julius. I would like to see him hitched, for his sake and mine.' They then heard footsteps coming down the stairs. 'Speak of the devil and he is sure to appear.'

'Ah, you are both here. Is all well?' Julius asked arriving at the bottom of the stairs and greeting his siblings.

Reggie spoke up, 'I heard your Miss Forrester was strikingly beautiful, Julius. Did you win her heart?'

Julius ignored him – whether he could not hear him or chose not to acknowledge his presence was not commented upon. Instead, he turned to his siblings. 'Shall we, Ambrose? There is a collection to do before a funeral at midday.'

'Did you have a good night at the dance, brother?' Ambrose asked not moving.

'Yes. Did you not ask me that question yesterday and I replied the same?'

'Would you like to elaborate? You look happy and we would like to see you that way,' Ambrose said candidly. He lowered his voice and said in a surprisingly emotional admission, especially for the early hour of the morning, 'We can look after you too and hope for your happiness, even if we are younger.'

Julius looked slightly taken aback and surprised. He regathered his features, his impassive countenance softened by his brother's admission and he gave a small nod of his head. 'I had a better time than I anticipated and three excellent dances. Then I saw Miss Forrester home safely. I hope to see her again... socially. Will that suffice?' He smiled.

'Excellent. I shall wait for you upstairs.' Ambrose smiled, pleased, and tapping his brother on the back with his approval, he strode past him and up the stairs. Julius exchanged a look with his sister.

'What has gotten into our brother? Has he become melancholy?'

'Perhaps, but do not think you have gotten out of it that lightly,' Phoebe told him. 'You are sharing a ride for many hours today; he is bound to ask for your next planned move and offer counsel.'

'He is more social than I, I might even take his advice,' Julius said in jest. 'Did Harland ask you to dance that I did not see?'

'No, but we enjoyed several pleasant conversations. I felt that he might but then Bennet joined us and Detective Stone was engaged in another conversation. Kate asked him to dance but I could not be so bold.'

'Is that so?' he asked studying his sister. The family never knew quite what to expect from Phoebe. 'Harland may not have asked you to dance, but every time I glanced your way, he was by your side or in proximity.'

'Perhaps,' she said. Then the thought occurred to her that the detective was studying her for a reason. 'Did you say something?' She looked alarmed.

'I told you I would not. But I did let him know that you regarded Bennet as akin to a brother and friend.'

'And does Detective Stone consider him a friend?'

'Yes, so you may need to reject Bennet's advances before Harland sees fit to express his interest. While they are new acquaintances, I believe Harland to be a loyal person.' Julius shrugged. 'Not that I am an expert on the course of love or matters of the heart.'

'No, but you have one. Thank you, brother.' She stopped him as he started up the stairs. 'If you have no objections, on your way this morning could you take me to the cemetery where Mrs Tochborn is buried? I would like to pay a visit and take some flowers.'

'Come along by all means. You are putting to rest the case in your head now that it is closed in court?'

'Yes, exactly so,' Phoebe agreed.

Julius sighed. 'And here I was hoping the flowers in the corner were from an admirer.'

Phoebe looked sheepish. 'They are. Emily's cousin, the solicitor, and no, he is not for me. But I am gifting the flowers to Mrs Tochborn. I can be ready in a moment.'

'Let us go then. We can wait for you at the cemetery if you like and bring you back.'

'No, but thank you. I shall have a brief walk and take the omnibus home. I feel I need it.' She felt Julius studying her for a moment.

'What is wrong with the pair of you this morning?' he asked, his brow furrowed with concern.

'Do not be concerned, I am not heavy of heart. As for Ambrose, I believe he feels the pain of unrequited love, but I did not tell you that.'

'Miss Lewis,' Julius said.

'Did you know she preferred you?' Phoebe studied him.

'No!' he said genuinely surprised. 'I only recently realised Ambrose has feelings for her.'

Phoebe gave him a wry look. 'Ah, men. You are such strange creatures.'

'I have not encouraged her. Is Ambrose angry at me for—'

'He is not,' she cut her brother off. 'But I think he would be happy to see you paired and perhaps she may notice him then.'

'I see.' He considered that for a moment and then turned and headed up the stairs.

'Ah, young love.' Reggie sighed and Phoebe grinned his way. She collected her hat, and the flowers, and farewelled her uncle as she ventured to see the lady at rest.

'Was it terribly romantic?' Mary asked and sighed thinking about the ball and the well-dressed couples. 'I bet you looked so beautiful in your silver-grey gown. I am sure Mr Astin could not take his eyes off you.' She measured two pieces of black lace against each other and was satisfied they were the same length.

Violet smiled at the young girl who had more experience reading romance novels than real encounters with romance.

'It was a lovely evening,' Violet assured her. 'The men looked extremely handsome and I was most pleased with my dress, especially as I purchased the fabric cheaply because it was marked, but I believe I hid that sufficiently between the folds. I danced half a dozen times or so, but was conscious that too much more might be unseemly given I am in mourning.'

'I agree wholeheartedly with your clever and dear departed, grandmother,' Mrs Shaw said. 'You are young and have mourned enough. It is time for living. Did you dance with Mr Astin, Mr Julius Astin?'

'I had the pleasure of dancing with both of the Astin brothers, and...' she looked at young Mary, 'they are both very good dancers.'

'I would die,' Mary said dramatically and then remembering her promise to Mrs Shaw added quickly, 'that is, I would be swooning, not dying.'

Mrs Shaw nodded with a smile. 'I should think so, young lady, we'll have no unnecessary dying around here.'

Violet gave a low laugh at Mrs Shaw's tone.

'What were the dresses like Miss? Was there one colour more favoured than all others?' Mary persisted with her questions and Violet indulged her, happy to fill their work time with a light conversation to make the morning enjoyable as they toiled.

But her head was filled with Mr Julius Astin. Beyond the wall, she knew he was present at this very moment. She had seen him arrive from her window table where she pinned a dress, and her heartbeat soared accordingly. So strikingly handsome, so strong, and so protective of those he cared about, an admirable trait.

Violet was feeling something she had never felt before and it quite frightened her. Love in all its truth and beauty. Raw, powerful, and distracting.

Chapter 31

I T WAS A LOVELY winter's morning in the South Brisbane cemetery. The sun was warm and welcomed on Phoebe's back, the breeze light and crisp, and Phoebe inhaled the smell of freshly cut grass. She mused that should she lie here in rest, she would be most content in these surroundings. Phoebe was only too pleased for the chance to pay her final respects to Mrs Henriette Tochborn and lay the flowers at her grave. On finding the grave, she saw the dirt mound had hardened and dried since the funeral and a small handwritten tag was pushed into the earth to identify the lady. A headstone was not yet ready for installation, nor would it be until the earth settled sometime in the future.

Phoebe placed the flowers, removed some of the dying bouquets and freshened the water in several vases where flowers still survived. Standing back, she bowed her head in prayer for a moment. Before leaving, Phoebe added, 'It was a pleasure to have met you in passing, Mrs Tochborn. Please take comfort knowing your final wishes were honoured and justice will be served. I hope you find peace now.'

She did not expect to see Mrs Tochborn in the cemetery nor anyone else for that matter, and she did not hear the lady's voice – she was gone as she should be. But a sense of peace prevailed over Phoebe. All was as it should be.

'Goodbye, Mrs Tochborn. Until we meet again.'

She made her way back to the gates of the cemetery only to see her brothers' carriage waiting there, and her mood lifted instantly. Phoebe hurried her step to reach them.

'You need not have waited but I am glad you did.' She smiled up at them as Ambrose reached down and pulled her up to sit between them.

'Julius was worried you were not yourself, a little low today perhaps, and suggested we should treat you, or rather he should treat us to tea and cake.'

She smiled at her eldest brother who added with a look of affection, 'I really just wanted to get you back at work earning your keep, but agreed to sweeten you beforehand.'

She laughed and playfully nudged him as Julius turned the horses and they departed.

'How delightful,' Phoebe said and inhaled the fresh winter's air. 'It is a fine day for the living.'

THE END

Next in the series, The Dastardly Debutante

M ISS PHOEBE ASTIN OF *The Economic Undertaker* has applied her mortician skills to many faces but a beautiful young debutante needed little work, or so she thought. When the debutante's spirit appears to her, insisting she was murdered and demanding Phoebe do something about it, Phoebe agrees. She has, after all, helped many of her ghostly clients before they move on to the next world. Aided by her brothers, Julius and Ambrose, Detective Harland Stone, journalist friend Miss Lilly Lewis, and her dear friend Kate who took a portrait of the debutant the day before her death, Phoebe finds time is running out to find the truth before the debutante will be laid to rest. For the Astin family, being dead is no excuse for letting crime go unpunished!

Author notes

I HOPE YOU ENJOYED this story and even though it is fiction, I do try to be as accurate to the era and facts as I can be. Fortunately, Trove (the National Library of Australia) is a wonderful resource and not a day goes by that I am not typing in a saying or expression to make sure that was in the lingo in 1890 Australia.

Asylums such as that which William Varsewell found himself in were very common in the 19th century and the Woogaroo Lunatic Asylum did exist in Brisbane in 1890. The admission numbers Gilbert quoted from the June report – 496 males and 369 females with three men and one female discharged – were indeed accurate for that week of reporting.[i]

The Tochborn claimant story is inspired by the Tichborne claimants' true story where a mother seeks her son, Sir Roger Tichborne, who was lost at sea. Two claimants came forward to be recognised as heirs and secure the estate. One was a butcher named Arthur Orton, and the other – William Creswell – was in an insane asylum.

My character of William Varsewell was loosely based on William Creswell who claimed to be Sir Roger Tichborne and was a 'resident' of the Parramatta Lunatic Asylum, in New South Wales. He had the support of brothers Edmund and Charles Horton who applied for his release on the grounds that he was their missing brother.[ii] The judge was not sure that "it would be for the benefit of the lunatic",[iii] William Creswell, to be released, regardless of his real identity. It was said by supporters of his claim that: "he possesses a number of distinctive marks, manners, and habits, which characterised Sir Roger Tichborne."[iv]

My second claimant, Arthur Horton, was loosely modelled on the real claimant, Arthur Orton, a butcher from Wagga Wagga, Australia. He spoke no French but did, in fact, suffer from the same genital malformation as the real Sir Roger Tichborne, which made him an interesting prospect. Some of the words spoken by my character Arthur Horton during the trial were words from the mouth of the real claimant, especially his belief as stated: "I was connected with a good family, and that I was superior to the position I was then holding."[v] The line by Mrs Tochborn were the true words written by Lady Tichborne before her death and believing so sadly, "I am certain as I am of my own existence, that the plaintiff is my first-born son."[vi] One can only imagine the hope she held.

Interestingly, the real Arthur Orton lost his case, went to jail for just over ten years, and when released took to the stage – he spent two years on the music hall circuit. On Friday 1 April 1898, Arthur died in his sleep but not without an ovation of sorts. More than 5000 people lined the streets and went to the cemetery to farewell the Tichborne claimant to his humble, pauper's grave.[vii] His dream to be recognised as Roger Tichborne was not upheld on his headstone, but "the coffin carried, with the permission of the Tichborne family, a plate which read 'Sir Roger Charles Doughty Tichborne'."[viii] My kidnapping story and the twin boys are fictitious.

I took some liberty with the saying "You wouldn't be dead for quids". The earliest use I could find was in the 1920s, but forgive me for using it in 1890, it was too perfect not to do so.

Some dressmakers did offer mourning wear with a family discount. Today, it seems so sad to think of wearing black for eighteen months and then moving to shades of grey, and not attending social events including weddings. Children were also expected to wear mourning clothes for one year after the death of a parent or sibling, especially in the middle classes.

When I discussed why the fictitious Mr Tochborn would not adopt because he did not know the child's genetic mix, I was truly surprised to find the concept of nature and nurture in newspapers in 1890 (the year I base my searches). I had always thought it was a modern psychological concept but clearly not, as one newspaper article featured a lecture by Professor Laurie in 1890 titled "The Teaching of Morality in State Schools" stating: 'We must seek to form the character, and to produce the habit of virtue. Nature and Nurture are the two great powers by which our lives are moulded. In the family and in the wider community of school the child acquires habits of thought and action, due in part to natural disposition, but in great part also to the influence of others.'[ix]

Thank you for taking the journey with me. If you find time to review my work (hopefully favourably) or spread the word, I would be grateful.

References:

[i] Commercial. (1890, June 25). *The Brisbane Courier (Qld.: 1864 - 1933)*, p. 3. Retrieved October 27, 2022, from http://nla.gov.au/nla.news-article3508354

[ii] The Horton-Creswell Trial. (1884, June 21). *The Sydney Mail and New South Wales Advertiser* (NSW: 1871 - 1912), p. 1182. Retrieved December 5, 2018, from http://nla.gov.au/nla.news-article164386958

[iii] The Horton-Creswell Trial. (1884, June 21). *The Sydney Mail and New South Wales Advertiser.* Op.cit.

[iv] Is William Creswell Sir Roger Tichborne? (1894, December 25). *Wagga Wagga Advertiser (NSW: 1875 - 1910)*, p. 4. Retrieved December 5, 2018, from http://nla.gov.au/nla.news-article101803124

[v] Arthur Horton's Confessions. (1895, July 5). *The Riverine Grazier (Hay, NSW: 1873 - 1954)*, p. 4. Retrieved November 19, 2022, from http://nla.gov.au/nla.news-article140005028

[vi] The Tichborne Case. (1871, August 28). *The Ballarat Courier (Vic : 1869 - 1885; 1914 - 1918)*, p. 4. Retrieved November 19, 2022, from http://nla.gov.au/nla.news-article191430362

[vii] The Tichborne Trials Archive, *Hampshire Cultural Trust*, 2018.

[viii] The Tichborne Trials Archive, *Hampshire Cultural Trust*, 2018.

[ix] The Teaching of Morality in State Schools. (1890, November 1). *The Argus (Melbourne, Vic. : 1848 - 1957)*, p. 13. Retrieved November 7, 2022, from http://nla.gov.au/nla.news-article8447252

- The Lineup Staff, The Twisted Truth Behind 10 Creepy Nursery Rhymes, The Lineup, 30 January 2018 from URL: https://the-line-up.com/creepy-backstories-nusery-rhymes

- THE DOWAGER LADY TICHBORNE. (1868, May 19). Gippsland Times (Vic.: 1861 - 1954), p. 3 (Morning.). Retrieved October 30, 2022, from http://nla.gov.au/nla.news-article61340951

- Mourning - Victorian Era, 21 November 2018, *Australian Museum*. Retrieved 7 November 2022 from URL: https://australian.museum/about/history/exhibitions/death-the-last-taboo/mourning-victorian-era/

- The real advertisement that Lady Henriette Tichborne ran in hope of finding her son, Sir Roger. Source: Advertising (1865, August 2). *The Argus*. Retrieved from URL: http://nla.gov.au/nla.news-article5775099

Also by Helen Goltz

Miss Hayward & the Detective Series (historical mystery/ romance set in Australia):

Murder at the Freak Show
The Artist's Missing Muse
Mystery at the Asylum
The Mortician's Clue
Murder in Bridal Lane

The Clairvoyant's Glasses series (paranormal/romance)

Volume 1 – A vision unexpected
Volume 2 – Time has a shadow
Volume 3 – Love has no bounds
Volume 4 – Fate comes to call

The Jesse Clarke series (cosy mystery):

Death by Sugar

Death by Disguise

Death by Reunion

The Mitchell Parker series (crime thriller):

Mastermind

Graveyard of the Atlantic

The Fourth Reich

Writing as Jack Adams (mystery suspense):

Poster Girl (stand-alone)

The Delaney and Murphy childhood friends' thrillers:

Asylum

Stalker

Cult

Hitched (coming early 2024).

About the author

After studying English Literature, Media, and Communications at universities in Queensland, Australia, and obtaining a Counselling Diploma, Helen Goltz has worked as a journalist, producer and marketer in print, TV, radio and public relations. She is published by Next Chapter and Atlas Productions. Helen was born in Toowoomba and has made her home in Brisbane, Australia with her journalist husband, Chris, and Boxer dog, Baxter.

Connect with Helen:

Website: www.helengoltz.com

BookBub:www.bookbub.com/authors/helen-goltz

Facebook: www.facebook.com/HelenGoltz.Author

Instagram: https://www.instagram.com/helengoltz1/